WHO IS SHIVA?

WHO IS SHIVA?

RAVITEJA GOLLA

ISBN-13: 9780692910375
ISBN-10: 0692910379

To Family & Friends

"Only enormous amount passion and patience can keep one's dream alive till it is achieved."
"The journey is always beautiful than the destination."

RAVITEJAGOLLA

CONTENTS

ACKNOWLEDGEMENTS

It took me eighteen months to complete this fascinating journey. There were different learning experiences and many memories to recollect throughout the process of writing this book. Without the support of a few people around me, my name would have not been on the front cover. They all deserve to be acknowledged and thanked.

My Family: Ramakantha Rao, Jayanthi, Arunima, and Sudhamsa: Highly capable and positive individual personalities who never objected my dream. They supported me throughout this project, even when I was jobless for a few months. Without their push and support, it would have been a rough and hard journey.

Friends: Faheemuddin, Manogna, Nandini, Vikranth, Veena, Shravya, Jyotsna and Anvesh, my friends who made the last 10 years of my life joyful. Those memories helped me write many sequences in this project very easily.

Prajwala, my friend who evaluated and advised my writing till the very end. Also, I would like to thank my many more friends who took the time to read my final draft and give their suggestions.

DevduttPattanaik, a well-established author whose writings are primarily focused on Indian Mythology. Reading his books made me write one of mine.

Christina Myrvold; for understanding my concept and coming up with a design for the cover page.

WHERE IS HE?

I was nothing but a man who was outgoing, down-to-earth and has always enjoyed everyone's company profoundly. People found me as a very jovial person and even if I am alone, it is by choice. But things changed when everything in my life took a u-turn. Never before had I felt the urge to want someone's company this badly. What had changed and who was the reason behind that change?

As my body sank into the rocking chair beside the big empty couch in my TV lounge, with loud music from a party next door piercing every vein in my ear, and the occasional laughter emanating from a comedy show that played on the TV but didn't have my attention, I looked outside the glass window, it was another very dark night.

The howling wind was making the trees sway as it slowly started to drizzle, but it didn't bother me. Amidst it all, the music, laughter and the wind's deliberate attempt to get noticed by blowing the curtains, there was an eerie silence all over the room. All I could hear was my heartbeat: Yes, my very own heart throbbing against my chest 79 times/minute was all I could hear. I tried to hold back my tears by taking long breaths, but I knew that I won't be able to keep that up for long.

I recalled something someone I met had said, "Worrying is like a rocking chair. It gives you something to do, but it gets you nowhere."

Of course I was worried, worried out of my mind to be honest! Never in my wildest dreams had I thought that this would happen to me. I never would have thought that Shiva, of all the people, would leave me. I had no idea where to look for him. You may find it ironic, and I don't blame you for it, that someone so close to me, someone for whom I was literally drowning myself in sorrow for the last couple of months, someone who had given me sleepless nights and taken away my appetite had left me, that someone who I could turn to at any point of time and in any situation of my life. Being friends, there were lots of amazing memories that we shared. Now, all I was left with were his memories and nothing more.

It had been a couple of months since I last saw him. I could still feel his presence with me. I wished to see him once to make sure he was alright. Oh god, how I would give anything to just know that he was okay and not suffering like I was. I begged myself not to cry, not again, but I couldn't hold myself any longer and the tears rolled out. Tears had yet again won the battle against the heart and like all prior times, I had failed.

I couldn't stay like this; I had to do something. I have to distract myself from having thoughts about him or they will, like every other time, make me cry incessantly. Perhaps a whiskey will help. The thought gave me some hope. I managed to get up from my chair and headed for the fridge. The whiskey was going to make my heart feel lighter, less burdened or it was going to completely fade away all my sorrows until I wasn't my own anymore. Those were always my 2 plans: Plan A rarely worked, but plan B always had my back. As I opened the fridge, a 750ml bottle of Royal Stag was staring back at me, waiting to be grabbed. It might have been a new year's present, or perhaps I brought it from the grocery store myself – I couldn't recall. I took the bottle out, placed it on the counter, and looked for a glass to pour the concoction in. After searching two cabinets, I finally found what I was looking for, along with a cocktail shaker which was definitely a present from someone.

I poured some of the whiskey in the shaker and headed to the fridge again to grab some ice cubes, only to find a chilled soda in the freezer.

Lucky me, I thought. A brief smile touched my lips as I pulled it out and placed it on to the counter of my very own little bar. I poured the half frozen/slushy soda in the shaker and emptied the whole can. My bartender instincts took over and I enjoyed the brief distraction. I put three big ice cubes in and started to shake. The noise, accompanied by my heartbeat's sound and the loud music made for a perfect harmony that only I was privileged enough to hear.

Once satisfied, I poured some of it into the glass and gulped it down in one sip. The almost frozen cocktail made every nerve in my body shiver, causing me to suffer from a brain freeze for a moment. Most people try to avoid it, but I, on the other hand embraced it. It eclipsed all the emotions of my memories and pain, even if for only a few seconds. Before I knew it, I was having my third drink and was again drenched in my own sorrows and emptiness.

I was on my way back to my rocking chair when I heard someone knocking on the door. It was followed by an echoing yet recognizable voice calling out my name.

"Aditiya? Adi? Are you in there?"

Another echo of knuckles tapping on the wooden door continued. I was neither in the mood nor in the condition to entertain someone. I heard the knocking again. Not answering the door made me feel that I was being rude. So, I went to the door and opened it.

"Aditya, what's going on?"

I have to admit, I felt quite dizzy but even then, I could recognize the face and the silvery voice that greeted me with genuine concern. I blinked my eyes a couple of times to clear my vision and there she was, my girl-friend, Nandini. The moment I saw her, I was lost for words because it had been so long since we last met, or maybe just because I wasn't expecting to see her.

Whatever the reason was, I just wanted to hug her tight and cry. It had been almost a year since I last saw her or stayed in contact with her and now, when she was in front of me, I truly did not know what to do. I walked back into the room, leaving the door open, expecting her to walk in. As anticipated, I heard footsteps following me in. I took up my glass for a next drink and sat in the chair, gesturing her to have a seat as well.

There was even more silence than before, even though there were two of us in the room now. The music had thankfully died down and it was just the two of us and the silence that had taken over. My heart was heavier than usual and I wanted to share everything that happened over the past one year without her. She sat on the couch next to me, staring at me without any expression on her face. But I did find tears in her eyes, and I had a strong feeling that those tiny drops of tears were for me.

I had never found the silence to be this deafening. Encountering it alone was another thing but experiencing it, even when around someone whom you love, was scary. I didn't want the silence to prevail like it was but I didn't want to be the one to strike a conversation either. Thankfully, she was the one who broke the silence and started walking towards me. The pounding of her heels against the wooden floor of my apartment made a screeching yet delightful noise.

I would have preferred to enjoy the odd sensation a little longer if I had not been slapped hard on my left cheek. It all happened so quickly that I had no time to react or make sense of the situation. A thousand bells rang in my left ear. She got down on her knees and burst into tears. This made me lose control and my eyes too began shedding tears. She had slapped me and for some reason, she looked in more pain than me. I couldn't bear seeing her like that. I joined her by dropping on my knees, hugged her, and started crying. It has been many years since I cried like this, but now I felt better and relieved. I felt very light.

"Aditya, what is wrong? What is happening?" She asked with a brittle voice.

I was still crying on her shoulder and couldn't control myself, no matter how hard I tried. After a few minutes, she asked me.

"Who is Shiva and where is he now?"

Hearing her utter his name, my heart skipped a beat.

How did Nandini know about Shiva? She couldn't have known about him as we hadn't spoken in over a year. In fact, none of our mutual friends knew who Shiva was.

"How do you know about Shiva? Did you meet him? How is he?"

A sudden chill of joy rushed down my spine. I asked with a sense of excitement, expecting that she would give me the details I was longing for.

'I do not know who he is?' She replied, in a wobbly tone.

"If you don't know who Shiva is, how did you come to know his name?"

"That is not important now, Adi"

"No, that is important to me at this point; tell me how you came to know."

I was quiet seriously expecting an answer this time.

"I visited your home this morning to surprise you and met with your parents. Avika shared with me what all happened."

"Oh!! She knew about him because everyone in my family knew about Shiva."

All that happiness and excitement that had surged within me, dispersed. I was once again left shattered.

I didn't have any more questions to ask Nandini. At that moment, I was feeling better after seeing Nandini. Because she looked so curious, I decided to open up about Shiva with her.

"Please get up, Nandu. Have a seat here." I pulled a bean bag from beside the rocking chair and requested her to have a seat.

"Let me tell you all that happened in my life after you walked away."

THE APPOINTMENT LETTER

I had no reason to wake up early in the morning. There weren't any deadlines to be met, deals to be made, projects to work on, or a schedule to follow. No one bothered what I did or when I did it. There was a time when I loved this boredom - the freedom of not having a job. But the same freedom didn't take much time to turn into anger and later on, into desperation. My insecurities grew and I forgot all about getting my dream job in my dream company. All I needed at that point in my life was a job —any job!

There were days where I got so bored out of my mind that I could actually feel my hair and teeth growing. I know it's an odd thing to say but I felt like that. It was one of those days when I heard a knock on my door.

Unwanted visitors were always around me! On my way to the door, I sneaked a peek at the wall clock. It was 44 minutes past 9. Who could it be this early in the morning? For a man without a job, it was very early in the morning. Had I not been awakened by the sound of the cranes working next door, I would have enjoyed my sleep for a little longer.

As I opened the door, I was greeted by a man in his 40s. He had a bag on his shoulder and was going through some envelopes in his hand. Noticing that his knock has been answered, he ceremoniously greeted me.

"Good morning sir! You have a mail. Please sign this form for me here", he requested, gesturing to one of the many columns on the sheet where my name was printed and handed me the pen.

He then handed me one of the envelopes he had in his hands. It was addressed to me. Strange! Who could have possibly sent me mail! No one wrote anyone mails, or at least that is what I thought. Who on earth could be writing to me? I received the mail and briefly ran my eyes over the logo. I instantly recognized it but couldn't recall where I had seen it before. I just knew I had; but when or where, my memory failed me. I closed the door behind me after the postman greeted me with yet another ceremonious "Have a great day sir". I came inside, still trying to jog my memory regarding the where had I seen this logo. I sat down on the couch and opened the envelope with part excitement and part inquisition. To my surprise, it was an offer letter from a company I had given an interview at not long ago. The letter congratulated me for having aced the interview and inquired if I would be able to join the company starting 11thof July. I wasn't expecting that. I reread the letter just to be sure. When it suggested exactly the same thing again, happiness filled me to my core. I felt relieved that I would have something to look forward to in life now. No more sitting idle at home all day!

I instantly felt like thanking God.

"Thank You God", I blurted out loud. There was no one in the house except me. So, I didn't have to worry about disturbing anyone. I thanked God because I knew I needed that job. Perhaps He knew it too. After remembering and thanking God, I paused for a moment.

Wait!!! I didn't believe in God; I was an Atheist. Why did I just thank him if I didn't believe in him? I felt stupid. I was praising a superficial being that had nothing to do with my achievement. It was I who had worked hard for it, had studied, showed up for the test and the interview and delivered. It was all my hard work and effort and if there was anyone to receive all credit for it, it was me. But that wasn't what troubled me. The thought about thanking God in the first place bothered me. But I didn't want to think about that then. All I wanted was to pick up the phone and pass on the good news to my family.

I called my dad's cell phone. He was a successful banker. All the while that the phone was ringing, I held the offer letter in my hand, looking at it one more time to see if it was delivered to the right address and to the right person. Aditya is a very common name in India and every other home in the country had one or two Aditya's in the family.

After the phone rang for the fifth time, he finally picked it up!

Hello Adi. Is everything okay?

"Papa! I got a job! I just received an offer letter", I couldn't contain my excitement any longer.

"Congratulations Adi! I'm very happy for you." He sounded so delighted with that news that I secretly felt a little too proud of myself.

"Let's celebrate your first job together at home with your sister and mother. See you at dinner this evening?" He said with a lingering tone of happiness in his voice.

"Okay Papa." I said and hung up as I didn't want to bother him when he was at work. Then I dialed my mom's number. My mom was a home-maker and a firm believer in God. She used to meditate whenever she had the time. She often called other ladies from the neighborhood to join her and soon, her small circle of friends started a weekly meditation class. As she knew a lot about meditation than any of them, she started delivering lectures too.

"Hello Adi. What's the matter?"She whispered. She was in between her meditation session.

"Mom, I got a job!" I shouted with joy.

"That's really nice to hear my son. I will call you back as soon as I'm done." She said with a husky low voice. I felt a little dejected. This was my greatest achievement so far. My first step into the corporate world, my very first break and no one was here to celebrate with me or share the joy I felt.

I didn't want to give the good news to my only elder sister Avika over the phone. I wanted to surprise her when she returned from her job in the evening.

Then, I shared the good news with some of my closest friends, mentors and cousins. A number of thoughts occupied my mind. This was it!

This was how my life was going to be from now on. I had bagged a great first job. As any B.tech graduate, landing a job in a reputable software house meant I was settled. I felt the next task was to immediately get married.

I waited for Avika to come home. Although Avika was older than me, her short height and slim physique made her look younger than me. In comparison, I was a bit heavier. She had always been like a second mother to me. Throughout my childhood, she pampered and supported me. We shared a very special bond.

It was almost 6:00 p.m. I was sure she would be home any minute. As I anticipated someone tried opening the door. She looked very tired as she entered. She didn't know that I was home and I didn't feel like telling her yet — not until she had some time to freshen up. She went into her room to take a shower and I decided to utilize that time to cook up some snacks and make tea. By the time she came out of her room with a towel wrapped around her head, I greeted her with the snacks and tea which I had placed in the tray held in my hands. Seeing me stand beside the dining table, she was taken aback; she wasn't expecting such a gesture from me.

"Wow!! Is that you? Did you make tea and snacks for me?" She questioned me, with a surprising look on her face.

"Yes Avika." I replied.

"So, tell me Adi, what was so special about today? You have never done this for me before. Do you need any favor?" She asked.

"Guess what Avika? I got a job!" I almost shouted as I was full of excitement.

"Awesome!! Congratulations brother, I'm so happy for you!" She gave me a hug while saying that...

I would have continued with the story had I not been interrupted by the loud sound of the wall clock. It reminded both Nandini and me that it was 2:00 a.m. in the morning. I looked at Nandini. She was still looking at me intently, trying to sense the extreme apprehension in my words. I wanted to continue talking but also craved for a little break from all the speaking. Before I knew it, my eyes started to shut and the image of Nandini started to blur.

Ding-a-ling-a-ling!!

I heard the loud music and jumped out of bed. That was my wake up alarm song. Seemed like my eyes had won over my heart the night before. As soon I woke up, the one thought that came to my mind was "SHIVA". I had a feeling that it was going to be yet another day without any information about his whereabouts. All of a sudden, I remembered some parts of my tête-à-tête with Nandini last night. I felt confused. Was Nandini really with me last night or was it just my mind playing tricks on me? I hoped it wasn't a dream and that she was really back. I was quite drunk last night to be sure if she was there, at least that was what I hoped for. I sat for a while, trying to think what had happened last night. But my head was moaning in pain.

Then, I walked to the restroom to take a shower. I walked very slowly, literally dragging my feet along the floor, and reached the mirror on the way and stared at my own reflection. My eyes were red, my hair was messy and I had an unshaven, non-styled beard which veiled half of my face. Something caught my eye and I looked at myself much closer. I was shocked to find three fingerprints on my left cheek. Seeing that, an instant flashback of the hard and loud slap confirmed Nandini's presence.

Where has she gone now? I immediately ran back to my bedside table to check my phone for any messages she might have left me. There was a message from her. I read that she would soon be back to meet me sometime in the morning.

Looking at her message, I immediately went to take a bath, shaved my beard, combed my hair and made some coffee for myself to subdue the effects of the hangover. Holding my coffee in one hand, I walked towards the farthest end of my room.

On the eastern side of my room, there was a big arched window with multiple grids that allowed light and fresh air to seep into the room. The base of the window had enough space to seat a person. That was my most favorite spot in the house to sit on as I could easily stretch my legs. I loved sitting there. The feeling of warm sunshine on my face was my kind of meditation. Whenever I felt low, I would just sit here and watch the people on the streets. All my tensions would just float away. The feeling somehow soothed me to my entire core and I could never describe or express how light I would feel afterwards. I was very fond of observing people.

As my apartment was near to a business district, the majority of the population that I viewed from the window belonged to the working class. The roads were always crowded. Some could be seen crossing the road while others waited for the bus, some could be seen eating samosas whenever I looked at any of them, I couldn't help but think how robotic their lives were. Getting up every day morning, getting dressed as per office rules, coming to job which most of them hate and going back to sleep I would often remember what Shiva once told me, "It makes your life easy if you earn money only for your living, but it makes your life miserable if you start earning to live better than others."I didn't clearly understand it back then, but I did now.

All that these men and women are striving to make a better living for themselves and their families. Now, even though I don't think there's anything wrong with that, where I think they defaulted was at their calculations. They always measured their happiness by looking at what their role models had, and they wanted to be like them. I always thought that if only for a single day had they been content with what they have, they might have been much happier and satisfied than they were now. I really hope that someday, they would start thinking if it was all worth it? Was it justifiable to work that hard for the things they didn't even need? Was it worth wasting the golden days of their lives working like a machine?

The buzz from the mobile in my pocket bought me back into reality. It was a text message from Nandini. It read, "Dear!! I have started from my home and will reach your place in an hour. Text me asap if you have some other plans for the day."

AN ANGEL WALKED IN

The word "Dear" in her text took me back to the first memory of hers. Nandini and I both went to from the same college. I still vividly remember the first time I laid my eyes upon her. It was the first day of undergrad college. I and some of my friends were sitting outside on our bikes, watching girls walk in and out of the school. We were young and misbehaving guys back then and like every other guy out there; we didn't shy away from passing comments on every girl, rating them on a scale of 1 to hot and making fun of some. Ilyas was with me too. I and Ilyas had been friends for many years now. We had attended the same school and lived just a few blocks away. Luckily, we had got admission in the same college too.

As we casually sat there, picking on girls, I saw a girl getting out of an auto. She wasn't like any other girl I had seen before. She had such grace in the way she walked that I couldn't help but notice. She wore a stunning white frock with embellishments on her bosom and some tassels that flew with the wind. She was bargaining over money with the driver, occasionally pulling a few strands of her thick, wavy and ombre hair behind her ear. I could still trace the shape of her earrings that kissed her jaw every now and then. She was the epitome of beauty. Everything about her, from her slim waist that her loose anarkali dress sporadically flaunted her pearly white complexion, from the way she was dealing with the driver in her soft crimson voice to her gorgeous big brown eyes… everything was just perfect. She was too beautiful to be true, just like an angel.

I have to admit, I was gob smacked!

As she walked past me into the college, I nudged Ilyas, who had surely missed her as he was busy playing games on his phone.

"Ilyas, I think she is the one for me." I could hear the excitement in my own voice.

"No, she is the fifteenth." He replied, still engrossed in his phone, not even looking up at me.

"I know I said that before but this time, I really mean it." He stopped playing and gave me an unconvincing look.

"I know I said this before too." I confessed.

"Dude, tell me one thing, how could you even dare to look at other girls even after getting rejected by fourteen girls? Where do you get all that confidence man?"

"I don't know. But this girl, there is something about her. It's… it's magical."

"Okay then… but if she too rejects you like all the other girls, I think you should try to hit on men. But keep me out of that list. I am straight and happy!" He joked.

I couldn't keep my eyes off her all the while I was in class. It was as if all my professors were on mute that day. I tried making eye contact so that she could notice me too, but she had this hesitant look in her eyes, as if she was frightened or felt unsettled. It bothered me a bit and I wanted to be just sure as to whatever it was bothering her. I wondered how beautiful she would look if she smiled. I waited for her outside the college gate in the evening. She came out with a few friends of hers who thankfully went the other way. I followed her for a while, juggling between whether it was good idea to introduce myself or not. I wanted to talk to her before it became quite obvious that I was stalking her like a creepy pervert. I was just a few steps away from her. Before I could call out to her to introduce myself, she turned around, looking frightened.

"Hi…" She managed to say. "Are you following me?"

"Hi. And no, I am not following you. I am Aditya. We are in the same class." I extended my hand for a handshake.

"Hi, I am Nandini; can I help you with something?" She hesitantly placed her hand in mine and plastered a fake smile on her face.

"Please, don't take having this conversation out of the blue in the wrong way. I happened to look at you in class today. You seemed worried, like troubled in your own thoughts. I just wanted to let you know that if there is anything you need or anyway I could be of help, please don't hesitate asking. You can count on me as a friend. I would love if I could be of some help."

I think I sounded genuine, and that changed her expression from one which portrayed the thought of being afraid to one which reflected peacefulness.

She smiled in return and thanked me for being so caring.

"Okay then, see you later. Bye!"

"Bye." She replied.

I felt a bit embarrassed that I had frightened her. I decided never to approach her again unless she came up to me. I thought that would never happen, but it did. I and Ilyas were having a casual chat one day when I saw her walking towards me.

"Hi, Aditya. How are you?"

"I'm good, Nandini. How are you?"

"I'm fine. I need a favor from you, if you don't mind?" She asked.

"Are you doing something important?" She looked at Ilyas, as if asking for his permission to budge in.

"No, we were just sitting." I eyed Ilyas so that he would excuse himself. He did, but not without giving me that "so now that you are with your crush, you will forget your friends" look.

"Can you come with me today after class?" She asked.

I had no clue why she wanted me to come with her. Anyways, without giving it any second thoughts, I agreed. I escorted her to the auto once all our classes were over and she came outside the college. I sat beside her with a sense of excitement.

Everyone knew that I was a very talkative person, even with strangers. But when it came to crushes, words would just get stuck in my throat. I wanted to talk, but I didn't as I feared I might ruin the moment.

"So, where are we going?" I finally decided to break the silence.

"I need some things for my hostel room. Since I don't have any good friends in the city yet, I thought I should ask you."

Wait, did she just count me as her good friend? Wow!! Butterflies fluttered in my stomach, but I tried to keep my calm and not make my excitement so obvious.

"Oh, that's okay; you can always come to me for help. If you don't mind, can I have your phone number? In that way, it would be easier for us to stay in contact."

"Yeah sure, sounds good to me. Here," she gave me her number.

We spent a good amount of time shopping for things for her room. All the while, we talked about studies, places she should visit, and markets that were cheaper than the rest. I enjoyed every minute of it with her. She was so much fun to be around. By the time I got home, it was almost evening. After I took a shower and changed into a clean pair of clothes, I decided to text her. But then, I decided against it. The dilemma of whether I should or shouldn't was too frustrating. It was true that we were good friends now, but wouldn't it look as if I was coming on a bit too strong if I texted first? Ah, the torture of not being able to make a simple decision. I feared her response or the fact that she would not respond at all. For almost half an hour, I just sat there in my room, with my phone in my hands and the keypad open. But the courage to type anything wasn't there.

"Hi Nandini. All good? I hope all the shopping didn't tire you out?" I finally typed in the text and hit the send button.

"It did. I'm exhausted."

"Well then, you must take some rest. See you tomorrow." I was desperate to talk, but decided to play it cool.

"That's okay. We can chat for a while." She replied.

After that day, we became really good friends. We started talking for hours, exchanged notes, holding combined study sessions, going for movies together etc. In a short period of time, we grew really close. I started to feel like I had known her for years. She understood me like no one ever did. She would always listen to my stupid talks and laugh at my silly jokes and fantasies about my dream job. My days started with a good morning text from her and ended with a good night text, again from her.

One day she told me about how much she hated the food served at her hostel's canteen and that she had started to skip breakfast. I got a bit worried hearing that and started bringing her breakfast to the college every morning. I would get up early and head to a nearby hotel to pick up breakfast for her. It became a usual routine, one which I didn't mind at all. I liked caring for her. I liked looking after all her little needs, even though she never asked me to. Doing those little things for her made me happy. After this went on for some weeks, until she asked me to stop it.

"Please Adi. Stop wasting money like that; you're making it a habit now. I will eat at my place; even it tastes much grosser than yesterday."

Deep down, I felt a little afraid that she might think of such gestures as an obsession. I had heard stories about how girls didn't admire over-protective and obsessive boyfriends. But I couldn't help it. I always looked after the people I cared for, and Nandini was no exception. I knew she valued my generosity. I knew she wasn't just number 15 for me; she was the one!

I kept bringing her food on and off so that on some days, she would get to eat what she really liked. Every day, I would wake up excited as I knew I was going to meet Nandini at college. She was my motivation then, as compared to my studies. In fact, I skipped classes whenever I could because I didn't find them very informative. Even when I did attend them, I would continuously yawn the whole time. Besides, I was never very enthusiastic about my studies, and neither were my parents. I had always been an average student my whole life. Thankfully, my parents didn't have any high expectations from me either.

I was a sports enthusiast and whenever I skipped classes, I would pass that time playing table tennis or basketball. On the other hand, Nandini and Ilyas were quiet serious about their studies. They would compete for the top position, but never really came first. I and Nandini would get together after she was free from her classes. I didn't feel exhausted from playing all day and we would sit together, wait for our bus, share a pair of earphones, and relax.

One evening on our way back home, we both were calmly listening to soft tunes when she started to feel sleepy. She placed her head on my shoulder. I wasn't prepared for that. True, we were close friends and it wasn't the first time she had done this but for some reason, it felt different. My heart started to race faster and my body instantly stiffened. I didn't know what to do. If I pulled away, she would have fallen head first to the ground and if I didn't, well, I didn't know what I would do.

"Nandini?" I tried to wake her up by tapping on her cheek with my left hand.

"Your stop is about to come." She woke up in a hurry and got down at her stop.

She lived just a few miles away from my place. We met almost every day, even after college. I would make up fake excuses to get out of the house just to go see her. Being with her for most of the time and talking to her gave me the feeling that life was incomplete without her. Sometimes, saying good night to her was very normal but on others, I would get overly anxious about keeping the conversation flowing.

I knew I loved her, but we had been such good friends since the last two years, the question of whether to propose or not kept buzzing in my head 24/7.

I couldn't take it anymore. My own thoughts left me restless. I didn't want to end what we had, but I also wanted to be more than just a *good friend*. I needed counseling so I reached out to the one person I knew would know what to do.

"Man, can I ask you something?" I and Ilyas were sitting on the roof of my house. We loved hanging out there. All alone, with minimum distractions and worldly chaos.

"What is it?" he asked.

"Which is more important to you, Love or friendship?"

18

"If the girl is beautiful or rich, then friendship is important. If she is both beautiful *and* rich, then love is important." He joked. It always took time for me to get him into a serious conversation.

"Shut up. I am talking about Nandini."

"Oh, I thought you two were *just* friends?"

"I thought so too. But the kind of giddy feeling I go through sometimes kills me." I continued.

"Giddy feeling?" He narrowed his eyes, indirectly asking me for elaboration.

"You know giddy… like sometimes it is hard to say good night or drop her off at her place. Like you don't want the conversation to end. You just want it to keep going for the rest of your life. We have shared both good and bad times together. We have been there for each other all the time. The moment that realization of love hit me, I started to feel awkward around her. The dynamics changed. I now feel goose bumps every time our hands touch casually… the same person with whom I sat for the past two years looks completely different to me now. I confess I had an infatuation for her since day one but only now do I realize that even then, it was more than that. Now that I see her in a different light, I love everything about her and how happy she makes me. Lately, I have started feeling guilty for pretending to be her friend, knowing that I have feelings for her."

"So, what are you asking me about when you already know how you feel about her? You know what the next step is, right?" Ilyas asked.

"What?"

"Propose her," he suggested.

"I am scared."

"Scared of what?"

"What if she says no? Then, I will lose her as a friend too. Things will become too awkward then."

"But you can't pretend to be her friend for the rest of your life."

"I don't know man, I am just confused."

"Look, I am not suggesting you to tell her everything right now, wait for the right moment. Maybe she feels the same way too."

I didn't know when that right moment was going to come. I just knew that I had to trust Ilyas's words then.

I was almost onto the last sip of my coffee now. The slow squeaking of the door pulled me out from my thoughts and I turned around to see who it was.

It was Nandini. Carrying herself with the same poise and grace as the first day I had seen her. I stepped down from the window and we greeted each other with good morning and a brief hug.

"Did you sleep well?" She inquired.

"I think it was good, but then again, I don't really remember when and how I fell asleep."

I really should apologize to Nandini. It was quite rude of me to act that way. I was quite drunk, I thought to myself.

"I am really sorry about last night", I finally gathered the courage to speak.

"It's okay Adi, let's not talk about that."

"Tell me, did you have breakfast?" I tried changing the subject.

"No! And I am starving; I thought we two could have it together like old times." I could see the excitement in her eyes.

"Cool, just give me half an hour; I'll see what I have."

My options disappointed me. All I had in the fridge were some eggs, orange juice and some bread. Well, when you don't have it, you just do your best with what you have. With this oddly motivating thought, I quickly beat up two eggs in a bowl, added some spices to it and poured the batter into a frying pan. While that cooked, I put slices of bread into the toaster and poured orange juice into two glasses. In the next few minutes, I had everything on the tray and I went inside my room, carrying it in my hands. Nandini was sitting on my bed, looking at an old photo album. Seeing me enter, she put it down and helped me place the tray on the bed.

SHREE AND TINU

"I have to say, this was one simple yet delicious breakfast. I didn't know you could cook."

"You mean cook an egg?"

"Yes! That takes skills too."

She laughed. I couldn't tell if she was genuinely complimenting me or mocking me. I thought it was the former as Nandini wasn't the kind to mock someone. She sipped the remaining juice in her glass and placed it on the table.

"Thank You, I guess!"

She sat right in front of me on my bed while I sat on the bean bag.

"So, tell me what happened next?"

"What?"

"Adi, what happened after you got your job confirmation letter?" She didn't hesitate in reminding me where we had left off last night.

I vaguely had any memory of last night and had absolutely no clue where I dozed off. Had she not pointed it out, I might have told her the whole story from the beginning again.

Okay, so I was really excited about my job at the MNC. I was finally going to start my career as a software engineer. As I had graduated with a degree in Information technology with a 3.5 GPA, remember? So I was curious as to what kind of work will I be assigned, what responsibilities will I handle and whether I will be able to prove my expertise or not. All these thoughts were the only thing on my mind for the next few nights. During the days, I would go shopping for office wear. I wanted to look my best. You may think I was overreacting but I just couldn't stop! After I was done, Ilyas picked me up from the mall and we went to have a look at my new office.

It took us a little while to locate my office. It was on the 10th floor of a high-rise glass building; on the outside it looked great. We still had to rate it from the inside. As soon as I stepped off the bike, I had this feeling of nervousness and excitement in my stomach. Within a few days' time, that was where I was going to spend most hours of my day. The excitement, that I was chosen among the many who interviewed for the same job position kept me up all night.

When my first day was just 12 hours away, I ironed my outfit for the next day and laid it out on my bed. I mapped my commute for the big day, set my alarm and checked it thrice before going to bed to get a good night's sleep.

The following morning, I woke up with jitters in my mind. I took more time than usual adjusting my tie, brushing my hair and making sure there weren't any creases on my shirt or dress pants. I then gathered all my important documents in a zipped file and waited for Ilyas to come pick me up. I decided against travelling by my own. Ilyas had always been my lucky charm and I didn't want anything to mess up today.

It only took me fifteen minutes to realize how bad that idea has been as when I finally looked at my own reflection in the little front mirror of his bike. To say the least, I had wasted about 20 minutes brushing my hair to perfection and now they looked like they had been electrocuted. With no combing aid to my help, I used my fingers as one and brushed them even. They didn't look the same as before, but looked comparatively better.

"Do I look okay?" I asked him.

"You look good dude." He told me.

"All the best, Adi" He continued.

"Thanks, dude" I replied, without wasting another minute, he sat back on his bike and was on his way to reach his own office which was just a few miles away from mine. I took a deep breath and started towards my office to embrace the future with a smile on my face.

"Can we see your appointment letter sir?" asked one of the security members at the gate.

"Sure. Here you go!" I showed it them.

"Please go inside to the reception area and let the receptionist guide you on your way to your office."

"Thank you", I said and walked in the direction he had pointed.

As I entered through the giant glass doors, I saw a girl well-dressed in business formals sitting at the reception desk. She looked extremely busy in some paperwork and kept attending phone calls. When she saw me walking towards her, she greeted me with a smile on her face.

"How can I help you today, sir?" she greeted me in her melodious voice, she seemed genuinely nice.

"Hi there, I'm a fresher here and today is my joining date." I told her my reason for the visit and handed her my documents.

She asked me to sign a few documents and led me into a room, which had a nameplate "Ekalavya" coined on it. It was oddly interesting to have a room named Ekalavya so I remembered its origin. It was derived from Mahabharata. It refers to an all-time sincere student. As soon as I stepped inside, the room was swarmed with students, all dressed in attire like mine, and seated calmly on their respective seats. There only remained one empty seat with my name tag on it. I felt embarrassed, even though I wasn't late. I started walking towards my seat and everybody traced my steps with their eyes. I sunk into the seat, thankful that the staring contest had ended. A couple of minutes later, we were joined by a group of people, many of whom looked more professional than the people in the room. One after the other they started introducing themselves.

"Hi everyone, we are the Human Resources team. We congratulate you in the first place and we welcome you into our family" one of them said out loud.

"Wow!!"

The majority of the HR team members were women who looked exceptionally well-dressed. They were all pretty good looking too. Most of the guys kept looking at them instead of listening to the lengthy speeches about compliance & governance, given by the senior members of the team. And for some reason, I couldn't blame them. They had such beautiful girls to look at in front of their eyes; it would have been foolish to listen to the old-age rules and regulations.

The guy who sat beside me was no shorter than six feet. He had broad shoulders and the fittest body I had seen any man have. He had a fair complexion, brown eyes and short hair. All in all, he looked one of the smartest in the fresher's crew, not because he was well-dressed but because he carried himself well. Since he and I were going to sit beside each other, I thought of it as the perfect opportunity to introduce myself.

"Hi, my name is Adi" I broke the silence between us in a very low voice as the speeches were still going on, but he looked least interested in them, just like I was.

"Hi I'm Shree Ram, but you can call me Shree" he said very politely, complemented with a smile on his face.

"We have a complimentary lunch for you guys today." the HR manager continued to speak. A few of the team members started distributing the coupons for lunch to everyone after the announcement. "You can leave for lunch now and we will meet here at 2:00 p.m. again," they concluded with a smile and left the room.

We started following one of the members who had stayed behind to lead the way. We followed him into the cafeteria. He asked us to form a line and wait for our turns. It felt a bit awkward to stand there holding a steel grid plate with multiple slots for different food items. When it was my turn, the person on the other side of the counter, the chef most probably, started filling my plate with different items.

He filled it with Jeera rice, Dal, Sambar, potato curry, a spoon of pickle and one papad. Shree was next in line after me. I waited for him so that we two could find some place to sit and eat together. I had already spotted two empty seats for us. As he joined me, he asked which college I was from.

"Mahatma Gandhi Institute of Technology. And you?" I couldn't resist not asking.

"I'm from CVSR College of Engineering" he answered.

"How did you like the first half of our first day?" he asked.

"When I first came inside, I felt like I had entered a workplace but after hearing those lectures for about an hour, I felt like I had just come out of an economics class."

"So I presume you hated economics?" he asked.

"I don't know but whenever my teacher started the class, most of the terms he used, didn't sound familiar to me. I tried to concentrate harder, but it only felt like watching a French movie with Chinese sub-titles. Everything just went over my head."

He laughed hearing my answer. I had a feeling he could relate to it too.

As we were casually enjoying our lunch, we were joined by a girl who just grabbed one of the chairs from another table and seated herself beside us.

She looked very enthusiastic with a smile on her face. She greeted the two of us. We greeted her back but with less zeal than hers. She was about 5 feet 5 inches, had a glowing skin with silky black hair that ended just below her shoulders. Her eyes were the same color as Shree's —brown.

"My name is Tinu", she wanted to keep the conversation going.

"I'm Adi…" "And I'm Shree". We had no choice but to introduce ourselves. Both of us hesitated as she had appeared from thin air. I didn't know about Shree, but I didn't recall seeing her in the training room. Maybe because I was least bothered about anything going on.

"Every mouth in the room is discussing about careers already. I got scared looking at them. No one seemed excited about their first day here. I saw you both were having a good time, so I pulled a chair and joined you. By the way, do you mind if I join you?" Tinu inquired.

"Well, I think that question came pretty late." I said with a very low voice.

"No no, we certainly have no problem." Shree covered up.

Once the day was over, I couldn't wait to tell my family all about the day's happening. I went home and over dinner, poured all of my excitement out. I told them about the interiors, the decors, the staff, my reporting boss, my tasks, my friends etc. They all seemed very happy hearing about it.

From the next day, Tinu started to sit with us. It took us some time to get along with her. After a few months, I started to realize that Shree was very different from the regular mass. He was a lot like me, more than I had anticipated. Just like mine, his mind too, was filled with questions all the time. And similarly, he loved chasing their answers. He was easy to talk to on any topic, be it work-related or another. On the other hand, Shree and Tinu were complete opposites of each other. He would have the answer to all the questions asked during a training session while she would stay quiet, rarely responding at all. Shree sat on my right and Tinu on my left and I enjoyed both of their companies alike.

Tinu was a charming and excited girl. Like every other girl on the planet, she loved to shop, gossip, chit-chat and play pranks on people. But all of it didn't make her less intelligent than the rest of us. True, she rarely raised her hand during the training session, but it wasn't like she didn't know the answers to them. She waited until no one in the room could answer and it was then, that she would raise her hand and shout the right answer with enthusiasm. All those tasks that no one successfully handled landed on her desk and she made sure they were done right!

Many a times, I felt really weird sandwiched in between two such people. Both of them were far more intelligent than me and I kind of felt left out when they would start talking about subjects I had little information about. There were times when I would be surprised to see them use their brains to such an extent.

One day, when we were doing the given assignment in the training room, the HR team stepped in and asked if anyone was interested in joining a group called Fun@Work.

"This is the team which organizes all the fun events on a monthly basis to make everyone step out of the pressure seats and enjoy for a while."

they described. It looked like none of us were ready, but I wanted to give my name. I wanted to ask Tinu and Shree if they were willing to join as well. I turned my head and looked at Tinu.

"I will join with you, if that's okay," Tinu said casually. I was taken aback by her response. She had answered a question that I was just concocting in my mind. Was she a mind reader or perhaps a witch? The former scared me more. Yes, I wanted her to join me, but I didn't know if she would be interested. I hoped that was a coincidence and not what I was thinking. I was surprised and responded to her with a shocking smile and looked at Shree to see if he was interested too.

"Sorry guys, you two go ahead." He replied.

"That's okay. No need to be sorry for that," Tinu answered.

We both gave our names and they requested us to join them for a brief meeting right away. We walked into the meeting room and I saw the room was filled with 12 members. None of them belonged to the fresher's lot. A discussion to organize a treasure hunt game for the coming week on each floor was in progression. We, being the fresher, had very little to do.

I was starving by the time the meeting ended. Though it was early, I thought of asking Tinu for lunch.

"Hey Adi, are you hungry? Shall we go out for lunch?" Tinu asked me. "*Hold on*" I thought. Was she reading my mind? She was saying exactly the same things I intended to say. How was that possible?

"Stop scaring me like that." Those words sounded very harsh in my head, but did not when they came out.

"What did I do?" she asked me like an innocent little girl.

"Whenever I think of asking something in my head, you spell it out and it isn't the first time it has happened."

"Oh shut up, that's just a coincidence." She replied in an absolute normal tone and started walking ahead of me.

I always felt that there was something special about both Shree and Tinu. I was glad to have found both of them at the very beginning of my career.

Our job training went along for three months. We all impatiently waited to get placed, but that never seemed to happen in near future and no further trainings were offered.

Meanwhile, we started playing Table Tennis, mastered playing UNO cards and aced online video games. I hoped we didn't make a security breach; but we even cracked down a few websites and started watching online movies.

HIS STUPID QUESTION

Tik – Tok, Tik – Tok!!

We were waiting for our turn to get the Table Tennis tables in the 60 x 40 air-conditioned recreation center, which had one TT table and two carom boards. Shree was the one with whom I played Table Tennis most of the time whenever we got the chance or whenever Tinu allowed us to play. She always wanted us to play caroms with her.

One day when Tinu was on leave because of some family event, we both almost did nothing except for playing Table Tennis. After sweating out our best, we walked into the cafeteria to have some tea and snacks.

We were casually enjoying our tea when Shree broke the ice between us. I had noticed that looked a little out of the place but I didn't ask about it. If something bothered him, I wanted him to be the one to tell me.

"Can I ask you one question Adi?"

"Yes sure, go ahead Shree".

"Which is more important to you, money or relationships?" I knew Shree thought a lot about such things, but he'd never asked me for an opinion before. It was a bit strange to ask for my opinion then.

It took me a while to come up with my answer. It wasn't a 'yes' or 'no' question. If Shree was the one asking it, I knew he didn't expect an answer as simple and naïve as that. I calculated the pros and cons of both and once I was sure what I would have chosen if I was in his place, I said, human relationships.

He looked at me for a second and then smiled, making me feel like an idiot. The expression on his face evidently showed that my answer was wrong.

"Don't just answer that question on the fly. Take your own time, Adi. Now, we've got nothing to do in the office and nothing at home as well. So think for the whole day and tell me the answer again tomorrow."

"But, I did!"

"No, you didn't. Think about it for a day and we will talk about it again tomorrow, okay?"

"Hmm", I got a bit irritated that he thought I hadn't given it enough thought. But like he had proposed, maybe I lacked a thought somewhere.

He knew that I couldn't withstand any questions in my head. All the while journeying back home, his question was all I could think about. I dialed Ilyas's number as soon as I got home.

"Hello, Adi How are you? How is your job?"He asked.

"Everything is fine. Are you doing something important? If not, then I have a question on my mind that has been boggling me." I blabbed out all this, not even giving him a second to respond in between.

"Okay chill. I am here. Shoot!"

"What would you prefer —*money* or *human relationships?*"

"And you need a quick answer, right?"He never got tired of irritating me.

"Yes, I do." I told him.

"It's simple. "Human Relationships" he said.

"And why did you choose that?" I inquired

"Well, Money can buy you all the comforts and pleasures of the world. People, on the other hand, can give you peace of mind. Minus that from the equation and you will never be happy, even if you have all the luxuries of the world. That's why I say human relationships." He said very firmly.

I knew Ilyas, he wasn't the kind who would just speak the first thing that comes to his mind. He always presented his case backed by practicality and logic. But somewhere, deep down, I still wasn't convinced so I dialed another friend of mine, an old school friend Manogna, whom everyone used to call Mano.

"I believe, money is more important to me now, Adi." she replied strongly without any hesitation. That was a quite frank reply and it made me more curious to listen to what she had to say in its explanation.

She elaborated, "I lent money to a few friends of mine when they were in need and I never asked any of them to return it back thinking they were my friends. I thought they would return the money whenever they had it. I just thought it would be impolite of me to keep insisting for it back as that would make them feel bad."

I could feel it in her voice; she was carrying some bitter memories and grudges.

"Then there came a period in my life when I was in need of some cash. I tried reaching out to a couple of my friends whom I had loaned money to in the past. But instead of giving me back my hard-earned money, they started ignoring my calls and texts. Some of them even straight out refused to pay me back. One of them completely denied that I had lent him any money in the past. Can you imagine that Adi? How humiliated I must have felt when he accused me like that? My own friends swindled me, the people I called my home, my family, my most dearest. They refused to have my back when I needed them the most and that too, by refusing to pay what was mine from the beginning."

There was a minute's pause before she continued.

"That was when I decided that money was more important than people. I had seen their true faces." She completed.

"But Mano, wasn't trusting them your own mistake?" I grilled more into the topic.

"Adi, trust is an important aspect in the human survival process. You *have* to trust someone —people, God or material possessions. Without trusting any of these, your survival isn't possible. The only drawback of trusting someone is that you don't realize it until someone breaks it and it's then when one really starts to rethink their priorities. But there is also a positive side to it, you learn from it. You take that experience and a meaningful lesson and build yourself stronger the next time."

"I'm still not convinced with your reasoning, Mano." I told her.

"Okay, let's assume that you have a friend who is very close to you. If he requests you for 100 rupees, you give him the money right away and probably don't bother about whether he will return it back or not. If he asks for 1000 rupees the next time, you still lend him the cash, but this time you probably expect him to return it, may be not soon though. Now, what if he asks for another 10,000? Being the good friend that you are, you might lend him the money again, a bit hesitantly, but this time you will surely expect him to return it back within a specific timeframe. But what if he asks for 100,000, what will you do? Would you lend him that too? No, you will most probably lie about not having the money even if you have it. I can still go one if you want but I hope that you must have gotten my point by now. So, now I ask you, who would you, value more?" Her question made me think.

Her explanation knocked some sense into me. She was right in her place. I might have done the same. I told her exactly that and we talked a little about our lives and I hung up the phone.

I was exactly back to square one. I had two strong cases but I only had to decide one side. I felt like a judge in the courtroom. Both the prosecutors had very validly presented their cases and were now expecting me to decide on the verdict. I needed some more evidences, consultations and time. I picked up my cell phone and thought of asking the same from another person. I wanted that this next person be someone who has had some experience in life and the first person that came to my mind was my uncle Padmarao, a very close family relative. Without any second thoughts, I gave him a call.

"When I was at an earning age, my primary choice was money, but I'm regretting it now. I think I valued it more than relationships and I am not very happy about it" He explained in a very low voice.

"What changed the opinion, what made you to do so? Please brief me, uncle." I pleaded.

"When I was working in America in my late 40's, I was earning quite well on my job. My parents wanted me to find a job in my hometown so that I could stay with them. They never asked for it directly though. But I refused to go back as my life was luxurious and comfortable there with my wife, children and their future.

I flew back to India, when my father passed away. I saw my mother break down into tears. After all the rituals were completed, I asked my wife and children to leave as they had their respective businesses. I thought of traveling back later with my mother, but she refused to come with me. I flew back to my family, but couldn't stay for long. The thought of leaving my mom all alone kept hurting me more day by day. I told my wife that I wanted to go back and stay in India for the rest of my life but she didn't agree because she didn't want to leave her children and come.

I knew her decision was quite rational. Who would want to leave their children, after all? I stayed confused for a very long time, in the dilemma whether I should go back or stay here. I finally decided to go back and stay with my mom.

After a couple of years, my children got busy with their own lives. It was then that my wife came back to live with me. All the while I was with my mom; I realized how bad a son I had been to leave her in the first place. No mother is ever happy to stay away from their children. Parents' staying with children in their old age is not a culture in America. Even if I wanted to stay with my children, I couldn't. Now it's only me and your aunt here. We have all the money that we need but miss being with our children. That's why I believe having people around you is more important than money or anything else."

I felt a little down after listening to uncle's story. It startled me a little. He always looked so happy. I never expected that he would feel this lonely and regretful. I recalled every time I saw him smile. Now I understood why his eyes always gleamed. They weren't tears of joy but tears of pain —pain of being away from his family.

"I'm so sorry Uncle Shankar, if my question disturbed you", I apologized.

"No Adi, that's okay, you're like my son. You can always ask me for anything" He said.

"Adi, always remember what I am about to tell you. Money can fetch you many technologies which will minimize the distance between countries, but you cannot buy the true essence of a relationship with these phone calls and video calls."

"Thanks for those wise words uncle, I will always remember them." I hung up the call.

There were a thousand thoughts that went around in my mind that night. Ilyas and Uncle were on one side but what made each of them pick relationships was different. On the other end, what Mano said was completely practical too. I couldn't sleep when I still had no answer to that question.

The next day, I walked into Ekalavya and waited for Shree and Tinu to walk-in. My head felt heavy and I wanted to sleep as I hadn't got any proper sleep last night. I just put down my head on the desk and rested. While I was almost slipping into sleep, I heard the sound of the door opening.

The man who entered the room was the same because of whom I now have this headache. I had never in my life felt this restless all because of one simple question. I felt like slapping him if he asked me the answer for it.

"Hey Adi, You look very fresh and happy. Looks like you had a very good night's sleep last night", he asked with a sarcastic look on his face. Initially, I felt like slapping him but then felt killing him would be more appropriate. The man was out outright mocking me.

"Yes, last night was the best sleep of my life, Idiot," I said with fury.

I wasn't going to be the one to initiate the conversation about that stupid question of his. I didn't want him to know what I had gone through last night. I wanted him to be the one to bring up the subject. I waited till the noon but he didn't bring it up. We talked about many things and played games, but the topic never came up.

"You guys proceed to the cafeteria; I will join you in 5 minutes." Tinu said as she was in between an important game with another colleague of ours.

"Sir, do you need a vegetarian or a Non-vegetarian meal?"

Every Wednesday, we would have chicken curry. The menu and the way we stood in line always reminded me of a jail's scene in the movies.

"Non-vegetarian sir," I said.

We collected our meals and Tinu joined us with her homemade meal that she occasionally brought in her pink lunchbox. Shree and I hated that color. Tinu and I started a discussion regarding different projects and stuff, until Shree finally spoke up.

"Hey Tinu, can I ask you a question?" I knew what was coming next.

"Sure, Shree," she said.

"If you were to choose from money or human relationships, what would you pick? Take your time and let me know your answer tomorrow."

"Poor Tinu" I thought in my mind.

"Why does that need a full day of time to answer? It is simple, I don't know", she replied smartly.

Shree just smiled and tried changing the topic.

"How come you don't have an answer for that question?" I didn't want her to simply escape from the question after what I had gone through to find an answer to that.

"Adi, we can't have answers for everything in this world. Not because we don't want to, but because a yes or no isn't enough to answer them. You and I might answer the same question differently because our back stories are different. We can only have opinions. And opinions vary from person to person, birthing more confusion and madness. Just because I have an opinion about something doesn't make it the answer. Opinions only result in dispute sand rivalries as we have our own experiences that caused us to think in a certain way." She replied and left the place to attend a phone call.

"Wow!!" For a moment, I stayed in shock. What Tinu had said wasn't something that just came to her mind. She had justified her point and left me wondering why people around me were so strange. Why didn't they have a simple outlook on things like me?

"Adi, did that answer your question?" He finally asked.

"It depends on the context." was the answer which I have given him, expecting that was the safest thing to say.

His expressions changed.

"So, I should assume that you too are like other people in this world. Who change their ethics based on the circumstances?"

Was he insulting, scolding or telling to me that I was stupid? I couldn't really judge form his comment. It could be any of them or all three; again, I had no idea. I looked at him blankly, waiting for an explanation for that abrupt accusation.

"Please, don't take my remark seriously. I just blabbed it out without thinking. I think everyone should have an opinion and I am glad that you have one too. Whether you choose money or relationships, it isn't my call to make, it's yours. I believe blaming a situation because of our own activities so that we can come out of them, thinking of ourselves as winners or losers doesn't make sense. We are all accountable for the things that happen to us whether we accept it or not. This is my subjective opinion and it need not to be objective." He closed with his short yet strong words for me.

"I agree with you Shree, but if we try to follow the ethics in the current world we live in, we will be exploited all the time. People will change their opinions when it comes to their ego and survivability. They change the moment they see us in our most vulnerable state. They run away so that they don't have to be the one to pick up the pieces or become a shoulder to cry on. "

"So, if we keep changing our ethics as per our comfort, what is the point of having them?"

"I don't know." That small conversation with Shree forced me to think.

"The reason most people change their ethics is because they want to show everyone that they are superior to them. They do so that they can supersede them. If you have ever observed a conversation between two people, you won't find it hard to interpret that both of them are trying to show the other that they are better. There is always a hidden war of ego going on. Like right now, both of us are trying to prove our points, secretly wishing that the other would just give up and believe in whatever you believe in, isn't it?

The discussion went for long but did not reach any conclusion.

MOST MEMORABLE DAY

"Shall we meet tonight at my place?" I asked.

"Why? Is something special happening?" Shree glazed.

"My family is out of town and I want to taste alcohol". I said with a sense of half excitement and half fright. I was excited because I had never tried alcohol before and afraid because I didn't want to get caught.

"You drink?" he asked with his eyes open wide.

"No, I have never. I just want to try once."

His pose of thinking reminded me of a scientist who was struggling to invent medicine for AIDS. He stayed in that pose for less than a minute before finally agreeing to come. I wasn't expecting him to say yes. I didn't have any idea he would be as elated with the idea as I was.

"Cool, walk-in at my home at 8:00 p.m.?" I was thrilled.

"Sure". He confirmed the time.

"What are you guys talking about?" We jumped a little as we heard a familiar voice just coming from inches away from where we stood. What made us more alarmed was the fact that both of us did recognize the voice well. It was Tinu. We turned our heads to greet her, but more importantly measure the distance between ourselves so that we can be sure she hadn't overheard our conversation.

"When did you walk in?" I asked, being a little despondent.

"Just now, you guys were busy discussing something about 8:00 p.m.," she said very calmly.

Seeing her expressions, we both relaxed a bit. I didn't want her to know about our plan because we had no clue whether she was going to like it or not.

"So what are you planning at 8:00 p.m. today?" she asked.

"Nothing much, we are planning to do a case study together at Adi's place" Shree said with an inexplicable expression on his face. I always thought Shree was not very good at double-dealing but this reason had confirmed me that.

"Oh, okay" she said very normally. I felt relaxed. I had no other choice to stand for the same thing. She seemed convinced surprisingly. I and Shree looked at each other and a mischievous smile crossed our faces. We had so easily fooled Tinu, which seemed like an impossible task to many.

On my way home, I stopped by the liquor store to shop for the brand names I was familiar with but had never really tried before. I was nervous about bumping into some familiar faces which was the reason why I kept my head all the while I was in the store. I didn't want them to judge me on the choices I made.

"Can I get some alcohol?" I kept my voice low as I headed for the counter. I couldn't decide on my own what to get so I thought the man behind the counter might help me out a little. If I were going to spend my money on it, I better get something of worth was the only thought that circulated in my head.

"What kind of alcohol do you need?" he was in a rush and I stayed silent for a moment.

"Beer, whisky, Brandy, Ram, Gin, Vodka what you need?" he became impatient. I was struggling between whisky and beer. I needed more time but the look on the counter man's face told me I didn't have much.

"Whisky" I finally said and he kept looking at me without fringing even a little bit.

"Which brand?"

Oh, now I had to answer that to. It wasn't like Shree and I hadn't done our research, it was just that I couldn't recall any names then. My mind went all blank. Maybe it was the fear of getting caught or the counter boy was just too intimidating.

"Jameson, Jack Daniel....." he started listing down the names in his frustrated voice.

"Ah, the Jameson," he fetched a bottle from the rack behind him. It was in a dark shade of green that looked really cool with the seal and everything.

"So you need that with soda or soft drinks?" I hadn't thought of that either. I started to think again, hoping he will help me out in any way to get rid of me.

"Try it with soft drink first, then you can try on rocks and neat later." I had no idea what he just said.

"Okay, get me coke" I finally uttered.

"3500 rupees," he told me with a sense of relief.

Wait, what? Even my car's oil didn't cost that much for a whole month and I was here, buying a drink for just one night. But now wasn't the time to change my decision. The man on the counter was eager to get rid of me and he made no effort to hide it. I took out the cash from my wallet and placed it on the counter. Meanwhile, the shopkeeper wrapped the bottle in a plastic bag and handed it to me. I collected the package, started my car and drove home.

Once home, I ordered a few chicken starters from a nearby restaurant.

I took out two anchor hocking rocks old-fashioned drink ware from kitchen, couple of forks to pluck the food, few plates and coke. I arranged everything in my room on the floor. Once done, I waited for Shree to ring the doorbell as it was almost 8.

At around 8:15 p.m., the doorbell finally rang. I walked to the porch and opened the door with a sense of excitement.

"Hello" she said. I went blank and my jaw dropped down.

"Tinu Hi, what are you doing here?" I asked her, blocking the entry-way completely so that's she wouldn't barge in.

"Umm, can I come in?" She asked me in her most genuinely sweet voice. I wanted to say no, but couldn't. I stepped away to make way for her. I knew the moment she saw the whiskey bottle, I me and Shree will be busted but it was too late for that now. She was already in my house and nearing my room. As she walked by, inspecting my house, she continued to make small talk.

"So, is Shree still not coming?" she sunk in into the couch in the TV lounge, making herself at home. I felt a bit relived that she had ended her journey on the couch.

"He is, but he is running a bit late." I was still standing near my bedroom door.

A few minutes later, Shree walked in. His smiling expressions changed the moment he saw the petite figure on the couch, scrolling through some fashion magazine that were placed in the centre table's lower compartment a few minutes ago.

He gave me a perplexed look. His eyes asked a thousand questions, most of them revolved around why the hell was Tinu in the house? Did I invite her? If yes, what was wrong with me? Was I in my senses? What were we going to do now? Had I already told her about our drinking expedition tonight? The list went on and on and I had to look away so that he would stop intimidating me. Sensing the odd silence in the room, Tinu looked up and smiled to find Shree standing by the main door with a few plastic bags in his hand. The odd quietness prevailed and thankfully Shree decided to break the ice by greeting us both.

We both responded instantly but in completely different tones. Tinu's was calm and composed and mine sounded like someone was trying to choke me.

"So, How much did your case study cost?" she finally inquired. This time, her voice was high-pitched and every little once of sweetness had vanished from it. She had overhead the conversation outside the office. She just hadn't told us until now. And we two had been laughing at our little accomplishment how we had fooled her with our made up story. Had she not been angry right now, we were sure she would have mocked us for thinking that we had doped her. We both froze. She stood there eyeing us with both her hands on her waist, like a mother how had just caught her two little kids eating from the cat's bowl. We had no other option than to come clean about it.

"3500 bucks." I finally gathered the courage to speak.

"How did you even think of doing this?" She started. I thought she did not like what we had planned. My head was down looking at the floor and so was Shree's.

"There is no wrong in drinking, but without me... is insane". Shree and I exchanged looks. Neither of us expected that answer from her. We were both individually concocting excuses in her mind to fool her, this time with some solid excuse. The absurdity of the situation made us all three crack. We all started laughing together.

"How did you know about this?" I asked with a sense of confusion.

"The guys who waste all the time in the world at office, how can they think of doing a case study, that too on late nights?"

"Oh, so Shree's stupid excuse gave you a clue" I said and looked at him blaming for everything.

"Shree's reason caught my attention there was something fishy going on. I had my guesses but none of them included alcohol. I would have never guessed, had I not used your machine today before leaving work as mine had hanged up. I went through your browser history for some file only to discover that you had done quite an awful research on alcohol earlier this evening.

"We both are stupid, aren't we?" I asked him.

"Oh don't even have any doubts about it." She laughed.

I felt a bit awkward to have my first-ever drink with a girl, but then again, they were my closest of friends and that one fact was enough to make me glad.

"Why can't we just start?" she said with much more excitement than both of us. She was unpredictable, that I knew, but this unpredictable, that, I hadn't anticipated. We sat down with our glasses, drink and coke, in hope of getting our appetizers soon too. We had camped in the TV lounge. It didn't feel right to invite Tinu into my bedroom. It would have been a different matter if it had been only me and Shree, but with Tinu, we wanted to keep things more sophisticated. We promised each other that each of us will only drink one glass as we didn't want to wake up with a severe hangover tomorrow morning. We were just making random conversation about office colleagues that the door bell rang.

We all froze. There was a chance that my parents were back early. The thought itself was enough to run cold shivers down my spine, if there was anyone home I feared the most, it was my father's anger. I had seen him lose his temper only a couple or more times in the past, but when he did, every wall in the house shuddered. If he knew what I was up to just now, he wasn't going to be very pleased about it.

The doorbell rang for the second time.

Adi... go!

Tinu poked me back into reality.

"Are your parents home early? But you said they won't be back until late."

"I don't know it could be them! They did say they would be late. Hurry, hide everything.

"Where?"

Shree finally spoke. His face has turned an odd color. He was freaking out like I was. Maybe, he knew if we were caught drinking with a girl, he too might be in trouble.

"Just cleanup everything from the lounge. Don't leave anything that might make them suspicious."

"Got it!"

"Tinu, you take the whiskey bottle into Adi's room, I will handle the rest."

But where to hide it in his room? Tinu was up and running with the bottle in her hand, asking for instructions on her way to my room.

We all were panicking, like a bunch of headless chickens bumping into each other, waiting for instructions.

"Hide them anywhere where they won't be found. Under the bed, behind the cushions, in the cupboard... you just figure it out, okay?" I couldn't come up with one single place.

"From which shelf did you take out the glasses?"

"Second, third... no, I think the fourth. Jezz, how am I supposed to remember? Just put those out of sight and no one will know."

Shree was obviously asking stupid questions.

I started heading for the door, mentally preparing myself for what was to come, even if my dad and mother didn't suspect anything odd, I was sure my sister would. She had an odd instinct about such things. Before twisting the door knob, I paid one last look behind.

Tinu came out of my room with my laptop in her hand. She jumped on the couch and landed in time to avoid falling onto the floor. She positioned herself comfortably and opened the screen of the laptop as if inquisitively looking for something. Smart move, I thought myself. In the next second, Shree was there on the couch too. Everything was back to normal, at least it seemed that way.

With trembling hands, I finally twisted the door knob and prepared myself to face my biggest nightmare: my dad's anger.

"Hello sir, here is your order." A petite-looking man with an even squeakier voice than his physique greeted me with a big smile on his face. The boy didn't look a day older than 25, wore a uniform with a hat and held my chicken wings order in a shopping bag with the restaurant's logo on it. I let out a sigh of relief, which reminded me that I had held my breath since the last minute. I moved a little forward to collect my food package and paid the bill.

"Thank you sir, enjoy your meal". He turned back and started towards his bike. I closed the door behind him without waiting another second. We could have been busted big time but thankfully we weren't. But just for extra precaution, I switched off the lights of the living room on my way back to avoid suspicion. It took us about five minutes to retrieve all those items we so haphazardly had hidden.

After we were all settled, Tinu poured the whiskey in put glasses. It was in a rich golden shade. I dropped three ice cubes in each of the glasses so that they could be as chilled as possible by the time we drank them. My very first thoughts were how horrible it smelled; it smelled of raw honey.

The glass still had some room before it was filled to the brim. To that, Shree added coke.

We all shared a *"cheers"* moment as we clinked our glasses against each other's carefully. We all counted till three and took the first sip. The very next second we all had our tongues out and a "yuck" cry. It tasted horrible even with coke. We all grabbed a chicken wing to get rid of that uncanny flavor in our mouth. Fortunately, the chicken wings subdued the effect with its tanginess and sticky flavorsome sauce. So this was how liquor tasted. I wondered why people were so mad about it. It didn't taste *that* good, I thought to myself. But since we had purchased the whole bottle and that too by wasting a lot of money, we weren't going to let it go into the dishwasher or bathroom sink. Besides, it was the first time we had tried it. Maybe the flavor got better after a few sips. With the help of a few more chicken wings on the side, I completed my first round of whiskey and felt it kick in my head.

"Hey, what excuse did you give your parents to leave home at this hour?" Shree asked Tinu.

"I told them that I will be working on a case study with my office colleagues." She said and laughed.

"You are crazy." Shree commented.

We couldn't wait to refill our glasses with the now-so-tasty concoction. After my second glass of whiskey, I felt like going to the restroom. I excused myself, got up and started to walk only to find that I couldn't. I could see the path clearly but my feet declined to receive the signals sent by my brain. I was unable to walk straight. That feeling of being out of control was awesome. I sat down once again and filled my glass with more whiskey, coke, and ice. Shree followed suit and Tinu too, after a little while. We all sat in complete silence until Tinu finally spoke: correction, she shouted.

"Why is everyone so quiet?"

"Tinu, don't scream! We are in an apartment. People will hear you and they will think that we brought you here without your consent. Please, I don't want the neighbors to come complaining to my mum tomorrow, saying that strange voices came from our apartment the last night. Keep it down please." I tried to calm her down; she was obviously very drunk.

"Then let's talk something interesting," she couldn't even make out the words right, but did she stop her gibberish? No! Sensing my panic, Shree tried to calm her down.

"Tinu please, Adi will get in trouble if you don't keep it down."

"Okay, I will whisper. Is it okay now?" She lowered her to an extent that it was almost impossible to hear what she said. She kept a finger on her mouth, gesturing that she fully understood what we wanted. She looked so funny that way. I always thought that she was so cool being herself, but watching her like this was way cooler and funnier too.

"Let's talk about love affairs, shall we?" she whispered, looking at Shree.

"Hahaha, Tinu do you think this fellow will ever have a girl in his life?" I remarked sarcastically.

"Hahaha you are correct, Adi" she laughed out loud.

"Divya," he said intently.

We all shared a momentarily pause amongst ourselves. I couldn't really deicide if part of that silence was because we were shocked to hear a girl's name from him or because when he said the name, his eyes were filled with tears. Before we could make out the tense situation, Shree burst into tears and hid his face in Tinu's lap. It all happened so sudden, that neither I nor Tinu had the chance to react. He continued to sob, louder by the minute until Tinu finally came back into reality and started to console him. He looked quite tired as if he was about to sleep. Besides, he had more to drink than the two of us, so we thought it was best that he slept. I stood up and walked to the kitchen. I still stumbled while walking, but I wasn't as drunk as the two of them. I thought it would be best that they both ate something. I took out the dish from the fridge, placed it in a microwaveable plate and put it in the microwave for three minutes. I got lost in a few thoughts until the beeper brought me back. I placed the dish onto a tray and put it on the carpeted floor where all three of us sat.

I had to feed them as they both weren't in the condition to eat themselves. Once done, I insisted that Tinu slept in my parent's room. She wasn't in a condition to drive herself home and even if she were, her parents would have been angry seeing her all drunk. After I made the bed for her, I came back to pick up Shree and we both rested in my room.

HIS BREAK-UP

I could feel the first few rays of sunlight peeking into my room. But my eyes felt too heavy. It felt like someone had put a grave burden on them. My head hurt bad too as if I had hammed it against the wall all night long. Every cell in my body was moaning with pain and my stomach growled like I hadn't eaten for days. It was the weirdest I had ever felt all my life.

It took all my strength to just open my eyes and the moment I did; I was poked by the harsh lighting of the sun. I immediately covered my face with my palms and gradually removed it from my face one finger at a time. I sat down on the bed, just looking around myself. Everything looked like floating in the air. I just sat there for a couple of minutes, trying to make sense of my surroundings just listening to my breath.

The first thing I heard was Shree's snoring. He lay beside me, snoring out loud. He looked so peaceful while sleeping. All the worrying wrinkles that he frequently wore on his foreheads were all gone. It was the first time I had looked at him with such inquisition. He was very handsome. No wonder all the girls swooned over him. The very thought brought a smile on my face. Shree always avoided girls. Even when girls were throwing themselves at him, he wouldn't care. I tried getting out of bed and moved my ass to the restroom. I desperately wanted to take a shower as I stank like the whiskey we had last night. Despite its great flavor, the smell was still a little unbearable for me to handle. I got into the shower and took my time just standing under the hot water to drain away the final few effects of the hangover. As soon as I came out, thinking how better I felt, I was instantly reminded of Tinu. She must have had an even severe hangover than I. After all, she had a lot to drink last night.

I rushed to see her room to check if she was okay. The door was half open so I peeked inside. The bed had been made and she was nowhere to be seen. I went inside to check the bathroom and she wasn't there either. I started to panic a little. What if she had left for her home in the middle of the night? It wasn't safe for her to go out on her own, let alone drive. I started running into my room to get my cell phone to check up on her when someone's voice stopped me halfway.

"Adi, here is your coffee" I didn't have to turn around whose voice it was.

"Tinu, don't you have a hangover. Oh god, for a minute I got so worried that you left in the middle of the night?" I asked her holding my cup of coffee.

"Nah, I just got up a little earlier than you. I did feel a bit tipsy for the first 10 minutes but after that, I felt fine." she said it all so causally.

"Are you sure that this is your first time taking alcohol?" I asked her, fully expecting that she would say no.

"Of course, it was. It was the first time I drank alcohol too, idiot" she said.

"Oh, so did you enjoy the last night?"

"It helped me to improve my mood regulations. I even forgot all my worries for some time. So I think I liked it, at least for that moment."

"That sounds disturbing, but it's good that you liked it."

"What is the first thing you remember when you think about last night?" she inquired.

The first thing we both remembered from the last night was someone named Divya. Shree was the one who had mentioned her name. Tinu too had found it strange that Shree was into a girl. Neither of us had seen him ever talking to her or meeting her. Did she really exist? There was only one way to find out. Tinu handed me my coffee and we both walked into my room and we positioned ourselves on the bed beside Shree. We kept murmuring between ourselves, trying to figure out who was Shree talking about. We both had nearly finished our coffee when Shree woke up and found us sitting beside him. I believe it was our mumbling conversation that woke him up. We both instantly stopped talking and smiled at him. He stretched both his arms, exhaling out a long breath.

"Good Morning!!" He said with a smile.

"Very Good Morning!!"

"So, who is Divya?" Tinu asked right away. She didn't even give him a minute to compose himself properly. She was obviously much more curios than me. Hearing Divya's name, I saw Shree's muscles instantly flex. His eyes widened in response as if he had been caught stealing. For a moment, he went completely blank, unable to move. He took a few more seconds before replying.

"Divya? Who Divya? I don't know any Divya."

"Don't act so smart Shree. You mentioned her name last night and then you started crying like a baby in my lap. Now don't pretend like it is the first time you are hearing her name." Tinu seemed a little irritated that he was straightforwardly acting like he didn't know anyone by that name.

I sensed that he didn't like the way Tinu had reminded him about last night. He obviously felt a little embarrassed. I wouldn't have barged into change the subject as I knew he didn't feel comfortable talking about it, but before I could, Shree replied.

"I can't talk anything about her now, please don't ask me guys." Saying that he fell back on the bed and covered his face with the blanket. I wanted to let go of the subject because he wasn't ready to disclose his personal life just yet. But Tinu wasn't the kind of the girl who would let it go. She reached for his mobile phone from the side table and started to scroll down the contact's list.

"Fine, don't tell me, I will ask your mother about it. Hi Aunty. Does Shree have any friend whose name is Divya?"

She pretended like she was on the phone with his mother. Knowing her, she could have done it in real too. Shree obviously believed her and instantly pulled off the duvet from his face and reached out for his phone to hang up.

"Fine, I will tell you, I promise, just hang up the phone." Tinu was fast and before Shree could even reach for the phone, she had jumped from the bed and was now standing by the bed post.

"Please Tinu…" he pleaded.

She pretended to cancel the call and handed the phone to me, I didn't know why she did that. I looked at the call log. She had dialed a number but it wasn't of Shree's mom, it was her own. Well, good for her I thought, she had at least gotten him to promise that he would tell us about Divya.

"Okay!! If you guys want me to tell you the story I have one condition." He said with a tone of disappointment.

"Anything you say?" we both spoke at once.

"I opened up that secret while I was drunk, so let me tell the rest whole story when I'm drunk again." At first, I thought that was a strange request to make. I would not have known whether I was able to drink again and wake up with a hangover like the one I had in the morning, but I couldn't do anything because in that very exact moment, Tinu left the room. It was odd, I thought, she didn't like the idea, but leave us like this without saying a word, seemed highly unlike Tinu.

"Hey Mom" I heard her saying that over the phone.

"The case study is not yet done. I will be coming back home tomorrow. Will that be okay?"

She asked in such a soft and made up tone that it was impossible to say no to anything she asked. If it had been my daughter who had asked me for the world in that tone, I swear, I would have brought it for her.

"I'm good for tonight again." she said with a smile which showed how excited she was to hear the story about Divya. How wrong had I been about her? A minute ago, I was already cooing up with ways to apologize to her about Shree's condition and there he was, lying to her mother about a case study that didn't even have a name or origin and getting away with it. The next thing I knew, Tinu was up for drinking again.

I did not expect that she would be thinking to drink again. I liked my first drinking experience. But Tinu was a girl. Even after such advancement in our society, a girl's drinking was still considered a taboo. But Tinu was different. There were so many layers to her that I and Shree still had to uncover. Another thing that I realized after my first drinking experience was that that once it started to kick in, it was almost impossible to stop. No wonder, it was seen as an addiction. The people who initially thought drinking is not good for health, after consuming it they change their statement to "drinking within limits is not a problem."

We were all set for one more night again.

"Divya was my classmate in my under graduation." He started after our first round then he continued.

"I liked her at the very first glance, the moment I laid my eyes on her, she was magnificent. But it was only her physical appearance that I admired. I didn't have a clue about her behavior and personality. I initiated the friendship as I wanted to know more about her. It was love for me all this while. When I could no longer suppress my feelings for her, I finally decided to confess my love for her. With the help of one of her friend, I finally arranged a meet up with her. It was the best night of our lives. We talked about so many things our likes and dislikes. I came to know that she wasn't a lot different than I. We both shared the same taste in music, we both agreed on the importance of healthy eating and fitness, we both even lived close by. After a few more meet ups and several speechless night of chatting, I finally gathered up the courage to tell her how I felt about her, I was sure she felt the same way as she had given me all the signs too."

"I Love You Divya." I told her on her birthday. There wasn't much hesitation in my mind; I believed that the answer I would guess be a yes.

"Why do all the boys always land up on love with their friends?" she sounded upset.

"Why can't we just be as friends?" Divya said with lot of displeasure.

"Divya, I never told you that I wanted to be our friend. My intentions from the beginning were that of love. I thought you already knew that." I responded very firmly, she was shocked and paused for a moment.

"Then why did you act like a good friend to me all this time?" she asked me.

"As I said I was in love right from the beginning, I was talking to you and spending time with you to know you better and giving you a chance to know me better." I thought I made my point pretty clear.

"Divya, just because I didn't express my feelings on the first night we met, doesn't mean that I didn't love you. Just because I didn't say so doesn't mean that I didn't feel it. And just because I didn't say it, does it mean that it can only be friendship? Didn't you see my love in all my gestures, the way I looked after you and cared for you? Did you, not for once, think that I was doing it out of love and not friendship? How can you count friendship as a default relationship if people just talk to you? Which, by the way is probably is the toughest relationship to express and maintain.

She didn't reply to that. She didn't have anything to say. She just sat in front of me and requested that I give her some more time to think about it. It was fine by me. The very next day, she accepted my proposal and we started dating each other. We spent the most amazing three years of our lives together. We both completed our under graduation program by then.

Soon after the graduation, she decided to pursue her Master's degree from the U.S.A. I felt I cannot live without her so I applied to the same university in Omaha state too. We rented a single bedroom flat and started lived together. We were in an intimate relationship for the first semester until things started to go bitter between us. There was an imbalance in our relationship. She started arguing. A majority of the times, it was her fighting with me over unnecessary things. I started to feel like she deliberately picked up a fight every now and then and it wasn't like her at all. I tried convincing her that I will change for her and become exactly like she wanted me to be. And I did change. But even then, things remained the same between us, we kept on fighting about little thing and arguing every now and then. We rarely talked.

One day, she moved out of the apartment and started sharing an apartment with a friend of hers. I felt alone in the apartment. I tried hard to convince her to come back but all my trails failed. She stopped returning my calls, didn't reply to my text and avoided meeting me. One day I came to know that she planned a sudden trip to India and got married to some guy, and moved to another university. I was shocked and hurt. I thought she just needed some time; a little break from us so that we both can sort out our difference, but hearing this broke me from within. It all happened so quickly that I didn't even have the time to react. The woman for whom I had left everything, loved to an unfamiliar state just so that I could be close to her had married someone else without even looking back once. I just wanted to know why? So I wrote her a message. She simply responded saying her parents found a nice and rich guy whom she didn't want to miss out on. I did not feel worthy to even reply back to that message.

Is Money that important than Human Relationships? Do people do anything for money?"

I could feel the pain in his voice when he repeated that question. The first time, he had asked me that, I knew it just wasn't out of the blue. There had to be something much deeper. Now I understood.

"At that moment when I was all alone, I remembered my mother crying on the day I was travelling to USA. I thought I was really stupid to move there for love and money. They weren't more important that my family. I packed my bags, travelled back to India, and shared everything with my parents. They were angry at the beginning but took it lightly. After I came out of that mood, I started searching for jobs and I landed up with you guys." Shree took a breath after blurting it all out.

As long as he spoke there was not even a single question or words from us. It was a different Shree I saw on that day.

IT's HER BIRTHDAY

"Hey Adi, would you like to go out for lunch with me like old times?" Nandini asked me. I was being a bit tedious with her about my stuff and I was aware of it.

"Yes! Sure, let me know if you have any venue decided for lunch?"

"Let's go to our regular place." She said with a smile. I nodded and picked up my wallet and car keys.

Would you like take your own car or would you like to in mine? I just wanted to be sure that she still felt comfortable with in my car like old times. Besides, she loved to drive, so I didn't want to give her the impression that I wanted to drive. If she wanted to, I was fine with it too.

"Can we take your bike?" she surprised me with that answer. I didn't recall the last time I had ridden my bike. It was parked in the garage for I didn't even remember how long; all I knew was that it must have been covered in all sorts of dirt and rust. I didn't even know if it would start now. But since she had made a request I didn't want to disappoint her. As expected, it was parked in the garage, covered in layers of dirt that hid its actual color. The look had most probably disappointed her. If I had been in her place, I would have insisted going in her car as I would have made an estimate as this was how she kept all her things.

"Do you still want to ride it?" I asked with a sought of question.

"Yes", she said.

Before starting the bike, I poured some water into it, applied a degreaser on some overly-dirty areas, wiped it off with a rug, sprayed the bike using a pressure pump to ensure no stain or dirt marks remained on it and lastly, wiped it one last time with a clean dry cloth this time to ensure it was all set to seat me and her. Once done, I glanced at my efforts and felt a bit proud of myself. The bike looked like it had just been purchased from a Honda Showroom. I then looked at Nandini, secretly hoping that she would complement me over it but she just smiled back and I thought that was enough. I started the bike, seated myself on it and waited for her to join me.

She sat at the back putting her both hands on my shoulders. That touch brought back so many memories with it. A lot had changed since then but her hand on my shoulder just reminded me, things weren't that different after all.

We reached our favorite spot, where we used meet and have our food back in college days. As soon as we entered, the restaurant manager smiled at us, which meant he remembered the both of us.

"What can I get for you to drink, sir?" A young waiter greeted us.

"Water without ice for both of us" She said. He placed the menu card in front of us. She didn't even look at the menu once. I had a feeling that she had already decided what she was going to order.

"Here is your water sir, Are you ready to place an order, Ma'am?" he asked.

"Yes please. Can we get two garlic naans with butter chicken, one vegetable biryani and two butterscotch ice creams later?" she said. That was the usual menu we used to have in the past. I was quite impressed and delighted that she still remembered the food we ate.

"You know what Adi? I see a different person in you. The Adi I knew was always fashionable".

"Fashionable?" I inquired. That word seemed a bit odd to describe someone.

"Yes, fashionable. Back then, you gave a lot of attention to your appearance even when you were about to go for a bath, but look at you now! You came in tracks without even adjusting your hair. Looks like you are least bothered about it now." She said with a lot of surprise. May be this is what she was expecting from me.

"Shiva made me realize that there is nothing in appearance. What matters is the way you think." I said.

"How did he do this to you?" she was fascinated to know. She continued.

"You still haven't told me about Shiva. I'm eagerly waiting to know who he is and how was he able to transform you into a different person altogether."

"I can straight away tell you who is he and our journey together but I want you to know why I was so attached to him and why I'm not able to digest the fact that he is not with me anymore. Until and unless you knew the circumstances of what led to all of it, you won't be able to approximate the impact he had on me or on my life.

"Okay, I will wait for that, but I'm very curious to know who this Shiva is?" she said.

"Here you go sir, your order is ready". He served us the biryani first which tasted like it used to a year ago.

"So, what are you up to these days?" I asked her.

"After completing 6 months of job, my parents suggested that I pursue MBA in Pune. I did, although the experience wasn't worth remembering. I had to stay in a hostel until I completed my degree and then I joined a company as HR."

"Are your parents living with you in Delhi now?" I asked.

"No, they are in Hyderabad, they moved there recently. I just travelled down to spend some time with them. I will be going back in a week."

"Oh that's good for you. Are you engaged?" I asked very casually. Deep within, I was frightened to the core.

"What do you think?" she asked.

"I hope not" I said.

"What makes you so confident about that?"

"If you were married, you would have not visited me late night that day, and I didn't notice you speaking with anyone over the phone since morning, which as far as I know or have seen, is the first thing women do when engaged or married. You know the whole "good morning" cute stuff thingy. These were the two points which made me guess that you are not engaged."

"Hahahaha, you got me Adi, you are right, I am not." She said and made a sad face. Only she didn't know how happy it made me inside. But then again who knew, she could be seeing someone. Maybe they weren't exclusive or anything, but there was a possibility that there was someone in her life, if not right now, then perhaps a crush. That question just flushed all the happiness I felt a minute ago.

"I'm just waiting for the right person to come in my life. Nothing dreamy or anything, but you know just someone who would understand me." She said very simply by not even looking at me.

She then looked away towards another table, where a guy was celebrating his girlfriend's birthday. The couple looked the same age as us and the way the guy was caring for the girl made Nandini smile. I reckoned, like every other girl, she too wanted her fairytale. She may never confess it outright but she did.

"Adi, do you remember how you celebrated my birthday?" She asked.
"Yes I do."

The very thought took me back a year ago, when I came to know about her birthday, just a week before her big day. It was on December 3rd which left me with exactly 7 days to plan something for her. I had never exercised my brain as hard before just so that I could come up with a decent gift for her. It wasn't like I had trouble coming up with things that she might like; the hard part was to decide what to go with.

2nd December, finally arrived.

I informed my parents that I will be going over at Ilyas's place for combine studies and will be back in the morning. I left from home in my car at 11:00 p.m. and parked it in front of Nandu's hostel at about 11:40 p.m. From within my car, I dialed her number.

Ring, ring, ring, ring, ring.

She picked it up on the fourth ring.

"Hello" her voice sounded like she was about to sleep or perhaps had already been sleeping.

"Hi Nandu, can you come out, I'm waiting at your hostel gate." I told her.

"Are you really? Okay, I'm coming down in 10 minutes. " she sounded a little excited. The blaring horn, squealing break and the revving engine sound was all turned down. For as long as the eye could see, the hostel's parking area was filled with immense darkness with only the sound of the cold wind crashing against the hostel's walls and the big old trees surrounding it.

"Hey, where are we going?" she asked me while crossing the road. She was wearing a blue jeans, a red color t-shirt and had a white scarf wrapped around her neck.

"It's a surprise, get in the car", I said. It was awesome driving on the lonely dark roads with her. It took me 30 minutes to reach a mid-night restaurant. Leaving the car at the entrance to the attendant for parking, we proceeded in.

The restaurant's ceiling was decorated in electric lights, depicting a starry night. It had been my idea. I knew Nandini was a fan of starry nights and wished she could count every star in the galaxy. I couldn't give her that, so I decided to set up a theme that would showcase my effort a little. With contrasting tables and balloons on the floor, to me, it looked like the perfect setup. It was just the two of us in the restaurant that night. I wanted to make it the most special night for her and the decorations and artwork were just the start. I pulled out the chair for her and lit the scented candle in the middle of the table. I then signaled a waiter and requested the special menu card to be presented to the lady. Hearing the word *special*, Nandini had looked up in excitement. She was feeling overwhelmed with the decorations. The waiter returned with the menu in his hands with a red bow on its cover. He handed it over to Nandu.

"I already had my dinner Adi. I don't even have any space in my tummy." She said holding the menu card.

"No, you have to order something. Just look into the menu and order something." I said a little firmly, giving her a clue that there was something hidden in the menu. Looking at the menu card, her eyes opened wide and then she gave a big smile "*seriously*". That Menu card was made by me that read.

ITEMS
Gift – 1   The very common procedure for birthday's, but in a different style for you.
Gift – 2   A gift of my choice which you may like or dislike
Gift – 3   A reel which can bring down happy tears in your eyes
Gift – 4   A toy you love the most.
Gift – 5   A gift which kicks off every day of yours freshly.
Gift – 6   A gift which may hurt you
Gift – 7   A memory to share with me.

"GIFT – 1 please" she requested the waiter.

The waiter signaled a few other waiters standing in the back and within the next minute, they pulled out a cart with a three –tiered pink cake on it. I had ordered the cake from her favorite bakery in Hyderabad and thankfully, it arrived on time. Maybe it was because I had called the manager of the bakery a thousand times to track the delivery of the cake. Seeing her smile made all the effort worthwhile.

All the restaurant staff gathered around us. The moment she cut the cake, everyone sang the Happy Birthday song. In that instance, her eyes were as bright as a full moon. She cut a piece of cake and insisted that I ate the first piece from her hand. She was the birthday girl after all. It was her day. So, I decided not to argue and let her. I ate half of the piece she was holding in her hand and took and fed her the remaining half.

"Can you please serve the remaining to the staff, sir" I requested the manager. They pulled back the cart and we sat down. Her hands were trembling holding the menu card. She placed it on the table ready for the next order.

"GIFT - 5" she ordered with excitement.

One of the waiters came with a wrapped gift and a small flask in his hands. He handed the gift pack to Nandini and waited for her to open the pack. It was a black coffee mug. She did not understand what was so special about it until the waiter poured in the hot coffee from the flask in it. As soon as it started to heat up, the color of the mug started to change. It turned all white with photos of me and Nandini together appearing on it. A soft tune also played. Seeing that, she was blown away.

She sipped the coffee and held my hand on the table, but didn't speak a word.

"GIFT - 2" she requested next. As soon as she said that, a waitress appeared from the back of the projector but without anything in her hands. A little inquisitive as to what was the gift, she looked at me for a hint.

"What is it?"

"See it for yourself."

"But…"

"Can you walk along with me ma'am?" The waitress asked Nandini. She looked at me and I nodded her to go ahead. After 15 minutes, Nandini walked out of a room in a gorgeous white dress that I had bought for her. The reason I chose that color was because I had seen her the first time in a white dress. That day, she had looked like an angel, but today she glowed in the dress like a star. She now had her hair pinned into one side with a few loose curls at the end. She was wearing light pink smoky makeup which went perfectly with her pearly complexion. Her mascara made her eyelashes even thicker than they already were, giving her a very stunning look.

"You look gorgeous Nandu" I couldn't come up with any other thing to say. Words defied me.

Even if they didn't, I didn't know if there was any way I could put into words how amazing she looked to me that very moment.

"Thank you, Adi."

"GIFT - 4" she ordered and started looking around for them to get something.

After a couple of minutes, two people carrying the big fluffy creamy brown-colored huggable teddy toy came out.

"OMG! What would I do with this?" she asked me.

"Hug it whenever you like to" I said.

She gave the teddy bear a big hug and seated it in the chair next to her. She looked at the menu another time to check which gift she was going to order next.

After a little deliberation between gift 3 and 7, she decided to go with former first.

"Gift 3, please." As soon as she uttered those words, all the lights in the dining hall went out and a video started to play on a projector screen in front of us.

That video was made by me. It was a compilation of her photos right from her childhood till date. I had tuned it with Sufi background music, as I knew she would love it. By the time, the video ended, she was all tears and held my hand as a gesture to say thank you.

"Adi, I can't believe you did all this for me."

"You can keep your thanks for later as there are a few more gifts left on the menu, go on and order something."

"But I don't need more gifts. You have already done so much for me."

"Nandini please, I insist."

"Okay". Wiping an unshed tear from the curve of her eye, she looked into the menu card again.

"GIFT - 7" she said. I stood up from the chair and stretched my hand to hold her hand.

"Now what?"

"Do you trust me?"

"Of course, I do."

"Then just follow me." I further stretched out my hand. Without a second thought, she placed hers in mine and I escorted her to the hotel's entrance. The valet brought me a bike that I rented for a night. We mounted on the bike and went for a ride at 100mph speed to the nearby lake.

"Wow! I have to tell you Adi, I have been here a couple of times before too, but tonight this place looks so much better and brighter. It just feels so good being here like this with you", she confessed while we sat at Necklace Road garden. We spent a good fifteen minutes there, just in abstract silence. I wanted to talk to her about so many things but I didn't want to spoil this odd yet beautiful silence between us. I realized I could spend the whole life with her, just like this, sitting by a lake and staring at her beautiful face.

We made our way back to the restaurant. All my way back, I was thinking only about the one last gift.

"Here is your bill, sir", said the waiter which I heard vaguely. When I didn't respond, Nandini looked up.

"What happened, what were you thinking?" Nandini asked me by tapping my hand. Her touch brought me back to reality. The lovey dovey couple beside us was ordering the check now. We finished our meals and drove back to my place.

HE IS NO MORE

"Wow that was one tasty Hyderabadi biryani. It had been so long since I had it, let alone this good." It was Nandu's way of thanking me.

"Yes, indeed it was really good." I was too full with the eating, that I just sank into the couch. She was right, the biryani was simply out of this world and there was a reason why I took her there. I knew she would love it.

"Adi you are in good state of mind than yesterday, but I still can see signs that you're thinking of Shiva".

She obviously wanted me to open up about Shiva, but I really didn't feel like talking about him at that moment. We just had an amazing time together and I knew that this topic would reap me off this brief happiness I was so comfortably enjoying. I preferred to stay quiet and thankfully, Nandini hinted the hesitation and changed the topic.

"By the way, where are Tinu and Shree these days? Based on what you have told me about them, they seem pretty close friend to you. Don't they visit you when you are feeling lonely?" she asked.

"Shree is no more" I felt wretched within myself saying that. Just the memory of that fact was enough to bring tears to my eyes. Nandini was right; Shree and I had been really close friends until that awful night.

"Oh Adi, I'm so sorry. I didn't know. What happened?" she was shocked hearing that.

"It was just a few days after we all three had our first drinks together. I and Tinu felt really sad after hearing about Shree and Divya. Although a few months had passed since then, I could still see the pain his eyes. And it wasn't just the pain of being cheated. It was a much deeper pain. He had really loved that girl from the core of his heart. He had imagined his whole life ahead with her and then one morning, all those beautiful pictures of their future together became a blur. He was sad, because he was no longer going to have that future with her, mad because she was starting her life with someone else and in pain that she cheated on him.

Why do all painstaking things happen to me? He had sounded really mad. I still don't know whether I will be placed in any of the projects, I can't get her out of my head no matter how much I try and there are so many family issues that I have to look after. Why is life so unfair with me? For once, I just want to forget all that happened and move on, but I just can't. I feel like I am going to be stuck in this pothole for the rest of my life with nowhere to go. Shree said with lot of hiccups, while he cried in Tinu's lap.

"Listen Shree, according to me, no one on this planet is free of troubles." Tinu said in a convincing voice. "Don't tell yourself or me all that shit so that I would feel sympathy for you and console you. Whether we admit it or not, we are all responsible for what happens to us."Hearing that, Shree got a bit irritated but didn't remove his head from Tinu's lap. Tinu started playing with his hair and said.

"Shree, if you ask me, I think none of us have troubles. People only have responsibilities that they are incapable or too fearful of handling. Instead of finding solutions, they prefer taking an out. They run away from them and therefore they begin to seem like troubles.

What she said made more sense to me; I believe Shree also agreed as he didn't have any comeback to counter that statement of hers. Once again, Tinu had me impressed with not just her wittiness but her wisdom. Although, she looked fun and childish most of the times, her philosophy on life was by far the most brilliant. Even Shree was sometimes taken aback by the opinions she had to offer. Right now, I couldn't contemplate if it was her speaking or the liquor she just had.

"You know in your heart that you have to forget her and move on, but you are so convinced that you can't do it that you aren't even trying. Everybody has family issues but only a few face them and clear them out, did you ever make an attempt to clear your family problems? All you need right now is getting yourself enrolled in a project and leave the rest to time. I guarantee it will be taken care of."

Watching these two in that moment I felt really happy. Happy because I had such good friend in life. Friends who genuinely cared about each other. Friends who despite being each other's competition in the office were so different and thoughtful outside the office walls. I couldn't resist the urge to rest my head in Tinu's lap either.

"Aah", she let out a little cry. Both our heads were obviously too much for her little lap to bear.

"Guys, I cannot bear the weight of your two heads anymore, get up." she insisted, but Shree and I had been liking it there so much that we didn't even budge a little.

After a few attempts to push our heads away, she gave up. Seeing her lose made us laugh. We spent the remaining day in my room too. We ordered an early lunch as Shree and I didn't have any breakfast. Then we watched an old comedy movie together and laughed some more. We later discussed our most embarrassing moments in college life and it was a bit hard to believe that Shree was a completely different man back then. Tinu was of course, the usual bubbly, running here and there.

The next morning, I was the first one to wake up. After we all freshened up, cooked ourselves some light breakfast and then I dropped Tinu and Shree at their homes and returned. By the time I returned home, it was almost mid day. All the while, throughout the journey, the memories of last two nights kept me company. I couldn't recall the last time I had this much fun. I also thought about Shree's ex-girlfriend "How nonsensical a girl was Divya to give up on a guy like Shree. I knew that if I ever saw her again, I would give her a tight slap." I kept thinking about Shree and Tinu sensitivities all the day.

As most of the people, I hated Monday mornings. I always felt why Monday was so far from Friday but bloody close to Monday. No projects or training programs were happening at the office. Some days, as I would wake up I would think about skipping office. But then, I was reminded of Shree and Tinu and I would decide otherwise. They became the reason of me not missing out office.

Thinking that, I kicked off my laziness and got dressed for the office. I was a bit late to reach, but no one there cared about that. We just spent the rest of the day recollecting memories of last night.

Everything was going good for a while. Tinu got placed into a project and she became very busy. We both waited on our luck to shine. One rainy night after I reached home, I got straight into the shower. I had been drenched from head to toe. By the time, I came out; I saw a few missed calls from Shree. We had just me half an hour ago; I wondered why he called me and that too, 4 times. I just called back.

"Hello Shree, tell me" I said with a little fear, thinking what made him to call me so many times.

"Hello, I'm a doctor from Care Hospital and your friend has met with an accident. Since your contact was the most recent and frequently dialed, we tried to catch a hold of you" a man on the other end said. His was no joke, his tone was serious.

This was much worse than all my fears. My hands started shaking. I couldn't believe what I had just heard.

"Sir, can you come as fast as possible to the hospital and inform his parents too" he said and hanged up the call.

It felt like the ground beneath me had started shaking or maybe it were my knees that could no longer bear my weight. I dropped down on the carpeted floor of my room in desolation. Then I remembered what the doctor has said, he had instructed that I call his parents too. Without further delay, I called Shree parents and told them all that the doctor has told me. I had remembered every sentence he had spoken to me.

"What are you saying?" Shree's Mom asked in a loud panicked voice.

"I have no clue aunty; please reach the hospital as soon as you can." I said and hanged the phone. I grabbed by car keys and rushed to my parking to get my car out. My phone started flashing again. The call was coming from an unknown number; I didn't feel like receiving it as I wasn't sure what I was going to hear was going to make me happy or sad. "Hello who is this", I finally picked it up.

"Hello, I am a Doctor from the Care Hospital. We are shifting your friend to the Banjara Hills branch. Please come visit him there. We have already informed his parents" he said. I thought I needed to inform Tinu. I had no clue how she was going to take it, but I had to do it, so I called her up.

"Hello Tinu, Shree has met with an accident and he is being taken to Banjara Hills Care Hospital" I said without allowing her to say even hello.

"What? How? When did that happen?" she asked.

"Please don't ask me any questions right now? Just start as soon as possible, okay?" I shouted.

"I will be there in 20 minutes" she said. I reached the hospital waiting for ambulance to arrive. Shree's parents were not there yet. Only I knew how fast I had driven here.

WEEEEOOOOWEEEEOOOO!! When reaching nearer, the sound of the ambulance siren nearly deafened me. I rushed out of the hospital. All the while, my heart kept pounding faster than my feet breaking into a run. I didn't care how everyone looked at me or thought of me, all I cared about was seeing my friend. As soon as I reached the entrance door, I saw the hospital staff open the ambulance door. It was Shree —his white office shirt covered in blood patches. The two male nurses pulled the stretcher and started walking towards me, it was then that I saw that it just wasn't his shirt that was covered in blood; the left side of this head was, too. The stretcher walked passed me. I felt like I no longer had the strength to move my feet for a moment.

"Sir, will you please come with us?"

One of the male nurses, carrying the stretcher called behind me. It was then that my mind finally came back into reality and I turned around and started running once again.

"Shree, I called out to him to make sure he doesn't lose his consciousness.", but he didn't respond to my words, his eyes were half open which meant that he could at least make sense of the surroundings. I continued to tap on his cheek over and over again shouting his name out.

"Shree.... Shree, come on man, wake up... Open your eyes Shree, look at me" my voice was becoming thinner. We were half way to the emergency ward when Tinu joined me in too. I felt a little relieved as I knew she would somehow keep him awake. Although, he didn't respond, but he didn't close his eyes either. Both of us didn't let go of his hand until his stretcher was taken into the ICU ward and the doors closed behind us.

A few minutes later were joined in by Shree's mom and dad. We all sat together outside the ICU theatre, waiting for some news —*any news*. Seeing my clothes covered in blood, his mother almost fell to the ground. As I had held his hand, there were significant patches of his blood on my shirt. I helped her sit up and then rushed to the bathroom. I felt like puking, the image of Shree kept coming back to me. When the doctor has told me on the phone that he had been in a motorbike accident, I hadn't expected it to be this bad. The reason Shree wasn't able to respond as because he had lost so much blood. Once again, the image of him danced in front of my eyes. My hands were red too. I instantly opened the tap and tried cleaning off the blood. I then looked at my own image in the bathroom mirror. I looked wrecked. I busted out crying and fell to my knees. Tears started to flow like water from my eyes.

I don't recall how long I stayed there, just crying until I no longer could. It was then that I was reminded of Tinu. She too, like me, must have been devastated seeing Shree's condition. She was all alone out there, in a desperate need for someone to hold her and tell her that things were going to be fine. I had to be that person. We had to be each other's and Shree's parents strength. I washed my face so that she wouldn't see my crying face and came out of the bathroom, I saw Tinu sitting next to the reception desk all alone with her head down to her knees.

"Tinu" I placed my hand on her shoulder. She stood up, hugged me tight and broke down into tears.

"Don't cry dear, nothing will happen to him, it was just a small accident. He will be okay, don't cry." I consoled her and myself. Four hours, passed and we had no news of him. Many doctors and nurses went in and out of the ICU but they all said that they were doing their best.

There was pin drop silence all around me in the hospital. The silence was frightening. Nobody spoke a word and nobody slept all night. I asked aunty if they needed anything to drink or eat but every time, she refused. Of course, I couldn't force them. I forced Tinu to come along to the hospital cafeteria with me so that she could at least have a cup of coffee and a sandwich if not a full meal.

As we walked into cafeteria, I saw the doctor who was handling Shree's case.

"How is Shree, doctor?" I rushed towards him and couldn't stop myself asking about Shree's condition. Having heard a lot about him, I fully expected him to say that he was going to be fine and recover quickly.

"We cannot say much right now." he said. It nearly broke my heart.

"What happened, actually?" I asked.

"That was a bike accident, where he fell on the construction rocks that were placed on one side of the road for the metro trial construction."

"Why the hell were the rocks placed in the middle of the road?" Tinu shouted. After hearing the doctor's words, both of us didn't fell like eating or drinking anything. Shree's father convinced the both of us to have some lunch and come back in the evening.

I took Tinu to my place; we took a bath, had a cup of coffee and went back to hospital.

Shree was still in the ICU and the doctors still said the same thing. I remember the clock ticking 12.

I fell asleep on the bench near the ICU.

"AhhAhh" I was awakened by someone's weeping. It was Shree's mother who was bawling like a kid and Shree's father and nurse was try-ing to calm her down. I was still a little asleep and couldn't make of the situation until she finally collapsed on the ground. I instantly rushed to her side as Shree's father and the nurse needed some assistance. I landed on the floor beside her, asking the reason behind her cries.

"What happened, Aunty?" I asked her but she didn't respond. I looked at Shree's father to inquire. Although, he did not speak a word, his eyes told me all. Shree was no more.

"My son...my dear son, Shree... the love of my life..." Aunty was crying her eyes out. It looked like she had just lost her senses. And why not, she had just lost her only son in an accident —the only breadwinner of the family.

I looked for Tinu and spotted her standing at a little distance from her. She too had fallen asleep and had just woken up by all the noise. She looked too frightened to walk to us and know the fact.

"Tinu" I started walking towards her and hugged her tightly in my arms.

"Shree is no more" I told with a heavy heart. She started to shout then cry and later tried to pull herself out from my tight grip.

"Tinu, please... Come out of it." I shouted without letting her out of my arms. She broke down into tears.

That was the first most heartbreaking moment of my life and second when I realized that I have missed out on another friend —Shiva."

MISSING GIFT

I was not mournful remembering Shree passing away, but after sharing that with Nandini I was just on mute thinking it would have been really good if he was alive.

"It's okay Adi, situations like these hit everyone once in a lifetime. We have to be brave enough to face them." Saying this, she came to sit beside me, placed her right hand over my shoulder and patted me. I did not respond to her. There was nothing I could say more that would have made me felt better. Sensing my sadness, Nandini decided to change the topic.

"Okay, I'm feeling very cranky for this weather; let me go and freshen up a little. By the time I finish, try to come out of these thoughts please." she said and left for a bath. She had come well-prepared to stay here. According to her, my apartment was a much better place than her hostel room with her annoying roommate. In her bag, she had an extra pair of clothes, her toothbrush and a few other essentials. She took her clothes out of her bag and walked into my bedroom. I was still remembering my days with Shree and Tinu.

CREEEEEEEAK!

I always got irritated with that sound of my bathroom door. She finished her bath and came out wearing a blue-colored dress. She had my towel wrapped around her hair. She then let her hair go free and using the towel, started draining the last few drops of water from her hair. I kept looking at her momentarily.

A reflection of light caught my eyes. I turned to look at it. It was a ring which Nandini was wearing in her ring finger.

I took me few seconds to recognize that ring. "Yes" that was the same ring I had presented her. On the night of her birthday after all the six gifts were done and only one remained, it was this ring. She had asked that she be presented the GIFT – 6.

All night, I had been fearful about that moment, the moment when she would request the Gift #6. But it wasn't that I wasn't prepared for it. Before disclosing what the gift was, I thanked the restaurant staff for a fabulous dinner.

"Thank you so much for the surprises, Adi" She told me in very happy tone. I simply smiled because I was a little tensed to give her the next gift. We drove to a place where there was enough light on the streets but no one was there.

"Get down" I asked her.

"Okay," She was too excited to even question why I had stopped the car in the middle of an empty road. I got out of the car and ran towards her side of the door to open it. After opening the door, I pulled out my hand for her and she gladly took it. She followed me to the front of the car where she leaned against the bumper, looking here and there, and eager to figure out what the next gift was. Only, she had no idea what I had in mind.

"I'll be honest; I'm actually a bit nervous about this gift."

"Why?"

"You said it would hurt me, but I am sure you would never do anything to hurt me." She answered the question herself before I could even open my mouth.

"But more than that, I'm excited too" she said. She was really poor at hiding her nervousness. And there I was trying to calm my nerves, thinking how not to ruin this moment after the wonderful time that we had together. I didn't respond to any of the things, correction, I barely heard any of it.

"Can you close your eyes and not open them until I tell you to?" I asked her nervously. She did as she was told.

"Whatever I am about to say, can you promise to listen to it all before opening your eyes?" I specifically mentioned that again.

"Okay, I promise. Now just say what you want to say, without wasting any more time. You know how much I hate suspense." she said. So I began.

"Based on what I'm about to say, you may think that nowadays, all guys say this to their best friends or friends. Yes, I agree and I know that people aren't the most delighted when their friend confesses their love for them. People may think it is just an attraction or it is a misconception of friendship. But Nandini, it isn't, at least not for me. I may not be able to prove my love for you and you might think of it as an infatuation, but it isn't. I have had this strange feeling about you since the first time I saw you bargaining with the auto driver. I won't lie to you, as then, I didn't know what to make of my feelings, but the more I got to know you, the more I felt in love with you. I want to spend my rest of my life with you, if you feel the same way about me too. The only thing through which I may be able to feel my love is by the trust you have over me." She was no longer smiling which was enough to make me sweat like a pig even on this cold night. Maybe I hadn't planned it through; maybe I had been a fool to hope that she thought we were more than just best friends. But since I had already taken such a bold step, I wasn't backing down now.

"Now, you can open your eyes," I was on one knee holding a designed yellow gold ring which included a beautiful cushioned gemstone with a band of smaller cut artificial stones on its shoulder band. The moment I had first laid my eyes upon the ring, I imagined how pretty Nandini would look wearing it, her slender but long fingers were going to make this ring pop out. The ring wasn't too ornamented. It was a simple and pure design just like our relationship.

She opened her eyes as I had requested and her eyes went straight to the ring I had in my hand. Before she could open her mouth, I confessed.

"I LOVE YOU NANDINI" There was a pause for a couple of seconds.

"Please get up Adi," she said. That wasn't any of the answers I had expected to hear. She looked panicked; like she'd been caught red-handed stealing something valuable. I felt a little disappointed as I knew that it meant it was a no from her side.

All of a sudden, she smiled and hugged me.

"I LOVE YOU TOO" she said and stretched her left hand, signaling me to put the ring in her finger. I was a little stunned by her reaction. It took me a moment to realize what was happening. More importantly, was it all true? Without letting these thoughts cloud my mind, I placed the ring on her left ring finger.

I could see how happy she was. Her eyes filled with happy tears and her smile hadn't ever looked half as pretty as it looked in that moment. I felt like the luckiest man on earth, as I slid the ring on her finger. I had always seen it in the movies, a hero would tell the heroine how he could see the love in her eyes but only that day I had found that symbolism to be true. Her glittery eyes and smile made her look more beautiful than she already was and I was so glad to know that I was the reason behind it.

"I knew that you had feelings for me Adi, but I never thought you would propose this early and that too, this extravagantly. I thought you had so much to look forward to right now in your life that this wasn't important to you."

"Nandini, I had decided that I wanted to spend my life with you long before you even knew how I felt about you."

A shy and brief smile crossed her lips. There were so many questions in my mind at that moment; I wanted to ask her when did she fall in love with me, why did she say yes to my proposal? Was she too, in love with me since a long time etc. But I didn't want to ask them then. Knowing answers to all of those questions might make me judge her, which I didn't want to. That night was the night to celebrate and to be happy together. I didn't want to ruin that moment by doing anything stupid.

"Let me drop you at your hostel, it is already very late" I said.

She didn't want to go. She didn't put it into words but her gesture showed it. She wanted to cherish that moment some time longer, but I knew that if we didn't leave right then, her hostel in-charge might raise an issue. I opened the car door for her and she followed me. We started the journey back to her hostel. I felt a little jealous that she was giving the ring in her finger more attention, but also happy that she valued it this much. She even kissed it twice and I couldn't help but smile.

"What made you love me?" she broke the silence between us.

"Let's not get into the reasoning right now. Can we please just celebrate us? We'll talk about the rest tomorrow" I said in a pleading tone.

Within no time, we reached her hostel. I helped her carry all the gifts to the elevator. After that, I waited for her to drop off all the gifts to her apartment and come downstairs to say goodnight. She took her time and came back after a good 10 minutes but the moment she stepped out of the elevator, I knew why. She had changed into her night clothes and had her hair in a messy bun—just like the way I liked it. As soon as she saw me, a pinkish blushed settled on her cheeks. She walked towards me and I met her half way, we were the only ones in the empty parking lot.

"So, what now?" she asked.

"What do you have in mind?"

"Why did we have to leave so early? We could have stayed there for another hour or so. I wanted to spend more time with you?" she asked in a very cute tone.

"Because it was already very late and I didn't want you to get in trouble with your hostel in-charge. We'll meet tomorrow, I promise."

She remained silent and I could sense that she wasn't overly happy to hear that. She didn't want me to leave then too. She made the puppy dog face she often made when she wanted to get her way, it was just irresistible. She looked at the ground, waiting for me to change my decision and not go. I pulled her into my arms and let her rest her head on my chest. We had hugged multiple times before but this time, it felt special. She made me feel like I had someone in my life I could rely on, love and be happy with. The rest of the worries or fear didn't matter anymore. We stayed like that for another couple of seconds before she looked right into my eyes with a smile on her lips that reached my soul. I placed both my hands on her cheeks, pulled her a little further and kissed her on the forehead.

"Why are you so down? I promise that I will come to meet you tomorrow." I said.

"I don't know why, I feel like I cannot stay away from you for even a minute." She said.

"You won't have to, I promise." She seemed a little convinced this time. We entangled ourselves in a brief little hug again before she started to walk towards her hostel door. I stayed there for another 5 minutes until she reached her hostel room and turned the lights on; just to make sure she had reached safely. After all, she was my responsibility now. I got into the car and let out a sigh of relief. All the things I planned had gone the way I had imagined. I couldn't keep all the excitement inside me; I had to tell someone and that was when I decided to turn the car towards Ilyas's house. I couldn't have gone home as I had told my mom that I would be staying the night at his home. My mom was really good at guessing my mood and seeing my elated face, she would have questioned me. It was too early to tell her though. It was past 2 a.m. when I reached his home.

"Knock!! Knock!!!" Ilyas opened the door.

"Guess what?" I was excited to tell him.

"Apparently, you don't sleep anymore?" he said.

"What? Shut up." I knew he would make silly guesses if I let him.

"Nandini said yes."

"I knew it… I knew her friend was a lesbian? What else did she say?"

"What? No… No you idiot."

"She said yes to my proposal."

"Hey good for you buddy, Congratulations." But I wasn't going to sleep in peace until I told him about everything that had happened between me and Nandini tonight. I made him listen to each and every word, despite the couple of yawns he faked, trying to tell me that he wasn't really interested in the details, but he was my only friend then and I needed to tell it all to someone. I needed to get all that excitement out so that I could sleep.

FINAL DAYS TOGETHER.

I lay restless on the couch in Ilyas's room, unable to take Nandini out of my head. I should have stayed a little longer with her like she had suggested multiple times. But it would have only led to the conversation I wanted to avoid. I just wanted my proposal and her acceptance of it to be the only happy thing about the night; I didn't want to get into the details of how we were going to take it forward, what future plans we both had. There was a little part of me that still thought that it was all a beautiful dream. I had always come across people who had their hearts broken when the person they loved didn't love them back. I had been the luckiest. I had dated a few girls before her; but I didn't have a serious relationship before. Nandini had been my exception to the rule —the one person who ruled out all the others. Unlike many others, I could feel what it meant to be loved back by the person who loved me.

The warmth on my face from the rays awakened me. I had to open my eyes very slowly so that I wouldn't be blinded by the bright light. When all the darkness left my eyes, I took note of my surroundings. I was in Ilyas's room. Ilyas was sound asleep, snoring. I didn't wake him up. I just sat there, trying to contemplate that all that had happened last night wasn't a dream. Was it true that Nandini had accepted my love? A little part of me kept telling me, I have had the most amazing dream of my life. Before letting that thought sink in, I looked for my mobile phone. There was a message from Nandini. With a little fear, I opened the text and it read, "I Love you, Adi". A big smile crossed my lips. It was really happening for me.

I wanted to wakeup Ilyas but he was in deep slumber, setting a loud background score with his snoring. I left him a message on his mobile before heading home. I kept smiling all through the drive, replaying the previous night's memories.

I couldn't be like this in front of my mom. I always believed that mothers could easily guess what was going on in their children's life by just the kind of behavior they depicted. I knew that I looked anything but normal. As soon as I stepped inside my house, the whole house smelled of freshly prepared Puri and Chole. I couldn't resist the strong aroma and my stomach was already growling. I walked right into the kitchen.

Ahh!! "My favorite food." I said and went to stand beside my mom in case she needed any help.

"Do you need any help, Mom?" I asked.

"No Adi, go and get ready for college, I will set the breakfast on the table" she said.

I spent more time than usual in front of the mirror, trying to look my best. The thought in my mind was that we have to pretend in front of many people that we are still friends. The hide & seek love. I was excited.

"Adi, your breakfast is ready", my mom called out to me from outside the room.

"You look a little different today. Is something special?" my mom asked me while serving me food. I knew my mom was going to notice. It was almost impossible to hide anything from moms, I thought.

"Nothing like that mom, just wanted to see how I would look if I really dressed well." I had no clue if she believed my stupid reason or not. I knew the longer I stayed there, the longer she would continue to pry. As soon as she turned around to get tea, I slipped away saying that I was already late and would have tea in the college. I hadn't lied. I missed the bus just by a minute. By the time I reached college, she was already waiting for me on the park bench.

"Why aren't you in class?" I asked.

"Because I won't be able to concentrate on anything even if I were in it."

"Shall we go?" I asked

"Umm…. Okay" she took a while to answer that.

"But where shall we go?" she asked.

"Let us think about that on our way out," I said.

"Can you take us to Lime Restaurant?" I asked the auto guy, who was waiting outside our college.

We both sat in the auto with only a few inches of gap between us.

"I didn't expect it that you would accept my proposal" I said with a sense of surprise.

"Why wouldn't I, if a person like you proposed," she blushed. I smiled back. She lifted my left hand and entwined her right hand with it.

Our palms touched each other's. Her hands were really warm. I was speechless, my heart started to race. She then placed her head on my shoulder. I didn't look at her as I was blushing. When I finally did, I found her sleeping like a baby. I didn't feel like waking her up, at least, not until we reached the restaurant.

"Nandu...Nandu" I tried to wake her up by tapping on her cheek gently.

"Oh hmm" she woke up; we paid the auto service and proceeded into the restaurant.

It wasn't a very big or fancy restaurant. It had tables set closely, which was the only thing that I didn't like about the place. The dining hall wasn't big either, but there was something about the ambience that I really liked. The dining hall had very unique artwork in the form of murals and paintings on the wall. All the paintings and murals were of lemons and lemonades in different colors. We were shown a table by a really humble server. We sat down.

"Adi, I will be right back," she excused herself to go to the restroom.

"Hi Sir, what can I get you for a drink?" The waiter asked me.

"Can I get two lemonades, please?" I said.

It took the waiter about 7 minutes to get the drinks. After the drinks arrived, so did Nandini from the restroom. She looked wide awake right now.

"Adi, Can I ask you a question?" she asked.

"Sure go ahead," I said.

"What made you to propose me?"

I knew, sooner or later she was going to ask that question. I just didn't understand why all girls needed an answer to that after they had accepted the proposal. It would have made sense if they asked that question before the guy proposed or when he did. Asking it afterwards didn't make any sense. I had seen many of my friends who said a lot of things which they didn't mean and then failed to maintain that. I didn't want the same happening to me and Nandini.

"Let me be very frank with you," I started.

"I liked you very much from the moment I first saw you. But it wasn't love at first sight. Sure, I was attracted to you but most definitely not in love." I saw the excitement in her slowly dropping down after hearing my answer. I carried on.

"After we became friends, we stayed in touch almost every day through calls or texting, which made me realize that I won't be able to live without you. Then some time later, I realized it was just an infatuation because we had become so habitual of each other." After saying that, her expressions completely changed but she still remained silent, which led me to continue.

"Then one time I thought how it would be like to get married to you. I started seeing you in that perspective. Only then, I found out that you were highly compatible with me. Qualities like simplicity, ability to decide between right and wrong, are you mature enough etc., etc. There were a couple of things which I hated too, but that I can go easy with them." I completed expecting her to respond.

"I'm not happy with the answer, that's for sure, but I am glad that you are being frank." She didn't have a smile on her face when she said that.

"What are the things you hate about me?" she asked.

"It doesn't matter, because I know that I can compromise on them. If I tell you what they are, you will try to change them and that is exactly what I don't want. Adjustments or compromising shouldn't happen. It should happen just like a magic."

"Did I hurt you, Nandu?" I asked in a very pleasing voice.

"Sir, here is your drink," the waiter interrupted.

She kept looking at the glass and didn't raise her head to look at me. I felt she did not like the way I answered.

"Nandini, please look at me." I tried to make some conversation with her by holding her hand.

"Right now, you may think that I am like every other guy on the planet. First like the girl, then be friends with her and then give that friendship a new name —love. But it wasn't like that, at least not for me. I liked you in our friendship, but it took me sometime to see each other as husband and wife. It was a tough battle for me to choose between a friend and a wife. I decided only when I was confident that I can get along well with you for the rest of my life."

I waited for her response, but she continued to stare at the glass and not me, so I carried on.

"There is something that I want to tell you Nandini, and believe me, it is the most important thing of all the things I said earlier. My life may not have begun with you, but I wish it ends with you! I promise you that we will be very happy after the marriage."

Still, she didn't respond. Then after a few seconds, I felt her grip under my hand harden. She held it tightly and this time, lifted her head too. When she looked up, I noticed tears in her eyes and a smile on her face.

"Why are you crying?" I got a bit worried.

"I just feel so lucky to have you. I never expected someone to be this frank with me but I am really glad that you are. It is so nice to hear you say that "we" will be happy. I liked the word we. Guys who proposed to me in the past always said things like "I will make you happy forever"; "I will never let you cry"… blah blah. By saying that, you just proved that my choice was right after all.

"I Love you, Adi," she confessed. I instantly stood up, pulled my chair beside her and sat down holding her in my arms. I placed my fingers under her chin, lifted it up so that I could see her beautiful eyes and brushed my lips gently on her forehead to give her a kiss.

MY JEALOUS FEELINGS

Everything continued to go well between me and Nandini or so I thought, until one day, a cousin of hers visited town looking for a job. I had woken up with a feeling of uneasiness in my chest. I went to take the shower, assuming I didn't get enough sleep last night and would feel better after the shower but it didn't leave me. Something wasn't right; I felt it in my bones. I picked up my cell phone and looked for Nandini's good morning text. Because she got up a little earlier than me, she always left me a good morning text to wake up to. Surprisingly, there wasn't one from her that day. Thinking, maybe she just forgot to send one, I typed a "good morning love" text. I waited but received no response, which made me feel a little irritated. She rarely did that unless she was really busy with something. I felt a very little rejected and ignored.

"Good Morning, Adi." As I walked to the dining hall, I saw my mom setting breakfast to the table. As I sat on my chair, she started to serve me.

"Poha??? Mom, you know how much I hate Poha!!!" I became furious.

"Your dad and sister like it, this was the only thing I could make in such a hurry." she was frustrated with my answer.

"I will have something in my college cafeteria, then." I picked up my bag and walked outside the front door in an irritated mood.

While waiting for my bus, I glanced at my phone again. She still hadn't texted me back and it was starting to make me worry then. I tried to convince myself that she must have gotten up late and had no time to check her phone, but even I knew that wasn't like her. The horn of the bus approaching brought me back to reality and I got onto it. I sat down on our usual seat and reserved one for her.

As the bus neared her stop, I didn't see her standing at her usual spot. She must have been running late but then she would have surely texted me to keep the bus at a halt until she arrived. But she hadn't done that either. I knew if she missed that bus then, she would also miss her first lecture. We still were a minute away from the stop so I quickly grabbed my phone and dialed her number.

"The number you're trying to reach is switched off at this moment" the lady on the voicemail told me. Startlingly, I had never despised the lady's voice from the other end until today. We were then at her stop and two other girls got on. But there was no sign of her as far as I could see. My worry started turning into panic. Where was she? Why hadn't she contacted me since the morning? Was she alright? Was she sick? I thought of getting down from the bus and going to her place, but before I could even get up from my seat, the bus driver changed gears, and the bus was on the move again. I tried calling her again, but still got no response.

Not having her beside me felt awkward. It felt like the longest bus ride ever. As I got off, I made my way towards the classroom, again trying to call her on the way there. The class was about to begin and I knew if it went inside, I would be trapped for at least an hour before I could know where she was or be able to meet her. I peeked from one of the windows to see if she was already there in the classroom, but she wasn't. Thankfully, I had the thought to call her roommate. Why hadn't I thought of it before, I hit myself gently in the head. She would know where Nandu was. I dialed her number, but to my surprise, even she didn't pick up her phone. After several tries and no response, I felt as if the whole universe was conspiring against me today. No one was picking up their phones.

"Can't talk right now! In class, text me what is the matter?" I got a text within no time from Nandu's roommate.

"Do you know why Nandu didn't come to college today?" I asked.

"She went out with some guy called Vicky, and "he is her cousin"."

Finally, I had an explanation and fortunately, it was much better than all the things that were going in my mind. But that happiness was only short-lived as I didn't know who this Vicky was, why was here and why Nandu was ignoring me because of him.

Then another thought crossed my mind. Why had Nandu's friend told me that she as with her cousin when I hadn't asked her? She could have just said that she was going out. Why had she emphasized on the word cousin and written it in inverted commas? Did she know about me and Nandu? We hadn't told anyone yet but what if she knew. Maybe I was over thinking things or maybe Nandu had told her about us.

I leaned into a chair in the cafeteria, placed my head down on the table and covered it with my hands.

"Adi?" I raised my head immediately, as I knew whose voice that was.

"Where have you been? Even your phone was out of reach." I started shooting questions at her.

"I'm sorry, Adi. I got a call from my cousin out of the blue saying that he was standing outside my hostel waiting for me as I was getting ready. He had come to the city in search of a job. Being new in the city, he rented an apartment near my place and wanted to buy few books. Because he didn't know about any good bookstores, he requested for my assistance. We went to Koti and got what all that he needed and here I'm. My phone was dead because of low battery."

"By the way, how is he a cousin to you?" Ignoring all that she had just said about all the "fun" they had together and trying not to think too much about it, I asked her the one thing on my mind.

"Oh, he… He is my Aunt's son".

"Aunt? Your mom's elder sister?" I was hoping to be so.

"No no, she is my dad's elder sister." She calmly replied, leaving me all restless.

That meant there was a possibility of the two of them getting married. I should have thought about it as now I had no control over the images that concocted in my mind. Him and Nandini getting married, having kids, enjoying life together etc. but I didn't want her to know that I was feeling jealous.

"Oh that's okay; I was just worried about you. You didn't respond to any of my calls" I said, completely ignoring to acknowledge her cousin's mention. Even though I didn't know a single thing about him, I had, in my mind, already started to hate him. Maybe I was just being possessive of her, but I wanted the conversation about him to end as soon as possible.

"Did you have anything for breakfast" I tried changing the topic.

"Yes, we both went to a restaurant on our way back and had breakfast there." I was stupid to have asked that. I should have already known. Instead of trying to deviate from the topic, I had inadvertently *brought it up myself again.*

"Oh, okay" I didn't say much as my blood was boiling listening her say his name over and over again.

"Are you okay, Adi? I totally get it that you are upset with me. After all, I didn't take your calls since morning because my phone was dead. I can imagine how worried you might have been. But please don't be mad and try to understand my situation here. I couldn't have said no to him. He is my cousin." I thought she sensed my jealousy from my tone. She tried explaining her condition.

"No I'm perfectly alright; it's just that I was a bit worried." We then went to attend the remaining classes and were finally done at 4 p.m.

"Nandu, would you like to go see a movie?" We hadn't had enough time to speak to each other today; I thought that would give us some much needed time. And since it was Friday, we could have even planned to stay out till late.

"Sorry Adi, I already promised Vicky that I will accompany him to dinner tonight. He asked for my recommendations about some good places here. I named a few and then he asked me if I would like to go out with him as he would get bored and possibly lost too, in the city. I couldn't say no."

"Would it be okay if I join you guys?"

All those images that I had to literally shun out of mind in the morning started returning. There was no way I was going to let Nandu go alone with that guy. I didn't like the idea. I didn't want to stop her because then she would have thought that I was being overly possessive. But I also didn't want her to go out in the night alone with him.

"No!!" I had barely completed my sentence before she abruptly cut me off.

"Why not? Am I not your fiancé?"

Yeah, but he doesn't know that. And I don't want him to know. He might tell my parents and it's too early to tell them about us." she placed her case. She was right. Even I didn't want to involve the whole parents' thing at the moment.

"Okay" was the only reply I gave her, and she didn't seem very pleased with it.

"Are you feeling bad? Please try to understand Adi" she hugged me by tightly wrapping her arms about my back.

"Please... please..."

There were two things Nandini used to do when she wanted me to do something she wanted. She would look down and make a puppy dog face which was simply irresistible or this. She would cuddle around me and won't leave until I agreed with her. And how could anyone not? I had never heard about or seen any guy on the planet who would say no to anything his girlfriend wanted when she was holding him in a tight death-like grip. It was very rare that Nandini hugged me like this and I would be lying if I said that I didn't like it. Her soft smooth skin touching mine, and her chamomile-scented conditioner driving me mad; I would have done much more than just that, had she asked for it. It felt like I had just been granted a one way-ticket to heaven.

"Yes, I fully understand your circumstances Nandu," I told her by unwillingly plastering a fake smile on my face. That evening I did not even feel like texting her, because I didn't knew when she might be with her cousin. I was in a dilemma. A part of me wanted to know where she was, what was she doing, was she enjoying her dinner with him or not and the other wanted that I didn't think about it at all. It was really hard to control my urge to text her. I stepped outside my room to go into the lounge to watch TV. I needed some distraction and I was sure some old clippings of a cricket match between India and Australia was going to sidetrack my mind from the entire buzz that was going on inside me.

"How are your studies going, Adi" the voice of my father from behind me gave me a shiver.

"Not bad, daddy" I replied. He came to sit beside me on the couch and waited for me to switch on the TV.

"Will I never get to hear that it is going really well?" Not again, I thought. I already had so much going on in my head. There was no room left for taunts and sarcasm from dad.

"I will do well in the things that I am interested in, I'm not interested in the course I have chosen and there is no option to change it now so I'm just making sure that I don't fail." There was no reply from him, for which I was thankful. It was the perfect window of opportunity to escape the room and the oncoming taunts, so I got up and left without even giving him a chance to continue with his conversation.

I knew my answer was irrelevant, possibly rude too, but I said what was true. I kept playing games on my cell phone, waiting for sleep to come but it looked like even it mocked me. Was I stupid to have allowed her to go alone or just jealous that there was someone else in her life with whom I had to share my Nandu with. But she hadn't asked for my permission. She had just informed me; I felt like a couple she should have discussed it with me before accepting the dinner invitation. There was complete silence in the room. I even heard the tick tock of the clock. After making sure that dad had left the TV lounge, I once again headed outside, had an early dinner and went to bed.

LUNCH WITH VICKY

"**B**uzz buzz" my phone vibrated. It was asking me to look at the text message. I rubbed my misty eyes and grabbed it to read the message.

"Good Morning, Dear" A smile crossed my mind but stayed there only for a brief second as I recalled everything about last night.

"Good Morning, Nandu. Can we meet today for lunch?" I asked, hoping that we two could meet today. I could see that she was typing something big as it took her almost half a minute to finish the text. Only I knew how hard those 30 seconds had been on me.

"Sorry Adi, We can't meet today. I already have plans for a lunch and then shopping with Vicky. Can we meet a day after that? I will be free Sunday afternoon. I can imagine how you must be feeling, but please try to understand."

Understand… my foot! She was outright ignoring me for some other guy… her own family-oriented fiancé. I literally wanted to shout at her but I knew I couldn't do that. The harder I was trying to be with here, the more difficult she was making it. Why all of a sudden had that Vicky become so important? How could he have taken my place in just two days? I and Nandu hadn't even eaten together once in the last two days or had a peaceful chat. It had been him and Nandu.

"Where are you guys planning to go for lunch?" I couldn't keep my curiosity to myself. Besides, I had a right to know where she was going and what she was doing. If I had been in her place, I am sure, she would have asked me to text her every half an hour and tell what I were doing. I hated that about girls. They always valued their independence but when it came to a guy, they wanted him to follow them around like a puppy.

"New Hyderabadi Chef's near Malaysian Township" she texted back.

"Okay enjoy and take care." I didn't feel, like chatting with her anymore. All I really wanted to do was grab my keys and go to that restaurant.

It wasn't like I doubted Nandini or anything, I doubted Vicky. Nandini had everything. She was pretty, intelligent and humble. It was hard for any guy to not fall in love with her, and that was what I feared the most. Vicky didn't know about our relationship and there was a chance that he might begin to have feelings for Nandini. I knew that if I followed Nandini, she might not like it but then again, I wasn't going to tell her that. I just wanted to look at the guy once and try to see what was going on in his mind.

I had this weird habit. If any idea or thought popped in my head I wouldn't be able to think about anything else until I did it. It didn't matter if the idea was good or bad I just had to do it. The idea to follow Nandini was one. I knew it wasn't right and she would be super pissed and hurt if she came to know about it, but I also knew that until I did it, I won't have my peace. It was still 9 a.m. in the morning. I decided to start at 11 a.m. as I knew it would take me about 45 minutes to reach the restaurant. I was all ready by the time the clock ticked 10. I went outside to watch some TV to pass the time.

"Adi, Can you take me to the hospital for my blood test?" My dad, who had just finished reading the newspaper at the breakfast table asked. Are you seriously kidding me right now? I thought to myself.

"Dad I can't, I have to go out for lunch with my friends. "I replied

"Why don't you take the car? He asked.

"I will take the bike" I said.

He exhaled aloud, ensuring that everyone heard it before heading back to his room to get ready. As soon as he closed the door of his room, my mom came out of the kitchen, holding a big spoon in her hands.

"Why don't you take him? He is going for a blood test. He won't be able to drive back safely right after. You can postpone your plan with your friends for some other day," she whispered but in a dominating tone. I was sure if I said no, she would hit me with the spoon in her hand. I did feel bad for my dad after what my mom had said. I stood up and went up to his room. After knocking on the door once, I peeked into the room; he was setting his hair in front of the dressing table.

"Dad, let's go. But we will take the car, okay?" I smiled wickedly. There were very few occasions when I was allowed to take the car on my own.

"Okay" he replied without looking back at me, still adjusting his hair.

"By the way, where is the hospital dad?" I was curious to know so that I can calculate the time it would take us and whether I will still be able to make it at the restaurant during lunch hours.

"It is just in front of that new restaurant Hyderabad chef's near Malaysian Township." Hearing that, the antagonist within me awakened and smiled a bit... All the while I drove; I had this wicked smile on my face, like I was going to catch someone red-handed. As we were just about to reach the hospital, I tried convincing my dad to try out the new place.

"Shall we go for lunch to that restaurant after your test?" I asked.

"Sure Adi." So my plan was still on. In fact, it had just gotten better now with dad by my side. I no longer would have to peep from the window or anything. I was going to look at him more closely. The blood test hardly took 15 minutes of our time and we were out of the hospital by 12. I called my mom to tell her that we planned to have lunch at the restaurant.

"If you had plans to eat out, why didn't you say so earlier? I am almost done with cooking. Now tell your father that he will have to eat the same at dinner tonight. And you Adi cancel your plans with your friends, okay? Don't leave your father alone." She sounded frustrated but didn't let go of the sarcasm. Dad had already heard most of the conversation through the speaker. We both looked at each other and smiled guiltily.

We were just waiting to get dad's medication from the on-ground pharmacy. There were a few people before us in the line which allowed me to scrutinize the restaurant's building from the other side of the road. It was a single-storey building with brownstones stoned into its walls. There wasn't enough parking-space in front of the restaurant. Not more than six cars could park there and enjoy their meals. But why did I care about it? I knew Nandini and her cousin would arrive any minute. I wanted to go in there before they arrived. Luckily, the person in front of dad had an urgent call and he left the queue to attend it. The following minute, dad and I were on our way to the restaurant.

We were greeted humbly by the guard who opened the door for us. He was wearing a traditional Hyderabadi dress. Upon entering, I quickly glanced inside to ensure that Nandini hadn't arrived. She hadn't. A number of tables were already reserved while others were filled with married and single couples, some even with their kids. The restaurant manager seated us on a table beside a waterfall which was kind of nice. By the time we placed our order; all the tables around us were filled with more people who came after us. I felt a little sad.

"Hi madam, how many people?" the waiter asked some lady.

"Just the two of us, please." I didn't need to raise my head to see who she was. I recognized her voice. It was Nandini. I didn't want to look up until she had settled down. The waiter led her towards one of the empty tables that was reserved for a couple. I stole a quick glance at her and had a mini-heart attack. She was wearing the same dress I had gifted her on her birthday. As always, she looked absolutely breathtaking with that hairdo and even wore matching earrings to go along. I could see that all the single men in the restaurant stared at her while she so causally placed her bag on the table and sat down. Had my ego not intertwined in the middle, I too might not have been able to take my eyes off of her. I then turned to look at the guy who accompanied her. He was a tall guy with broad puffed up muscles. His complexion was fair like mine but his features made me envy him.

I could see that they were having a good time. Everything that the guy said, made Nandini laugh out loud. She looked happy which I didn't like. I started doubting all the times we had eaten out. Did I make her laugh that much? Did she have a good time with me too? I felt like getting out of there. I could no longer see her giggle like that with another man, even if he was just her cousin as she always put it. I knew I wasn't going to be able to stomach another bite. I looked at my dad who seemed to be enjoying his food. He was almost done eating, so I requested the waiter for the bill.

After paying the bill, we both got up quietly and started walking towards the exit. As we neared the main gate, I felt like having one last look at her. I shouldn't have but it was too late. As I turned around, she unexpectedly looked in the same direction too. Our eyes met. I would have loved to look into those eyes longer but the reaction on her face made me decide otherwise. She looked unpleased and disturbed. And then shocked and angry. It took her a second to realize what I had been up to and she didn't like it. I knew it from the beginning; I knew she wasn't going to like it because I knew it was wrong. I rushed outside, making it more obvious to her that I had indeed, been spying on her. I left her thinking that I doubted her loyalty and sincerity towards me. How stupid was that of me. But what had been done, had been done, and there was no way to bring back time. But I wasn't the only one at fault then. She too, had been ignoring me. As her boyfriend, I just wanted to see who she was spending most of her time with. I had asked her to introduce me to this Vicky but she was the one who had refused.

"Adi, can we meet for breakfast tomorrow?" I got a text message from her the same night. I knew why she wanted to meet me. I had my reasons, but I wasn't sure she would be in a mood to hear them out.

The next morning, as she had requested I went up to her hostel and waited outside for her to come down. I left her a text saying the same. When I didn't get any reply from her, I decided to call.

"Hmmm", she picked up.

"I am waiting outside your hostel for you."

"Okay". That was the only word she said before disconnecting the call. It felt like a tight slap on my face. After a minute, she came out of the elevator, walked towards me and without saying a single word sat on the bike. I was too scared to start the conversation or even say "hi". I just started the bike and drove to the nearby hotel.

"Tell me Nandu, what do you want to talk to me about?" I pretended to be innocent.

"I can understand that you love me a lot, but we are not married yet. We still have our own private lives. There is a thin boundary between love and possessiveness and I feel that until we get married, we should value the boundary." Her tone made me realize how wrong I had been. She wasn't angry at me. By doing what I did, I had humiliated her.

"I did not doubt you Nandu; I just wanted to see who this Vicky was." I clarified.

"I never said that you doubted me. I know you would never do that, whatever you did was out of possessiveness."

"Let me tell you one thing Adi, I will marry no one except you. I can't even imagine someone other than you beside me. Yesterday, when I went to meet Vicky, I wore the same dress. Do you want to know why? It was because I was missing you so much. It felt wrong not to have you beside me. It felt wrong to laugh at someone else's jokes. Wrong and unreal and I didn't like it a bit." She said all that in such a pleasant tone that I had no choice but to believe her.

"BTW, I was actually glad that you were in that restaurant yesterday. It was the second time I had worn that dress and you were there to see it."

"I am sorry Nandu. Just the thought of you being with someone else made me lose my mind a little there. I knew from the start that what I was doing was wrong; I even knew that I might hurt you, but I did it anyways. I am really sorry. Can you forgive me?" I genuinely felt like apologizing to her.

"Already did!" She smiled and it made my heart melt.

Everything from then onwards went smoothly between us. We cleared all our doubts the same day and promised to never doubt each other's feelings. We also decided that we shall talk about such stuff before going to such lengths and I felt relieved. Relieved, for I knew that Nandini loved me from all her heart. Relieved because I knew that no matter who came between us, we were always going to be together. Days passed by and out little world remained happy. We continued to date secretly until our last semester's exams were near. It felt like the time had been fast forwarded. We had spent 3 years together.

She got a job at a very reputed MNC, while I still tried to find one. We were sad that she had to travel to other city and I had to stay here without her. I was half sad and half excited that finally I won't have to study anymore in life. No more assignments, exams and boring classes to worry about.

The thought of Nandu leaving town soon was horrible to say the least. I wanted to spend some time with her, before she left. The only thing that came to my mind was to plan a trip. We had gone on long drives a hundred times, but the idea of going on a trip together sounded more romantic and thrilling.

"Nandu, can we both go for a trip for a couple of days?" I asked her the day before our last exam.

"You sure?" I inquired.

"Yeah why not? Will there be a problem?"

No, I'm okay with that." She said giving the idea another thought.

"That was quick. You don't even want to know where, when and how?" I was in a shock.

"I have no problem roaming around with my would-be. I trust him." Her bold expression of her love made me blush.

WE BOTH ON A TRIP

"**M**om, some friends and I are planning a trip to Araku after the exams on Friday, can I go?" I asked her in the sincerest tone ever, hoping that she wouldn't say no.

"How many of your friends are going?"

"It's sort of a class get-together. I, Nandu and some other buddies from class." I said in a trembling voice. I knew that if I told her that it was only I and Nandini, she would refuse. I felt bad lying to her, but I badly wanted that trip with Nandu. She gave me a look as if she had caught me.

"You can go, but be careful." Something from her expressions and tone told me that she knew that I and Nandu were going alone on the trip. But she still agreed. I realized that you could lie to anyone on the damn planet but never cheat your mom. She knows everything, she just pretends she doesn't.

"Thank you, so much. She was the hardest to convince at home. Now all I had to do was convince my dad, which was a piece of cake.

It was the last day of college and I had mixed emotions. I was going to miss all my friends badly but I was also super excited about the trip with Nandu. But I also knew that after the trip, she would have to leave town, which kind of made me sad. With so much going on in my mind lately, I had barely prepared for the final exam. I entered the examination hall and sat down on the seat with my roll number on it. The invigilator started distributing the answer sheet and it was then when I first truly felt like I should have prepared more for the exam. After all, it was going to decide my future. Luckily, Ilyas was seated next to me. The subject's professor then started distributing the question paper. I said thank you to him after receiving it. I took a deep breath and looked at it.

I was taken aback a little. My eyes widened. Although, the question paper was in English, I was barely able to understand any of the terms on it. I felt like it was the first time I was introduced to them. I was so sure I was going to fail. My only option was to rely on Ilyas to help me clear the exam. I shifted my seat a little on the right so that I could be near him. The professor looked at me furiously but I didn't say anything. I pretended as if I was picking up something from the floor casually like boys did during exams. After being sure that he was no longer spying on me, I tried getting Ilyas's attention.

"Hshhhhh" After getting no response from him, I looked up at him. He was looking at me with the same blank expressions that I had on my face. We both knew we were screwed. I knew from his expressions that he was going to be of no help and I had to save myself. I tried recalling all that I could and proceeded with the questions. I knew that half of the reasoning I wrote didn't even make any sense, but I just couldn't leave the paper all blank. Getting a single mark on a question of 10 marks seemed hopeful. The paper was of 180 minutes but I was out in 45 because I had done all I could and sitting in the examination hall, seeing other kids engrossed in their papers and asking for extra sheets made me more anxious. I waited outside on the bench till 12 p.m. when the final bell rang. Nandu came out with a bunch of her friends discussing answers. Many of them looked happy and excited as it was the last day of college. I sat there for another couple of minutes as she said goodbye to all her friends. I knew that we had to leave in the next 15 minutes as the train was supposed to leave at 2 p.m.

We wanted to meet all our friends, spend some time together and take some group pictures, but we didn't have time for all that. We had a train to catch. I got up the minute I saw her walking towards me. We both made it to the exit gate before anyone found out that we were missing. We hailed a rickshaw together.

"How did your exam go?" she asked.

"Well, all the questions were correct."

"Very good" she responded.

"But I am not sure if I answered them correctly too." She took it as a joke, but I had meant it.

"If the evaluator tries to understand what I have written, he will fail me. However, if I succeed in confusing him as to what I truly mean, then I might pass." She laughed some more and started looking outside. It is getting late; I didn't want to miss the train. I had already booked the ticket last night so that it saved us both from standing in a long queue at the ticket counter.

"Can you drive a little faster?" I requested the driver.

"Don't worry Adi; we will not miss the train." She looked relaxed.

''May I have your attention please! Train No: 2612 will leave in next 20 minutes." The lady through the speaker announced. Listening to that announcement we ran through the toughest crowd and made into our compartment.

It was a regular train with sleeping couches for each passenger. That was a houseful crowd in our compartment. The smell of sweat all around us annoyed me very much. After the train's final whistle, our journey together to the Araku began. All the while, we saw India in its raw beauty. Men and women working in the rice fields. Lush green gardens, mills, small villages with children waving at us in delight. Although a couple, we pretended to be friends to avoid attention from everyone. Instead of sitting together, we sat opposite each other, talked casually about college and our professors so that others won't judge us. Not many people were open to the idea of an unmarried couple going on a trip alone. I didn't want anyone eyeing us on our relationship.

"Are you hungry?" she asked me.

"Not much. Are you?" I asked.

"Yes" I had been stupid to not pack any food with me. I should have bought something from the many stalls at the train station. Our only hope then was the salesperson with snacks who visited every compartment after half an hour.

"You can share with us, if you don't mind." Listening us talk about food, an amid-aged lady sitting right in front of us offered her food. It was such a genuine gesture that I felt bad saying no.

"That's okay Aunty, thanks for asking." Nandini replied before I put forward my hand.

"Common young man, looks like your friend is hungry. At least ask her to have it." She was looking at me. Nandini looked at me and my expressions said that I wanted whatever she had in that box of hers.

"Thank you very much" she took the box which had a few bakery biscuits. Nandu ate a couple of them and had some water. After an hour or so, packed meals were being sold. I immediately bought two for us.

The rice was packed in an aluminum tray with two plastic containers, one with curry, whose consistency competed that of water and other with Raita that smelt sour. I didn't feel like eating it and I stopped Nandini from having any too. I couldn't risk her getting sick on the journey and spending most of the time inside the hotel room vomiting. She had just opened the pack and had a few bites. I told her to wait a little as we were just about to reach the next stop. We would have surely gotten some better food then. As soon as the next station arrived, I got down and grabbed a few snacks and a bottle of water.

"Are you both friends?" The man who sat beside the lady who had offered us food asked me. I assumed he was her husband.

"Yes uncle" I didn't feel comfortable disclosing to strangers about our relationship. I didn't want to give them an impression that we both were eloping together. Saying otherwise would have given heed to more conversation on the topic I wished to avoid. I thought of sleeping for a while.

Nandini, would you mind if I go up and sleep on the top shelf for a little while?

Sure, I don't mind. She smiled.

Since we hadn't paid for the top shelf, it was only fair that I asked the lady and her husband too if it was okay. They didn't have any problem so I climbed up and rested for a little while. I had been up since last night —partly studying for the exam and partly thinking about the trip with Nandini. Nandini too excused herself and climbed the steel handles to rest on the upper bunk opposite mine. She too fell asleep in no time.

Only a couple of hours remained before we reached our destination. By the time I woke up, Nandu was sitting on her couch. I stretched my legs and let them fall in the air.

I felt relaxed after the dreaded exam. Today had been an eventful day. First the exam, then running for the train and then the lunch thing. It was finally dawning on me that I was going on a trip with Nandu alone. I smiled looking at her. She smiled back but also raised an eyebrow, inquiring what made me smile like a mad person. I jumped to her couch lowering my head from the fan which was so close.

"Why were you smiling?" She asked.

"I can't believe that we are actually going for a trip." She leaned her head on my shoulders and cuddled her hand in mine.

"Do you think our parents will agree to our marriage?" she asked.

"I'm not sure about that" I replied honestly. She didn't like the answer. She immediately unbundled herself from my shoulder and looked straight at me in shock.

"What happened?" I asked.

"You sounded like you don't want this to happen?"

"You know your parents well, you should be able to tell whether will they accept or not." She asked.

"In that case, tell me whether your parents will agree or not?" I asked her without any delay.

"As far as I know, they would not agree in the beginning, but I think I will be able to convince them after some time." She said. Her answer made me smile.

"What does that smile mean now?" she was not in a mood to joke.

"Till this date, I had never seen my parents discuss the topic of my marriage. How am I supposed to know if they will say yes or no? What If I tell you something now and it doesn't happen? What if I say they won't have any problem now but when I discuss it with them, they do. Then what? Wouldn't that make me a liar" She looked a little confused as I started explaining.

"In any relationship, people always have unexplored scenarios, where you never know how they would react to something unless and until that scenario occurs. That is how relationships work, you discover something new each other all the time, and it is a never ending process. You can never know a person completely. We gain experience as time passes in our life. Our opinions change all the time which is an unconscious process. The person you see this year will behave differently in 3 years. You should always re-discover the other person be it a partner or parents. So I never know how my parents will react." I elaborated my earlier sentence so that she would understand better.

"You talk very well about relationships, how come?" she asked with a sense of astonishment.

"I keep thinking and analyzing about life and relationships all the time." Before we could have led that conversation further, the train whistled, reminding us that I was time to get off the train. We collected our baggage, got down from the train and walked out of the station.

It was 2 a.m. in the night and not many people got down. As we stepped out to get a cab, there were hardly three. Two of the cab drivers were sleeping in their car's back seat. We had no other option but to go with the guy who was awake.

His pricing was very decent. We were so tired then that as soon as we entered the hotel room, we landed on our beds and went to sleep.

ARAKU VALLEY

"Adi, Adi wake up" she continued to tap my shoulders until she got a response from me.

"Hmm, what time is it?

"Let me sleep some more" I did not even try to open my eyes.

"So you planned a trip with me just to sleep?" She obviously sounded offended. She was right, the reason I had planned this trip was to have some alone with her. I wanted to spend every second of the trip with her and make the most of it. The thought of her leaving in some days dawned on me and I woke up immediately.

"Let me show you something" Nandu, holding my hand dragged me to the balcony.

As soon as I stepped down from the bed, the coolness of the tiles sent shivers down my spine. I was fully awake now. As she opened the sliding door of the balcony, chilly breeze entered the room. Nandu touched her body against mine. Although, a small gesture, it made my heart race ten times faster. I rubbed my palms and placed on my face for some warmth. I had just puffed out a warm breath of air when I finally laid my eyes on what she was trying to show me. My heart skipped a beat. I had never witnessed anything that beautiful in my entire life. Thick clouds floated just a stone's throw distance from us. Much lower than what I had always imagined. It looked like they were playing hide and seek with us. Hiding from us the beautiful sight of the faraway green mountains, dressed in white snow, touching heaven. Beneath those mountains were rich lush green gardens as far as the eye could see. I had never seen such a pure shade of green before. Nandini told me that those were parsley fields. I had never before; observed parsley this closely, even though we used it abundantly in our salads and yogurts. I would have loved to observe it more closely, but the space between the sky and the ground was covered with thick fog. With Nandini beside me, I felt like never leaving this place. She was all I needed and this view was more than what I could have wished for. I knew I would never get tired of this view even if I lived all my life here. This was nothing short of heaven on earth.

"This is so beautiful, isn't it?" she asked me.

"Yes, it is," I said rubbing my palms again and again. I was literally speechless. That was all I could say as a response.

"Ting Tong" the doorbell rang and Nandu walked back into room to see who it was. It was room service. The man had a tray in his hand. Nandu opened the door further to allow the man to drag the tray inside. The scent of freshly-brewed coffee filled the entire room. Closing the door, she started her walk back to the balcony. On her way back, she stopped near the tray, poured coffee in one and started towards me.

"But you don't drink coffee." I asked her. All the times we had eaten out together or went to get some snack, she always ordered tea. I assumed she didn't like coffee. Maybe she was making it for me. The thought of her caring for me like this made me smile.

"I do" she said, I was confused. She did like coffee. By filling only one cup with it, she was expecting me to make my own. She then placed the tray with the cup in it on the oval coffee table in front of me. She wasn't done then. She went back into the room again and grabbed the blanket from the queen-size bed and walked back into the balcony. "Have a seat" she pointed to one of the chairs available.

"Can you hold this blanket?" I wasn't sure what was going on inside her head. As I sat down, she too accompanied me, but not on the empty chair next to me —on the right side of my lap. I was a little startled. This was one daring move but also one that was utterly romantic. She didn't weigh much so I felt comfortable. She then wrapped the blanket around us, not just herself but *us*. She then placed her head against my chest and moaned a little which sent shivers down my spine. She wasn't done then either. Taking one hand out of the blanket, she grabbed the cup filled with coffee and presented it to me.

"Have a sip" she told me.

I signaled that I can't as I was holding her and the blanket.

"Here, let me…" she brought the cup closer to my lips for me to take a sip. I did as I was told. She then, from the same mug, took a sip from the same side that I had drunk from. I had seen the same in many movies and commented how cheesy that one move was, but now that it had happened with me, I didn't find it cheesy at all. It felt good.

"You are so romantic today, can I know why?" I asked looking at her.

"One of us should be romantic, right?" she raised her eyebrows.

"Wait, do you think I'm dumb?" I started tickling her sides and she jumped out of my lap.

"Oops, I'm sorry Adi" The entire coffee spilled on me.

"See… If you try to be romantic, this happens" and she laughed.

I would have loved to show how passionately I loved her but I hadn't come here to spend the whole weekend indoors. There was a reason why I had chosen this place in particular. Nandini loved the outdoors and this place was full of greenery. I wanted to take her out, enjoy local food, meet new people, and go by the waterfalls and more.

"I think we should get ready and go out to see a few places. I will go freshen up first" Because my shirt was all wet and sticky then, it was only fair that I took the bath first. I walked back into the room, opened my suitcase and took a new shirt and jeans out. I stepped into the washroom, opened the hot water tap and took a steamy hot shower. As I came out of it, the mirror had fogged up. I wiped it with my hands only to find a smile settled on my face. I didn't believe it at first but when it didn't go away, I knew that with Nandini it was going to stay like this.

"Now, it's your turn" I came out of the shower saying that. I still had the towel in my hand and was drying my hair.

"Here, let me do that for you." she took the towel from my hands and tried her level best to reach my hair by standing on her toes. Every time, she did that, she lost her balance. Seeing her struggle like that, my heart warmed up and I landed down on my knees so that she could easily do what she was so eager to do. I wrapped my arms around her waist and gently rested my head against her belly. She went all still for a brief moment but then came back to reality a second later and started drying the hair on my nape. It was such a pleasant feeling; her belly was softer than any pillow I had slept on.

"Enough now, let me go and get ready." she said and started picking out clothes from her bag.

"Let me know if you need any help showering. I can come in and help you." I tried flirting with her in a husky tone as I crashed into the bed and laid one-sided watching the subtle sway of her hips as she made her walk towards the bathroom.

"I know you are trying to be romantic. But no thanks." she didn't even turn around to face me while she uttered those words. Lying back on that fluffy bed and looking at the ceiling, I just lived in the moment. After a while, I heard the shower turn off and a few minutes later she came out weaning a light pink colored kurti with white very beautiful intricate embroidery on it with a white trouser. She smelled heavenly and her long wet hairs were enough to drive men crazy.

"What are you looking at?" She inquired.

"Just You!" I hadn't lied. Even if there were a dozen other girls in the room, I was sure that my eyes would have followed her everywhere. That was what made her unique. Right then, she wasn't wearing an ounce of makeup, didn't even have her hair combed and yet she looked absolutely breathtaking.

"So, I assume it is going to take you some time to get ready?" I asked.

"Can't you see I'm almost done?" she said.

"I know pretty well that when guys say the same, they actually mean that. But when girls say that they are almost ready, they are lying. Every time they are reminded that they have forgotten to put Kajal, mascara or whatever that is they put in their eyes" I joked.

"Shut up, I don't need to impress anyone. Unlike other girls, I don't want any boys chasing after me. I already have you, I don't need anyone else." Her words sounded honey to my ears. This was exactly what every guy needed to hear. I got up from bed and hugged her from behind.

"Do you really think we are made for each other?" She asked looking into the mirror for a while.

"Yes, of course" I told her. We kept looking at each other in the mirror, our pair looked very cute. Nandini was slim enough to perfectly fit in my arms. I couldn't control myself from appreciating her beauty. Her scent was maddening. I couldn't resist smelling. I pulled some of her hair back and gently brushed my nose against her then open neck. I knew I shouldn't have done that because now that I had, it was hard to let go. I placed a warm kiss on her neck as I pulled her a little closer to myself.

"Stop it now. Did you order any breakfast for us?" she pushed me back on to bed and asked while she got ready.

"Yes Madam, if you must know, I did, it should be here any minute. I teased her by imitating a receptionist's voice. Less than a minute later, the waiter knocked on the door with a breakfast tray. After I received it and closed the door behind me, Nandini was done getting ready. We both sat down beside each other on the big bed and started unpacking the breakfast. We both ate from the same plate and Nandini even fed me a couple of times. Anyone who saw us would have thought that we were a married couple on our honeymoon because we were acting that way.

After finishing the breakfast, we both went out to see Araku. We rented a cab for the day and started our journey together. Since we had arrived late last night, we had missed all this beauty lush greenery surrounded us. The roads were very narrow as they had been made by cutting between the mountains. One side of the road was covered with trees in different shades of green, orange pink and purple. The valley on the other side of the road was covered in thick fog. Every now and then, we would get a glimpse of the sun shining bright. The breeze was chilly. With Nandini on my right, admiring the views of Araku, I wanted nothing more from my life. It was, by far, the most romantic date I had ever been on and I knew nothing was ever going to top that. We hardly chatted amongst ourselves as the picturesque beauty had us awestruck in the moment. We had decided to go see Borra Caves first.

After a journey of 45 minutes, the two-way road ended and merged into one. The driver took on one end of the road that had been constructed specially by clearing trees from the path. The road was based with red mud. The road kept narrowing as we went further and I was surprised to see two-way traffic running so causally. There were many potholes on the road which turned the ride a bit jiggling at times but I was too astonished to see how the cab drivers were driving so effortlessly and not caring about traffic coming from the other direction. I was completely blown away by the driver's skills.

When the movement of our bodies finally stopped, we stepped out of the car and stretched our muscles in all possible ways. In front of us was the gate of Borra Caves. There was a horde of people who were entering through the big gold entrance gate. There were many who were enjoying local food at the many street vendors who had their kiosks up near the entrance. I had researched about the caves before. I knew that a lot of walking was involved so I instantly purchased a water bottle from one of the kiosks for myself and Nandini and lined up in the queue for tickets at the ticket counter. Borra caves were India's largest caves. It had a very massive opening about 100m horizontally and 75m vertically.

"The caves were created by the flow of river over the limestone area. The pressure was exerted by the Humic acid in the water on the mineral deposits and the limestone dissolved in the water. The dissolved limestone trickled down drop by drop forming the different shapes in the cave." I heard a tourist guide explaining to his troop in a very loud voice.

The insides of the cave were lit up with colorful lights that gave the caves a colorful and vibrant look.

"It looks like we are going to a disco party, doesn't it Nandu?" I joked.

"Sshssh... it isn't the time to make jokes, Adi" She replied.

She hadn't spoken a word since we had entered. She had been gob-smacked. She wasn't in a mood to joke. There were many tour guides who had brought their tourist groups and we decided to follow in their tracks and hear all the interesting facts one of them was occasionally telling his group. As we caved in further, the line narrowed and formed a queue. We kept waiting for our turn and when it finally came, we saw a stone that resembled Lingam around which the crowd had gathered. Lingam was the notation of Lord Shiva.

"Join your hands and pray that our marriage happens." I knew she was a firm believer of God, so to respect her feelings and to tell her how absurd that was, I did as she said. She put a 100 rupee bill into the dona-tion box and rubbed her fingers on the Vibhuti bar and painted it hori-zontally between my eye brows. Once when we were out of the caves, Nandu requested that we visit the Lord Shiva temple which was near the exit gate. There, she donated another 100 rupee bill. To me, it looked like bribe, corruption and black money. I was tired of walking all the way around the cave. After walking for another 15 minutes, we were back from where we started —the front gate.

"Can you see the monk sitting under the big banyan tree?" she asked me. Looking towards where her finger pointed, I saw a big banyan tree and a monk sitting calmly underneath it. If the monk had been there before too, why hadn't I seen him? Forget the monk; I hadn't even noticed the big years-old banyan tree.

"Yes I see him," I replied while still in shock.

"Shall we go and talk to him?" Before I could have said anything she had already started dragging me towards him by pulling my hand. As I moved closer, I saw the picture becoming clearer. The entire feel was different.

The man looked like he was in his mid-sixties, had messy hair that were loosely braided at the end, with a couple of Rudrakshamala's around his neck. His whole body was covered in Vibhuti but it didn't hide his petite physique. The beaded necklaces around his neck hinted me that he might be a devotee of Lord Shiva. He had three distinct lines on his forehead in between his eyes horizontally and was parted from the middle with a red mark. The only piece of clothing he wore a saffron-colored dhoti. He looked like he was in deep meditation. He had both his legs crossed over one another, which was a very difficult position to hold. But his face expressions showed not an ounce of effort or pain. He had both his hands held in midair in front of his torso with only a few fingers joined. It was a strange pose to rest in but he seemed calm.

"Swamy" Nandu tried calling in a very low tone. For a while, he didn't seem bothered.

"Let's go, maybe he is in a deep meditation" I tried convincing her because I didn't feel like wasting time on that shit then.

"Om Namashivaaya" he opened his eyes, chanting that mantra of Lord Shiva twice.

"Swamy, I'm a deep believer of Lord Shiva. I have had a few questions on my mind for a while now; I would like to ask you". For starters, I didn't know Nandini was a believer of Shiva specifically. Secondly, I was in no mood for a spiritual lecture then. I knew that if I didn't pull her away from there then, we were going to waste a lot of time there.

"Sure, go ahead" his voice was very clear sharp and catchy.

"What is that we should look up to in Lord Shiva?" Nandu asked the Swamy. He took a deep breath and changed his posture as any regular mediator.

"Shiva has many qualities. So many that it is impossible to keep count." He replied in a very calm tone.

"Can you tell which of those can make a human's life peaceful?" She had never looked that curious about anything before. I didn't understand why she was talking about peace and other stuff at this age.

"Destroy fear, see the truth, be wiser than the rich, experience ignorance and recognize the boundaries. These are the five things which can make a huge impact in our lives. Let me elaborate them for you" he continued.

"Every human emotion has its own counterpart like Need/Greed, Acceptance/Ignorance, and Love/Lust. There is a certain limitation which is a very thin line between any of these two. If you are conscious enough to identify the difference between these things, the things you call and see as trouble today in your life will go away. Ignoring certain things in life is also an important concept for which you again need to be conscious about your activities and its effect along with your needs."

"Are these written anywhere?" I didn't know why I intertwined in between by asking that stupid question. But I was curious for a moment.

"Haha, Shiva doesn't tell any philosophies directly. Everything about human wellbeing has been protected in the form of stories in our mythologies. You just need to decode them."

"It was really nice interacting with you, Swamy." If I hadn't tried to end the conversation there, I was pretty sure he would have started telling us those stories.

"You never told me that you are a devotee of Shiva?" I asked her while we were travelling to the Katiki waterfalls, which were at a distance of about 4km from the Caves.

"I never knew it was an important detail to tell. Besides, the topic never came up." She replied very causally.

"Okay, let me tell you one thing right away. I'm a non-believer of God but I don't have problem with your beliefs." I didn't hesitate telling her that. I thought since we were going to spend the rest of our lives together, it was only fair that she knew that about me.

"Does anyone in your family believe in God?" she asked.

"Everyone except me." I said with pride in my voice.

"So, something is wrong with you." She mocked.

LAST DAY OF TRIP

On our way back from the Borra caves, we stopped nearby a waterfall that was crowded with foreigners. We found ourselves a spot on the big bumpy rocks. There were many who cooked food on portable stoves while others enjoyed a cool splash from the waterfalls. It was a really refreshing sight but I wasn't in the mood to get wet. I was already feeling pretty tired after that long walk at the caves.

Can we go a little closer to the waterfall, Adi? "I want to feel the water drizzle on my face." Nandini asked excitedly.

"But I don't want to get wet, Nandu" I told her.

"Please just a little closer. You can just sit and see. Please, please, please…" Seeing her insist so much, I grabbed my backpack and followed after her. The sun was shining at its brightest now. It was after all, afternoon and unlike in the city, there wasn't pollution to veil us from the harsh sun. It was right at our heads and I wasn't admiring its presence very much. After walking a few steps, I knew that I couldn't anymore.

"Nandini, I can't walk anymore." I said.

"Shall I go and come back." She answered.

"Okay, but be careful" I let her go.

Waving at a few kids who were there with a family, she started walking towards the waterfall. All my attention was on her usual. As she neared, she took off her sandals and placed them on a rock, gesturing me from the distance to keep an eye for them. I nodded as a response and she turned round and started her walk again. She tied her scarf in a wrap around her waist on one side so that it won't come in the way, bent down to pull her trouser a little up so that it won't get completely wet. As she further neared the waterfall, the rocks became slippery and a couple of times she almost lost her balance, giving me a near heart attack. But every time she would regain her balance, she would look back at me to reassure that she was fine. She was a bit childish that way. I was starting to worry as I knew it wasn't safe. She could have easily hurt her feet on the rocks. After another minute of careful walking, she reached the waterfall. No one had gone that far and she turned around and gestured a victory sign using her two fingers shaped as a V.

"Nandini, I think you shouldn't go any further, it isn't safe." I shouted from behind.

"Adiii, One more stone close, please" she shouted trying to dominate the volume of the waterfall. I had no choice but to show her a thumb up, but deep within, I was shit scared for her.

But I think she didn't hear me properly as the next thing she did was try leaping onto another rock. The distance between the rocks she was standing on and the one she wanted to jump to was bigger than the earlier ones and before I could tell her to stop or rush towards her, her foot slipped; she lost her balance and fell down the waterfall. It took me a millisecond to get up and reach where she stood. I didn't care about how much my feet hurt as they rubbed against the uneven surface of the rocks. All I wanted to do was get to Nandini. A crowd of people had already started running towards the waterfall, many shouting, some crying and others hiding the face of their children so that they won't see what had just happened. I had covered a minute's distance in about 10 second or less. By the time I got to her, I saw her head hit one of the big rocks on the bottom of the waterfall. She lay unconscious and within the next second, I saw a pool of blood forming around her.

"Nandini," I shouted at the top of my lungs.

I woke up covered in sweat. My heartbeat was faster than a bullet train. My breathing was out of order. The room was pitch-dark. I switched on the bedside lamp and turned onto my left to see if Nandini was there. Sanity finally returned when I saw her comfortably snuggled in the blanket beside me. It was the worst nightmare ever. I rested my back against the bed post and started to stare at the ceiling. I was afraid to close my eyes, let alone sleep. Was that nightmare a sign? I knew she was going to leave town after some time and I hadn't feared the long-distance relationship thing ever before. But then, I did. Even if something were to happen to her, I was going to be miles away from her. How was I going to keep her safe? My eyes filled with tears. This was our last night together. Tomorrow morning we were to go back and Nandini was to leave right after. I didn't know when again, were we going to be like this.

Without a second thought, I stepped out of my bed and went to sit on hers. I saw her face and she seemed peaceful. She looked so beautiful even in her sleep that I couldn't help but wonder why she chose me.

The way we took care of each other and behaved with each other, it felt like we were already married.

I gently caressed her face and adjusted a strand of hair that had settled on her cheek. I bent a little and placed a soft kiss on her left cheek that woke her up.

"What happened, you haven't slept yet?" she asked me in her drowsy voice. Her eyes were still shut.

"A bad dream woke me up and I realized that this is our last night together. I will miss you so much Nandini" I told her and laid next to her, holding her hand in mine. She adjusted to give me some space and covered me with the blanket. She then curled up against my chest with her head resting on my shoulder.

"Nandini, you mean the world to me, I have never loved anyone before the way I have loved you. I don't know if I will be able to live without you. I don't want to lose you at any cost." I told her all that was in my heart. I choked up a few times in between and Nandini just rubbed her left palm over my heart to soothe me. That little act eliminated the ache at once. I traced the outlines of her hand which made her to open her eyes and look at me. With her looking at me with such passion-filled eyes, I couldn't resist kissing her. Our lips interlocked and she didn't pull back. To my surprise, she started imitating my moves which made the kiss more passionate and wild. I wanted to keep kissing her, even if she fainted by going out of breath. I wanted to memorize this as that was going to be the only thing she would leave behind with me when she moved away. We left each other's lips for a brief second. Nandini was almost out of breath and I could hear my own heartbeat as loud as if it was beating in my ear.

"Nandini..." was all I could manage to say.

I kissed her again with more passion that had built up within me, she reciprocated. My hands went down her chest as I tried pulling up her shirt. I wanted more of her to feel and love. As soon as I did, Nandini almost froze. Worried that she might have fainted in real, I set her free from the interlock and looked at her with concern.

"Let's not cross our limits" she pushed me a little away from her by pressing her soft hand against my chest. Guilt was fairly visible in her eyes.

"Okay, I'm sorry." My mind was not in a state to work. That was all I could manage.

"Don't be. We both started it. I just feel this is the not the right time for this." She said.

"Okay" My manly core felt a bit dejected but I completely agreed with Nandini's decision to stop. We just cuddled and slept.

I woke up around 8 a.m. the next morning, moved myself out of bed and opened the curtain.

Nandu groaned a little as the first beams of sunlight touched her face. "Urrgh, it can't be morning already" she muttered in her sleep.

"Where are we going today?" she asked while we were getting ready.

"We are not going anywhere today" I told her my plain decision.

"Why? Are you planning to complete the pending work from last night?"She teased me for last night.

"No, just wanted to spend the remaining time with you here." I didn't feel like going anywhere and waste time. I just wanted her to stay close to me. I was feeling emotional then. We just passed the time by talking, playing cards, watching TV and eating together.

A few hours later, we were parting our ways at the railways station. We had packed our luggage and reached the station 30 minutes before the departure time. As soon as the lady announced that the train will reach the platform in the next 15 minutes, we held our hands a little tighter. As we sat there on one of the empty benches watching people say good bye to their loved ones, our hearts sank more. In those few minutes at the railways station, we saw so many happy and sad endings. Some waved off the love of their life, mothers praying for their sons, fathers giving away their daughters to their newly-wed husbands, children sending off their father to the army and more. Ours was a similar love story too. We too were to go our separate ways and who knew when we were going to see each other's faces again. Despite telling myself a thousand times that long-distance relationships work, I knew that letting Nandini go was going to be hard.

"Bye, take care. Will see you soon. I Love you…" those were the last words she said after kissing me on my forehead. An hour later, I boarded my train and started back to Hyderabad.

We were on calls most of the time, but it reduced as she started her new job.

I was still trying to get into sleep that night, when I got call from Nandu. It was around 1 a.m.

"Hello, Nandu…" Seeing the time in my watch, I got a bit worried.

"Hello, Adi" she sounded brittle.

"What happened, is everything alright?" my heart started pounding fast.

"I told my parents about our relationship" She paused for a few seconds after saying that.

"What was their reaction?" I sensed that her pause meant that they had rejected the idea of her marrying me but I still wanted to hear it from her. More importantly, even if they did say no, why was Nandini calling so late to tell me that?

"Today in the evening when I came back from the office, my mom was discussing about a matrimony profile for me. I thought it was better to come clean before she started approaching respective families."

"They are not happy with my decision." she told me in very low voice.

"Ok, but why are you crying, did they beat you?" I got worried.

"No, they would never do that. It's just that they all are treating me like an alien and it really hurts. They don't want me to talk to you anymore."

"So, what are we going to do now?" my heartbeat started to build up.

"I just want you to trust me and listen to what I am about to say." My attention was completely on her words.

"I Love you and I will marry only you. Just trust my words. Wait for me. It will take time to convince my parents, but do wait for me. Till then please don't try to contact me. If anything happens, I will call you myself, ok?" She instructed.

"Are you sure that everything is fine with you?" I couldn't make of the situation. It was all happening too quickly.

"Yes it is Adi. I never knew they would behave this way. What you said was correct. You can never know a person's reaction when he/she is exposed to an unexplored situation. Adi, do you trust me?" she asked me very firmly.

"Yes I do." I was very much confident about that.

"Then just wait for me, I may not be sure of how much time but I will come back for you as a bride."

"And I will wait to become your groom." I said.

"Okay bye Adi. Take care. Know that I love you a lot." She said and hung up.

Days started to pass slowly. I couldn't get Nandini out of my mind. No distractions worked for me. I started staying alone most of the time. I would walk on the road for hours just thinking what she might be doing, was she missing me too, was she fine, were her parents treating her well etc. I felt invisible even when surrounded my many people. I got fed up on thinking of ways to fight the loneliness but nothing seemed to work.

A few months passed and she didn't contact me —not even once. When one day, I could no longer take the pain, I called her up. A lady picked up on the other end.

"Nandini?"

"Umm, who is this?"

"Is Nandini there? I could have recognized Nandu's voice even in my sleep. That wasn't her.

"Wrong number…" before answering my question, the lady cut the call. It then dawned on me that Nandini had changed her cell phone number, as soon as that thought crept into my head, along came all sorts of trashy thoughts. May be she didn't want me anymore, maybe I was just a pass time for her, maybe she found someone better than me, maybe she even got married… But the only thought that shushed such ill thoughts was that she had promised to return to me as a bride. When and how, I didn't know. All I knew then was that Nandini hadn't lied when she said that. Even if I had to spend all my life waiting for her, I was going to because she had promised me that.

After such a long gap, she had come back to me, but I wasn't sure as why? As a friend or something else? So much had passed since we last talked and I hadn't expected her to show up like this one day. It wasn't like I had forgotten about her; I had just given up the idea of me and her getting married. I hadn't brought up the topic of what happened to us yet; I wanted her to be the one to open up and tell me why she didn't contact me or changed her number.

THE DAY WITHOUT SHREE

I saw her getting ready in front of me. Her ring had brought back so many memories. I was in shock that she was still wearing it.

"Adi...Adi..." she called me to make sure that I wasn't thinking about Shree or Shiva.

I moved my eyes from the ring and saw her. She still looked beautiful as before.

"Would you like to have some tea?" she asked me.

"Yes sure" I replied and she got up and headed to the kitchen.

"What happened next?" she asked me in a loud tone from the kitchen. I was not in a mood to tell my story in that loud tone. So I got up, walked towards the kitchen and stood by the door, watching her make tea. I didn't speak a word for long.

"Adi...what happened next?" she distracted me.

I started speaking. "I was not ready to go to office where Shree wasn't there. Sitting at home didn't help me to come out of it, so I decided to go back to the office. I still remember the day when I woke up, got dressed and headed to the office. It was going to be hard to not see Shree on his usual seat. Hard to not hear his irritating yet convincing theories about life and humans. Hard to not eat lunch together. As I got off at my building,

I felt afraid to go into the Ekalavya room. But I also knew that I couldn't stand there forever.

I entered the room and saw that no one was there, which was more horrible. I walked and occupied my usual place. I couldn't stop turning my head and looking at the seat right beside me.

"He is not here anymore" That fact sent shivers down my spine and broke my heart every time I reminded myself that. I couldn't sit there for long. I walked out and looked for Tinu. She worked on the 5th floor left wing; I took an elevator and reached her desk.

"Hi Tinu, are you busy?" I asked her in a very low voice, standing against her desk.

"Yes Adi, I have a meeting to attend now." we shall meet for lunch, she said.

"Okay I will wait for you." I said and moved back to my room.

I didn't feel like sitting down for some time. There were still 2 hours before lunchtime. Everyone in the room was either busy working or chatting amongst themselves. I didn't feel like joining any conversations either so I just started working around a little. It was then that my eyes went on to the bag that lay on the floor. I knew that bag inside out. It had belonged to Shree. He might have deliberately left it at the office thinking he would collect it tomorrow morning. If only he knew, he wasn't going to see the next day's light.

I instantly picked it up from the floor and brought it to my desk. I knew it was wrong to go through someone else's personals but I just wanted to make sure that there wasn't something too valuable in it. If there was, it was my responsibility as a friend to return it to whomever it belonged. I unzipped the bag and started to look inside. There were a few notebooks, a couple of stationary items and a pen drive. None of these things were of much worth so I decided to keep them to myself instead of returning it to his parents. It was almost 1 p.m. when I got a call from Tinu asking me to join her for lunch at the cafeteria if I wasn't busy with anything. I told her that I will be there a in a few minutes. Any place was better than there. When I reached the cafeteria, Tinu was already waiting for me.

"Hi Adi, how are you?" Her voice sounded broke like mine. I instantly knew that she hadn't recovered from the big loss either.

"I'm trying to come out of it" I said.

"We need to come out of it Adi. We can't stay in the past forever. I know it must be more difficult for you as you two were very close, but that is the only way you will find peace within." she said.

I knew she was right. It was going to be really hard to get ever the fact that Shree was no more, forget about his face, his smile and then his injured face. There were many momentarily pauses in between our talks. Whenever we all sat together, we were always the loudest in the whole cafeteria. But deep within, we both knew that was never going to happen. The only thing that bothered me was that Tinu was coming up with her loss in a much better way. Maybe it was her work, or responsibilities at home that kept her busy and distracted. I had none of those. The only thing on my mind was Shree and his bloodied face.

"I feel like if I got into any project, I will be better able to cope up with Shree's death that is all I keep thinking about all day and night." I shared my thoughts with her.

"Of course you will. This is exactly what has been helping me to come out of it. I am so busy with work all day that I don't even have the time the scratch my head. When I go home, I am too tired that I just have dinner and sleep. Same routine the following day." She told me. We then again shared a brief pause after which Tinu asked for a leave.

"Okay Adi, I will have to leave now. There is tons of work that I need to complete before heading home. Would you be able to meet me for tea after a couple of hours?" she said completing her lunch and made a quick move from there.

All the way back to my seat, there was only one thing that was going through my mind, I needed to get into some project or else I would go mad thinking about Shree. As I was immersed in my own thoughts, one of the HR team managers visited the Ekalavya. As the door opened, all eyes were on him except mine. I was looking at desk when the HR team member's feet stopped at the back of my seat.

"Aditya. Can you please go and meet Nisha Mathur", he said.

"Sure. Right away?" I asked.

"Yes please" He smiled.

With a notepad and pen in my hand, I started walking towards the HR wing which was located diagonally the Ekalavya room.

Nisha Mathur was the HR head for this Hyderabad branch and she was one of the most beautiful and nicest ladies among the many others in the office. She was comfortably seated in her chair typing an email draft, as I entered her room.

"Nisha, you wanted to see me "I asked.

Hey, Adi, how are you doing?

She asked me in the sincerest of tone and I felt like putting my heart out. Of course I didn't. If I had told her that, she would have had me admitted into a psychiatric ward.

"I am good. Thank you for asking." I tried keeping the conversation professional.

"Adi, I am really delighted to tell you that we have a new project on the 4th floor and the manager has requested for a fresher. Seeing your progress report of the last few months, we believe you are the perfect candidate for the project."

"Really? That is really good news for me. I didn't expect it to happen so soon." I told her bluntly.

"You can join the project from tomorrow and all the details regarding the project and team will be emailed to you by the EOD. Sounds good?" she asked.

"Perfect actually. I can't wait to start. Thank you so much Nisha", after thanking her I walked back to the Ekalavya. This was what I expected would happen someday but I hadn't anticipated that the day would come so soon. Technically, that should have been the first step in my career but for some reason, I wasn't able to feel that happiness, not an ounce of it. The immediate person that I would have loved to share that happiness with wasn't there.

Beep... beep. My phone buzzed.

"I will be coming down in 5 minutes and then we both will go out for tea, okay? Read the message from Tinu.

We walked to a Tea stall which was in front of your office building.

"Nisha got me into a project and tomorrow will be my joining" I told her as we waited for the tea.

"Wow, that is really good news. We had just spoken about it in lunch." She seemed a bit surprised.

"Yes, I guess, I got lucky" I plastered a smile on my face.

"You don't seem happy. Do you?" she asked.

"I am happy... it's just that Shree is not there"

"Common Adi... You need to come out of this, things will hit you hard in life every step of the way. It doesn't mean you get carried away by their effects. Have you ever noticed how ripples form in the water when you throw a stone? The effect of such a simple gesture makes the water lose its calmness. But only for a little while before it restores it. I am certain that you feel the same way, you just need to give it some time."

"Yes, maybe I need some time to come out of this." I said.

That evening as soon as I reached, I placed Shree's bag in my cupboard's drawer and closed it. Tomorrow was going to be a new day for me and I needed to prepare myself for it both physically and mentally.

PROJECT ASSIGNED

It was my first day of the project, after completing all the paperwork at the HR desk; I finally headed to the 4th floor. The entire floor followed a specific theme. The entire floor was divided into little cubicles of red color, each for single person. There was a work desk with a few drawers, a PC, a revolving chair and a dustbin to throw away any paper thrash. The cubicles weren't big but people had decorated them with plants, notice boards with sticky notes on it and additional drawers to put important files and folders. I stood there for a minute before the manager came and introduced himself and showed me my desk. He also introduced me to all the existing team members.

"And here is your seat, Aditya." He pointed towards an empty cabin which looked like it had been recently refurbished.

Finally, I had my own desk and a machine that I could use for work and not games anymore. I was excited to start my job but also a bit nervous as all those people and the surrounding was new for me.

"Hi, Adi" a man in his early 30's, sitting right next to me greeted me.

"Hi, sorry I don't remember your name?" I said in an apologetic tone.

"That's fine bro, my name is Naresh." He smiled.

"If you need any help with anything, just let me know, okay?" he added. I felt a little relieved when I saw that he was trying to be friendly.

After a few minutes, my Team Lead visited me and summarized about work and project.

Luckily, on the first day of my new project, all my team members left a little early which allowed me some time alone to go over the different aspects of my job, including previous project details, and understand the working of the machine. I had already been given training on how to handle the technical tools which were used in the project. 45 days I had practiced on it and thankfully I was able to manage all the work on time. I was so occupied that day that I hardly had any time to think about Shree.

In the following days Tinu and I met regularly. Sometimes one of us had other lunch plans so we would meet for tea in the late afternoon. But that too ended as our workload increased.

Even on some Sundays, I had to go to the office to complete the work. It was one such Sunday when I went to the office to complete some pending work that had to be submitted by Monday morning.

I went to my cubicle and sat down to work. I would have started work if it hadn't been too hot in the office; the air conditioner wasn't on.

"Hi security, can you turn on AC in 4th floor?" I dialed the security and requested.

I was able to finish my work by lunch time, but did not feel like going out for lunch or home. I just emailed all the work to my team lead and sat idle on my chair at my desk. Everything had become so systematic. Or maybe I was the one who got a bit mature or boring to put it more correctly. I always said no to all those people planning a hangout, I refused party invitations, stopped meeting my friends, even Tinu sometimes, who was in the same building as I. All such thoughts started running through my mind. Why had I become so boring? Why didn't I feel bad when I isolated myself from everyone on purpose? Did I not need anyone anymore?

After an hour I switched off my machine, grabbed my bike keys and started back on my way home. Those thoughts did not get out of my head so soon. I started observing my own life.

Every Monday, I woke up at 6. a.m., freshened up, ironed my work clothes and got dressed, I would have breakfast and leave for my office.

There, I would reach my desk, switch on my machine, work like a robot and leave for home after 5 p.m. Then I would spend an hour stuck in the traffic, go home, take a bath, have dinner, and then sleep.

The next morning, I would again wake up at 6 a.m., freshen up, iron my clothes and get dressed. Then have breakfast and leave for work. Come home after 5 p.m., take a bath, have dinner and then go to sleep.

That was everything I did throughout the week. Everything on time, like a robot. There was nothing else and every day was the same. This had been happening for many months and I hadn't even realized it until today. The saddest part was that I saw no change in the routine in the future either.

Was that all there was to life? I saw my life in a straight line, without any ups and downs, thrills or adventures, happiness or sadness… Everything was just stuck at a point, I was moving forward but in that straight line only. And a straight line on the electrocardiogram meant death.

If I already knew that I was going to repeat the exact same thing over and over again, what was the point of doing it in the first place? It wasn't making me happy, just rich in the monetary sense. Was that motivation enough to continue what I was doing? But then again, what other choice did I really have? There were times when sensing the quietness in the office; I would just want to scream at the top of my lungs. I had started to feel trapped in my own body and I knew there was no getting out. Was money all I needed in my life now? Weren't relationships of any worth? I was getting promoted but that only put extra pressure of work on my shoulders which equated to less time for me and my family. Ironically, I was getting richer but also poorer at the same time. As all these thoughts piled up in my mind, I started to hate my job. I rarely got any time to spend with my family or friends. There weren't any emotions left inside me. Unlike old times, nothing excited me up or broke me down. As days went by, my hatred for my job increased. Everyone else was so busy in their lives or to put it right, I had deliberately pushed them out of my life and I had no one who I could talk to.

"Hi Tinu" I called her over the weekend.

"Hi Adi, how are you? Looks like you are very busy these days?" She was being sarcastic.

"I was busy with my office work, yaar. It has gotten really tough and demanding. You aren't the only one who says that. I hear the exact same thing from my other friends and family members too." I said.

"Yes, I know stupid, no need to give any explanations. Tell me what made you to call me out of nowhere." She was surprised.

"I hate my life style, can you help me out." I said in a pleading tone.

"Why, what happened?" she asked.

"I see that I'm repeating the same things every day, nothing is changing, and I don't like it." I said.

"So, are you bored of your job?" she asked.

"No, it is not because of boredom and I'm not a sensation seeker." I continued.

"When I started observing consciously my daily life I was upset. I'm doing the same job every day. I'm not enjoying it anymore."

"Are you looking for a job change?" she asked, interrupting me.

"Even if I do some other job, after a few days I will be doing the exact same things again. What's the point of a job change then?" I argued.

"Adi, then what is your problem?" she asked me, in slightly high tone.

"Is that all we are supposed to do in our lives? Is it how it is going to be like in the next 10...? 20 years? Is nothing going to change? Shouldn't that be considered a crime? I was becoming emotionally dead inside. It's like I have restricted my life on an 11.4 km road from Mehdipatnam to Hi-tech city. Is it what others call living life to the fullest?"

"What do you want to do now?" she asked.

"I'm not sure about that yet, but I know that I don't want to do what I am doing right now." I said.

" Look Adi, to survive you have to earn, and if you have to earn, you need to work, which is nothing but doing the same thing again and again, right?" she questioned me.

"Yes you're correct, but life always needs a balance. You're earning but you're not enjoying then what is the point. "

"So you're saying you have earned enough and it's time for you to enjoy?" she asked.

"I won't stop earning, it's just that I want to take a break and do something different for a while."

"Any plan on what to do and all?" she asked me.

"No" I answered; I thought she did not have an opinion for me. There was silence for a moment.

"Can I ask you something?" she asked.

"Yes sure," I said.

"Is there a possibility that you weren't enjoying your job right from the beginning, it is just that you have realized it now? May be that is the reason why you seem so frustrated."

"I believe 90% of our generation opts for software jobs just because they don't know what else can be done to earn money. Only 10% of the population is passionate about something very different. I'm no different from the 90% lot."

"Then what is your passion?" she asked me.

"As of now, I have nothing." I said.

"Then what are you trying to say, Adi?" her tone was again high.

"I don't know Tinu, I just wanted to spill out my feelings with someone as I thought If I didn't I might die. So, I called you up because I assumed you had answers to everything." I said.

"Hmm, the only thing I can suggest is to give this job some time, there are always some deadlock situations in life where we feel this is it. This is how it is going to be for the rest of your life but time resolves everything. These situations don't stay the same forever. I am most certain that this is just a phase you are going through and will soon come out of it" I had no answer for that comment.

"Okay Tinu, I will call you later" I didn't feel comfortable enough to extend the call any longer.

Did I know what had to be done if not this job? Her question made some sense to me. I sat back for a while but nothing popped up into my head.

"This is it." I convinced myself and went to bed getting ready for the daily routine.

The very next day, I repeated the exact same routine. I got up, ironed my clothes, dressed up, had breakfast and left for work. There, I turned on my system, worked till 5 p.m., left work, got stuck in a frustrating traffic jam with everyone trying to get home as fast as they could. I did try to change the routine a bit by watching a movie but I was so tired then, that I went to bed at exactly the same time I did every day. No matter how much I tried, I was reliving everyday like a new one and it was killing me inside.

"Hi Adi", a message popped up in my system from my manager.

"Hi Dip, yes?" I knew something was going to come up my way as he rarely pinned me.

"Can you come to my cabin?"

I locked my machine and walked towards his cabin which was about just 20 feet away from my desk.

It seemed like he was on an important call over the speaker with someone. Looking at me, he waved his hand, gesturing me to come in. As I walked in, he pointed out his hand at the chair in front of him. I sat and waited for him to finish his call.

Even after 25 minutes I was sitting on the same chair like a fool, waiting for him to finish the conversation. If he knew that the call would take this long, why did he call me? I could have completed the task I left pending before coming to his office but he, being the manager, didn't care about that. He didn't care if I had to spend an extra fifteen minutes working overtime because he wasted my time. He was my boss and he didn't care about anything unless I left without completing my work.

"Sorry for the call, it was unplanned," the typical fake manager's smile on his face was a clear sign that he wasn't the least bit apologetic.

"Aditya, we have a few major activities planned coming weekends, say about the next 8 weeks or so." I had a strong feeling that he was going to ask me to repeat the same routine I did every weekday on weekends too. If he did, I was sure I would kill myself.

"I want you to attend them and learn so that you can lead the team under you whenever we have the same trainings the next time. I am positive that this experience will be very beneficial for you in the longer run. After all, one day you will take my place."

He had obviously bribed me by bringing up my career. Even he knew that the trainings were nothing more than a bunch of boring people giving lectures. He knew that by linking the importance of attending the training with my career; I wouldn't be able to refuse. Of, course I thanked him for the opportunity to give him the impression that I was delighted that he chose me from all the rest. If I had refused, I feared losing the good impression I had set on him. Besides, it was also about my job security. I knew that I was replaceable by the amount of new interns and management trainees the company was hiring every now and then. This was how it worked everywhere. The tough competition had made it easier for companies to discard all those people that didn't abide by the rules or were willing to put up with the extra pressure of work.

SHREE'S DIARY

The schedule from then onwards went from bad to worse. I worked 8+ hour shifts with no extra pay, rarely got to see my family, even on festivals, and hated the lifestyle I had become so accustomed to living. After the 6 weeks training, I got a two-day leave, for which I couldn't be more grateful. But those two days were almost over now. I decided to take a leave from work for two more days and figure out what I really wanted to do. On Tuesday evening, the last night of my leave, I was all alone in the house. My family had left town to attend a family event in a nearby town. I, of course, had the perfect excuse to make —work. I was home alone and feeling starved. I wasn't in the mood to cook or eat any of the frozen food in the freezer, so I decided to take a walk to the nearby restaurant to get something for myself. As soon as I got out of my apartment after locking my house, the first chill of the cold breeze reminded me that I was only wearing a sleeveless shirt and shorts. Too late to go back and change. I decided to continue the climb down the stairs in the hope that by the time I will be down, my body will be better adjusted to the outside weather.

I felt like having Biryani from Al-Sabha, a neighboring restaurant chain. Their biryani was my go-to favorite dinner when my mother had cooked something that I didn't like.

"Salaam waalaikum, Adi" the uncle at the billing counter knew me well, as we had been living in the same colony for many years now.

"Walaikum salaam uncle, khairiyat?" I wished him back.

"Alhamdulillah" he replied back saying everything was fine by the grace of God almighty.

"What happened, I don't see you very often nowadays?" He asked me.

"I have been working 7 days a week since last two months." I was tired even saying that.

"Don't work too much Adi, it's not good." He just said with a big smile. I felt happy as I was talking to someone after a long time that wasn't anyone from the office or may be because he is the one to say not to work too much. He said it will take about 10 min –15 min to get my food ready. While he was busy attending to other customers, I thought of having a cup of tea.

Altaf, an adolescent boy who owned a tea stall in front of this restaurant took my order for tea and said that he will have one prepared in 2 minutes. He had been running this tea stall since his teen years.

When he came back with the cup of tea in his hand, he tried to initiate a small chat with me.

"Adi Bhai. How are you? It has been a while." I didn't want to say it again so I just said I'm fine.

"Can I ask you something, Altaf?" he was almost closing his stall, no one was around.

"How much do you save per month?" I asked, looking at his same old clothes.

"Why this question now?" he asked me with a smile packing his things to shut down the stall.

"Just wanted to know." I said.

"It varies from 80,000 to 90,000 per month." he said, still casually continuing his work.

"Oh, that's good." Was the expression on my face, inside, all I could think was that this little boy earning double than me! I literally felt like laughing at myself. I had gotten admission in the best school and college;

my parents had invested so much money into my education, my grooming and my lifestyle. I worked my ass off 8+ hours —work that drained me out all my energy, work that I didn't even enjoy doing. And there, that little boy was making the most of what he knew and enjoyed doing, and was earning more than me at such an early age.

"Adi, your food is ready." The uncle reminded me with his loud voice.

"Okay Altaf, have a good night." I wanted to ask him many questions but I felt it would be awkward to ask about his income and stuff. I moved from there, collecting my food.

I enjoyed the chicken biryani as expected. I walked to the hallway and switched on the TV. I kept thinking that Altaf was earning much more than me. For a moment, I thought about opening a tea stall myself. But I knew even that wasn't going to be easy.

If money was the only thing that mattered then it didn't matter how anyone earned it. All that education and grooming had done for me was to make me a more sophisticated citizen. It had made me acceptable in the society of literate people. But was that doing me any good?

While I was watching TV, a reminder alarm popped up in my mobile, reminding me about tomorrow's meeting at 9 a.m. in the morning. Thinking about that only made me realize that I will be going back to the same routine from tomorrow morning, and it made my heart sink with both sadness and frustration.

Due to a sudden power outage, my entire apartment went dark. As all the window were closed not even a single beam of light from outside entered in. I grabbed my mobile and started to search for a battery-powered table lamp. Not sure where my mom kept that.

After passing almost all the rooms looking for it, I reached mine. I opened my cupboard and found it there, hidden behind my books. While I was about to close the door, something caught my eye. I saw Shree's bag which I had found in my office months ago. I did see that nothing important was there in it, but since I had nothing better to do then to wait for the power to be back, I decided to take out his bag and go through his stuff. I hadn't done that before because I had been too heartbroken then.

I placed the bag after emptying all its content on my reading table and lit the battery-powered lamp.

I started flipping through his notebook. The first few pages were some notes that he had noted down during our first few days at the office. Later it was filled by information about some raining session, computer model stuff etc. Closing it back, I went on to unzip all the pockets on the side of the bag. There wasn't much in the bag except for a few stationary items and sticky notes. I felt the heaviness of the bag as I placed it on my desk. I inverted it again and shook it, hoping that something would fall out. But it didn't. Then I turned it over and on the back side of it was a mesh pocket with a zip. I had missed looking at it the first time I opened it and discovered a small diary. I had never seen the diary before, not even with Shree. My curiosity urged me to open it even when by the looks of it; it seemed to be his personal diary. After a little hesitation, I finally flipped the cover. On the very first page was a heading written in Shree's hand writing, also signed by him at the end. The heading read DIARY NUMBER 8.

On the next page dated 12/07/2011 were a few paragraphs written. Before beginning to read, just out of curiosity, I flipped through the diary only to discover that the whole diary had just one note. I felt strange at first and then it dawned on me. The date on the first page was the day before his accident. This was Shree's very last note before his accident.

"I received a call from an unknown number yesterday. I recognized it was her right after she said hello. Divya had caught me unguarded like that out of the blue, I hadn't heard from her since ages. At first I thought of cutting the call but then I thought whatever happened between us didn't matter anymore, and greeted her in a friendly tone instead. We had both chosen our different paths and she was married now. There was no point holding grudges, I thought.

She told me that she was not happy with her married life and wanted me to help her out. I wasn't sure why she called me in the first place to tell me that. I told her that everything will settle down. All she and her husband needed was some time to sort out their differences.

But to my surprise she called in the morning today to ask if I was still interested in marrying her. I didn't know how to answer that. A lot had changed between us since then. I may still have feelings for her deep within me, but I also remembered how she had walked passed me and gotten married to someone else. So saying yes straightaway was out of the question but I feared that saying no would hurt her more. So the only thing that seemed sane was to ask for some time to think about the proposal. She agreed and granted me as much time as I needed.

The same evening, when I went home after office, I heard my parents fight; they stopped when they saw me enter the gate. But the silence only prevailed for few minutes, until it all started again. Every day, they would blame each other for ruining each other's life and I have had enough of it. All day, after coming from work tired, all I need is some peace of mind and they just can't give me that.

When I went to bed, there were a thousand thoughts running in my mind. Divya was still waiting for my answer and despite all the thinking I had invested into the idea of marrying her, I still had no answer. After spending 25+ years in the companionship of each other, my parents are still playing the blame game. Seeing them fight, I wonder if every marriage is like this. Not much is happening in the office either. I am not even sure when I will be assigned any project. If only I had been assigned to some project, I would have kept myself engaged. If only there was some way to escape all this. Some place I could run away to, leaving all the responsibilities and people behind. Like an unplanned trip where no one knows me and no one follows from behind. That is all I need from life now. A few moment of complete solace.

That was all that was written in Shree's diary. I hoped that by now his parents would have stopped fighting because he had done exactly what he had written in his diary. He had left them all alone. The power came back; I placed the diary on my reading table and walked into the kitchen to drink some water. As soon as I remembered that I was starting office form tomorrow, I decided to sleep in a little early so as to get the most sleep before waking up tomorrow for work.

As days passed, I started feeling more robotic than ever, repeating the same tasks every day. The feeling of being stuck in a rut further depended. I wanted to come out of it desperately.

A few days later, I received a call from my manager asking me to come in for a little word. Hoping that he would appreciate me on my work and dedication, I knocked on his cabin's door and after his answer entered.

"Come in and have a seat, Adi" he said without looking up as he was busy typing an email to someone important.

"I see you are working really hard to complete the given tasks but I came to know that you're missing your deadlines on a regular basis now. Adi, you can always come in and talk to me if there is any problem." It may have started with a little appreciation, but it didn't end on a good note. I'd had enough, I was working as hard as I could and trying my best to stay on top of my game, and instead of complimenting me on how hard I worked or how grateful he was that I stayed late after work hours to finish as much as I could, he was accusing me of being lazy.

"I'm not comfortable with the new technology in this project. I'm struggling because I haven't gotten trained on it for enough time." I bluntly told him.

"You can't say that. You aren't the only one who is new to the technology; there are many others who are learning it too. You have to be ready to get into any technology and learn it within the given time frame." His voice was little louder than before.

"There is a thing called interest Ganesh, if I'm not interested, it doesn't matter how much time I spend. The results are going to be blunt." This time even I raised my voice a little.

"I will give you a second chance to prove yourself or else there many people on bench who are desperately looking to get into this project. I don't like to point it out to you like this Adi. Please be careful next time."

How dare he give me a warning? I felt enraged but obviously couldn't express it in front of my boss. I needed to hold in my anger, at least, till I was giving the permission to leave.

"You can leave now." he concluded.

When I came back home and unlocked my bedroom door, I saw everything was kept where I had left it. My mom would have probably killed me if she saw the home in such a messy condition. I removed my shoes and socks from the living room, threw my bag on the couch and walked to my room and fell on my bed. Despite trying, I couldn't get the words of my manager out of my head.

I had two options at that point. First, to continue doing the same job despite hating it as it was the question of my livelihood and social eminence. Second, ditch it for some other job or career where my heart really was.

Should I be afraid and accept or should I be bold and take a step. I wasn't sure what to do, I felt my head might burst if I worked like this or thought about it over and over again. I quickly got out of my bed, undressed myself, took a towel and proceeded for a shower.

The warm droplets from the shower formed steam while I closed my eyes standing like a statue under it. The sensation of steamy water calmed me a little and helped to take things away from my mind. I felt fresh and every bit of air touching my skin felt like heaven.

I dried my hair with the towel in front of the mirror which had been mounted on my cupboard window. While I was getting dressed I saw Shree's diary through mirror on my reading table. I had already read that but I wasn't sure why I headed towards it to read again.

"Sometimes I feel like going for an unplanned trip somewhere very far from these circumstances." His last words got stuck in my mind when I opened it again.

MOM'S WORRY

The thought of going for an unplanned trip did not get out of my mind very easily. The words *unplanned trip* looked and felt exciting but scary at the same time. For starters, I wasn't; sure if my family would agree to it. They wouldn't understand my desperation to just break free. How much I needed that, they didn't know that.

It was my parent's 25th anniversary, so we all decided to dine out for the evening to celebrate. We all went to a fancy restaurant. While we were waiting for our ordered food I saw something printed under my plate on the dinning mat.

*"Change is a wonderful thing, but when ideas do not move forward into actions they die."*That quote on that piece of paper was a mind-awakening statement for me.

I always believed that books and quotes can influence one when they can connect with the circumstances and incidents themselves. Because I had read such novels where the protagonist had a choice to make, I felt like relating to the quote myself. It felt like it was put there for me to see and take note from. That was it, all the doubt that occupied my mind earlier vanished. I knew what I needed. The answer was right in front of me. I needed that unplanned trip so that I could decide what I wanted my future to be like. However, before telling my family or friends about it, I needed to pick a destination —the place that was going to offer me a new chance at life. A place that was going to refresh my mind, body, and soul. A place that would help me forget my past, about Shree's death, my dead-end job, and help me start afresh. All the signs were clear.

Me finding Shree's bag in the first place, then the diary in which only one page had been written, the page that fed my brain to hope for a change and lastly the dining mat quote, which boosted my motivation and gave it a direction.

The very next day evening as I was switching channels on TV to find something interesting, I paused at a channel which as showing an interview of Aamir Khan, an actor who inspired me in many ways. He was sitting amongst a group of college students and was being questioned about his success.

"If you want to experience most phases of life, just go for a trip with your friends from Kanyakumari to Kashmir."He told the students.

Was that an omen for me? Kashmir to Kanyakumari? Wasn't I the one looking for a destination? However, the trip he mentioned was going to take me months and I only had plans to leave for a few days. Therefore, I decided to cut down the trip from Hyderabad to Kashmir.

The same night as I was checking my Facebook profile, I saw a post from one of my friends who had been recently married. She had just spent her honeymoon on an island without any laptops or mobile phones. She posted that it had been the best experience of her life. Another sign I thought. That thought started feeding my brain. So, I was planning to leave my job and go for an unplanned trip from Hyderabad to Kashmir without carrying a mobile phone. It sounded both crazy and scary but the thought "I needed change" kept pushing me.

I knew discussing the idea with my dad or mom in the first will not work, so I decided to ask and convince my sister first because elder sisters are the younger version of mom.

"Shall we go out and have an ice cream?" I asked her.

"Looks like you need something from me," she said with a smile.

"Nothing like that" I did not want to give her any hints until we were out of the apartment.

"Okay, let's go." We reached a nearby ice cream parlor.

"I want to quit the job and go on a trip for a while." I came up straight to the point.

"Wait, what!!!!!" her eyes widened.

"Have you gone mad, why you would want to do that?" she asked me.

"I'm stressed with this job; I don't want this robotic life anymore. I feel if I continue in the software industry, I will end up with diabetes, lack of vitamin D and preferably a heart attack at such an early age. I don't want this to be my life; I want to explore it more. So I just want to take a break for a certain period, come back and then decide what my career options should be." I tried my best to brief her about my situation. She remained silent for a while, looking at the floor.

"I get your point. When I joined my job, even I did not like it but eventually I had to adjust to it. I think having a job is not the most important thing. You are just 22, Adi. You have lot of time to decide your career. It is good that you have realized at very early age." There was a sense of relief listening to her but I know it had just started.

"By the way where are you planning to go?" she asked taking the first bit from her ice cream.

"An unplanned trip to Kashmir" I said.

"What do you mean by unplanned?" she asked.

"I want to travel till Kashmir... not to Kashmir" I paraphrased my statement.

"So you want to go till Kashmir but stop at different locations in the middle?" she asked casually.

"Yes, you can say that," I partially shook my head.

"It looks like pretty much planned, then why were you saying it as unplanned?" She finally asked what I feared the most.

"I want to start the journey with only clue that I should go towards north. To which place I go for a halt or where I eat and I sleep everything will be instantaneous. I just want it to be exciting each and every second, minute, and day."

"What will you get out of this?" she already lost her cool.

"Look Avika, we were brought up under certain circumstances. We weren't financially-challenged and our parents worked their best to provide for the family. Within those circumstances, we came across many hurdles and dealing with them keeps us busy throughout our childhood. I want to experience other circumstances too, which we were not exposed to before."

She looked confused.

"Mom always cooked us food that we liked, we traveled in cabs because it gave us comfort and space unlike metro and buses. Similarly, every activity we did, we preferred to do it in our comfort zone. How would I react if I had only one meal available and that too something that I hated, how would I deal with a situation if I had to walk a few miles for food, will I be comfortable sleeping anywhere apart from bed, will I be able to live without AC? There are many people living without all these luxuries. I want to meet such people and get a chance to experience their life. This trip will help me to explore myself and life as well." I was done.

"I'm really amazed at the way you think at this age. This is such mature talk coming from you Adi, I appreciate that."

"Let's say if you go into a hotel on your trip and it is the most dirtiest and unclean room ever. You always have an option to take your mobile and look for a hotel with better reviews and go there." She brought up the scariest point. I just smiled at her.

"What does that smile mean?" she was angry.

"I know this would happen. This is why I want to travel without my mobile and laptop." I finally did it.

"Shut up and let's go home." She said without much hesitation and with much frustration. The way she responded, broke my heart. She got up from her seat but I didn't. I kept looking down at the floor not responding to her.

"What's your problem?" she sat back and asked me in a dominating tone.

"I want to do something and you are not letting me to do it." My eyes became wet, thinking that my trip will never happen.

"It's not like that Adi, we care about you. It's just that the idea of leaving behind your mobile phone and laptop scares me. How would we know if you are okay or not, where you are, do you need any help etc. if you don't carry your phone?" I expected that question from her.

"I will call you guys every day from the public telephone services. It's not like I won't let you know about my trip. " I knew it was right for her to feel worried about me.

"I'm okay for the trip but without your mobile phone… I don't think so." She sounded like it was her final decision.

"Will you support me when I talk to Mom and Dad?" I asked hoping that she would say yes.

"Okay I will but you have to carry your mobile. Deal?" That was her final offer and I had no option but to agree to that.

By the time we reached home, dad was reading the newspaper leaning against the bed's headboard and mom was folding laundry.

"Mom dad, Adi wants to talk to you guys." she initiated the conversation which made it a little easier for me.

"What is it, Adi?" mom asked, while dad looked at me.

"I want to resign from my job." I told them.

"Why are you saying it in bits and pieces? Dad and Mom, Adi is not comfortable with his current job, he has no clarity on what to do. He wants to go on an unplanned trip." she elaborated my thoughts about what trip and why unplanned.

"There is no need to go anywhere, if you want to quit your job, sit at home, take your own time and decide what you want to do next." my mom said. She was still doing the folding ad didn't even bother looking up. Dad didn't speak. I assumed even he had the same opinion.

"Mom, but I wish to go." I tried to argue with her.

"I said No." her voice had the intensity of dissatisfaction. I could feel that, so I went into my room.

I remained silent for the next few days because they hadn't agreed to my idea. One day, as I was browsing something on my laptop, dad walked into my room.

"Adi, I liked the reason for your trip but your mom is worried about your safety. You know how much we care about you. I hope you can understand how hard it will be for your mother to send you out on your own like this without anything. What if something happened to you and we didn't even find out about it? She is worried whether you will come back or not. " He said in a pleasing manner.

"I can understand that dad. I'm just bored of this mechanical life, and I want to explore more about it. I can understand mom's feelings." I really did understand mom's concern.

I had almost given up hope on the trip. Many young people like me may have had many dreams but the whole safe-side mentality became a hurdle. They could have done something extraordinary but no, they had to stay safe and continue with the same systematic life.

I was not obstinate about my trip anymore, but it was just that I didn't recover from that for days either. I didn't remain active at home, kept thinking about the trip all the time and that made me even more restless and lazy. I had once again started repeating my routine and hated it too but there wasn't much that I could have done then. Lava within me was just building up. I never knew when it would erupt.

One night when I was about to sleep, my parents walked into my room. Dad pulled a chair to sit beside my bed and my mom stood beside him.

"Why are so dull these days?" he asked me. Listening to our conversation, my sister entered my room too.

"Nothing like that, I just need some time to sync with this mechanical life." I said without bringing up the topic about the trip.

"How much will your trip cost?" a little shocked whether I had heard right, a smile crossed my face.

"Not sure daddy." I said.

"Okay, when do you plan on leaving?" this question made me even happier. I looked at my sister. I couldn't believe what was happening. She smiled back.

"If you say you two are okay with the trip, I will start this Saturday." I said.

"Okay, I will then deposit 2 lacs in your account and will give you some cash. Complete the formalities of quitting job. We will talk the rest on Friday."

"And you will call daily three times every day; if that's okay only then you can go." My mom firmly said.

"Of course mom, I will call you." I immediately jumped out of my bed and hugged her.

"Now go to bed. It's already past midnight." Dad got up from the chair, placed it back from where he had borrowed it and left the room.

"Finally you made them accept. Idiot!!" Avika patted me on my shoulder with a smile and went back into her room.

I felt really fresh in the morning with the feeling that I was going to do something super exciting. I was sure that this trip was going to be life changing for me. I was all set to quit my job. Most importantly, I was eager to see my manager's reaction.

"Mom, you guys meant what you said last night, right?" I just wanted to make sure before quitting my job.

"Yes dear." She said.

As any new trainee, I was the happiest person on my first day of job. I had been super excited then and even more when I finally got into a project. However, none of that was compared to the amount of happiness and excitement I felt going to the office for the last time. I was finally going to do it. Quit my job and go on the trip I had dreamed about for so long. I took my time, typing my resignation email, enjoyed deleting all the work and personal stuff from my machine. I had never felt that I could be this happy quitting my job. Even though, I had no plans, I was still excited for the unknown journey that lay ahead of me. It was around 5 when I finally sent my resignation email to my manager. Within the next few minutes, I received a call from him to come see him in the office. I had strategically chosen this time as I knew I would get off after 30 minutes and he won't have enough time convince me to stay.

Upon entering this room, he asked me to take a seat. He was fully attentive this time. There was no laptop, emails, or phone for him to hide behind.

"I just saw your email, what is the reason?" he asked inquisitively.

"I am not enjoying my work." I wanted to put it in simple way.

"What is the actual problem?" It was obvious that as a manager he knew what troubled me so much that I decided to resign.

"It is nothing from your end or the company. It is just that I need a change." I finished very quickly.

"When are you planning to leave office?" I expected that question.

"Today... because I haven't completed 1 year in the project so I am still on probation. No trainee on probation has to serve the notice period, right?" I tried reading the company's policy to him. He obviously knew that. However, I wanted him to know that, I too, had read the policies and that there was nothing he could do to keep me.

"Okay all the best for your future, then." He greeted me with a handshake.

That day, I had lunch with my co-workers, collected their contacts, surrendered my laptop, gave a little farewell speech and packed my bags. As soon as the clock stuck 5:30, I screamed a silent "YAYY, its closing time" chant, got all my things, rechecked my drawers for the last time in case I had missed something, said my goodbyes and left. I got a little emotional at the end not because I felt sad for leaving that place, but sad because I had made some really good friends there. I had met the two most amazing people of my life Tinu and Shree there. One had left me and I was leaving the other today.

The next morning I woke up with a smile on my face. Relaxation showed on my face. Finally, I no longer had to go to work and waste my energies. I decided to go shopping and buy a few things for the trip.

I purchased a 65L black travel backpack. I figured travelling would be easier if I had less baggage to carry with me. I wasn't going to stuff it with useless items like 3 pairs of shoes, a dozen t-shirts, a pair of jeans etc. I had already decided that I would take a minimalist approach to packing and only carry items that were the most essential. That way, I wouldn't even feel lazy or tired due to extra baggage. So my backpacking list had the following items:

* Four outfits
* A pair of clean inner garments
* My tooth brush and tooth paste
* A pair of sandals
* A water bottle
* And a diary for my travelogue

However, as the days neared, Avika handed me two books to read on the journey -"The Alchemist" and "All the Light We Cannot See". According to her these were books every sane man and woman needed to read and learn from.

Mom handed me a raincoat and a few basic medicines. A day before my journey, I was done packing and set for the trip.

"Adiii" I heard my dad calling me.

"Yes Dad" I came out of my room and reached into the dining hall.

"Come and have a seat here." He pointed out to sit beside him by tapping his hand on the sofa.

"Did you pack all the important things?" he asked.

"Yes Dad." I replied with a smile and a sense of pride that I had shown some efficiency.

"Carry your mobile and its charger, wallet which has your ID proof and your debit card."

I didn't want to carry my mobile but I knew I had to as I knew it would make them feel less tensed and worried. After all, they were my parents; they were bound to worry about my safety.

"I have deposited 2 lacs in your account and here are 20,000 in cash. Just keep a 1000 in your wallet and safe guard the rest in your bag." I felt the concern and tension in his voice.

"I will take care of myself dad, you don't have to worry." I tried telling him.

I was so excited for the trip the next day that I barely slept for half an hour. As soon as I saw the first dull reddish rays seep into my room from the window, I knew it was time to get up and get dressed. I wanted to leave early to avoid traffic. Besides, it was a bit chilly those days and I really wanted to feel that cold breeze against my body. I laid out the clothes I planned on wearing and went straight for a bath by grabbing the towel from behind the door. By the time, I was out of the shower; everyone else in my house had woken up. With a Quarter Saggy Pants, t-shirt, hat and running shoes I was all ready for the adventure.

"Adi come here." My mom called me as I was heading out of my room and towards the main door of my apartment. I had told my mother last night that I would be eating breakfast out so that she wouldn't have to get up early just for that. However, being the mom she was, she did get up, made my favorite breakfast at and insisted that I ate all of it. For the sake of her happiness, I gobbled up as much as I could in one sitting. Next, she went into her room and came back with a photo of Lord Shiva in her hand.

"Pray to God." She told me pointing at a photo frame. I closed my eyes, joined my palms pressed together, while my fingers pointed upwards. I didn't believe in god, but I didn't want to hurt my mom's feelings, so I did. Then she applied Vibhuti on my forehead and placed a gentle kiss. I could see her worry, as I started walking towards the main gate. I saw tears rolling down my mom's cheeks as if she was sending her son on war. Her love was so pure that even I had teary eyes.

"Mom please don't worry I will call you daily and will reach back safely. I promise" I consoled her holding her in my right arm.

"Good - Bye" I waved my hand, giving a hug to all three and went down in the elevator. I didn't know what was going to happen but the feel of my first step of my trip on road felt awesome.

UNPLANNED DAY ONE

The moment I left the house, the clouds were still pretty low. Since winter was just approaching, the roads were covered in thick fog. It was almost impossible to see the road clearly as a precautionary measure; I stayed close to the footpath. The wind was cool so I zipped my jacket up until my neck. The fog and the chilly winds were the perfect start of my journey. All of it felt invigorating to me. The bus station wasn't very far from my apartment which was why I had chosen to walk and not take the taxi or drive. As I reached the bus station, there were only a few elderly men wearing sweaters and mufflers sipping onto hot tea from a nearby dhabba. There was still some time before my bus arrived, so I decided to take a seat on one of the benches. They were freezing and wet —which I discovered after I had sat on one.

"Okay, which ever bus arrives next I will be on it." I told myself. This felt very new. Never before in my whole life had I done something this unplanned. I was letting things go by the flow, not knowing if it will be good for me or bad. After a while, number 5k bus arrived and stopped right in front of me. The doors opened right in front of where I sat and it felt as if they had opened just for me. Taking it as a sign, I picked up my b backpack and started towards it.

"Where do you want to go?" the conductor asked me. The man looked in his mid-forties, had a well-kept mustache on his face, wore a yellow uniform, and had saddlebag around his waist.

"To the last station." I said. The bus waited for other passengers to step on and then took off.

"It seems like you are going on a trip young man." the bus conductor asked me looking at my backpack.

"Yes I'm." I said with all the excitement on my face.

"Where are you going?" was his next obvious question.

"Actually I don't know." I knew my answer was going to raise some eyebrows and it did.

"What? Do your parents know that you are going for a trip?" he seemed a little worried. He might have thought that I was eloping.

"Yes they are aware of it." I tried to gain his trust.

"Do they know at least where you are going?" he still wasn't satisfied.

"No, even they don't know." I didn't feel like lying to him. He didn't ask any further questions from me.

By the time I reached the last stop, the sun dominated the fog, but the wind was still a little frosty. While I walked towards the Jubilee Bus Station, an appetizing aroma caught my attention. As I walked further, I saw a street vendor making fresh Dosa on his mobile cart. I couldn't resist so I ordered one Special Dosa for myself.

Dosa batter fried into thin crisp sheet with butter, stuffed with upma, chilli powder, served with peanut chutney was like being in heaven. They tasted out of this world. For the first time in my life I knew how it felt like to do things own way. The things you always wanted to do but never tried out of fear. My parents rarely encouraged the consumption of street food. This was the reason me and Avika never really tasted the true Indian food that everyone else talked about. Having a Dosa all by myself felt really good.

After having the Dosa I went back to the bus station which had started to get crowded. There was a line of buses, one after the other wit passengers getting on and off and stations boys carrying their luggage behind them. I had absolutely no idea about which bus to take. I didn't know where I was headed. All I knew was that I needed to move north. So I pulled out the country's map and folded it into a square sheet. In that very moment I felt like Indiana Jones in one of his movies with a treasure map but with no clue where it was hidden.

From where I stood, Medak and Adilabad were the two districts in the north. I started walking toward the bus platforms to see which one was going to take me there. I finally spotted a bus with the sign Medak on it, but it had already started wheeling away. I ran as fast as I could and finally made it into the bus before the doors closed or the driver changed gears.

"Where do you want the ticket for?" the driver himself had a machine for issuing tickets right in front of his gear rod over the engine box.

"Medak" I told him.

He took the money and gave me a ticket. Not many people were headed that way so there were many unoccupied seats available but none with a window view. I scrutinized the crowd and decided to sit beside a 6 to 8 year old boy instead of hitching a seat next to an elderly man. I had traveled with a few before, and all they talked about was politics and how astray the new generation was. I didn't want to get into any such debate —at least not on the first day of my trip. I figured the boy next to me might sleep during the journey and I would have some free time for myself to think about my journey and the routes I planned to take.

I placed my backpack under my legs and leaned back, still panting a bit. He looked at me. I couldn't draw from his expressions but they looked somewhere between anger and fear.

"Hello buddy" I greeted him.

"Excuse me" a woman who was holding a kid on her lap called me. I assumed she was the mother of the little kid sitting beside me.

"Oh hi" I thought she might need a seat change to be beside her kid.

"I'm already handling two kids…" She pointed at the other kids sitting beside her on the window seat.

"Okay…" I wasn't sure as to what she expected me to do.

"Can you make sure that my son doesn't peep out all the way through the window?" she requested.

"Yes sure". All her kids were at such a young age. I thought it was difficult for her to travel with three little fellows like that in a bus.

"What's your name?" I tried making eye contact with him but he was not at all willing to do that. He was just looking out from the closed window.

"Sai" her mom replied.

"Hey Sai, wouldn't you want to talk to me?" I tried initiating a conversation with the young boy. He just gave me a blank stare and didn't say a word. I was determined to not give up. I wanted him to feel comfortable sitting with me, if not talk to me. So I took out my mobile phone from my bag as I knew that was the one thing he couldn't resist. No kid could. Seeing me play Candy Crush on my mobile, I had his complete attention then. He watched every move made and judged me internally. Seeing him so engrossed and interested, I asked if he wanted to play.

He nodded his head happily.

"Friends?" I stretched my hand forward. He placed his tiny hand in mine, like I had just gained his complete trust.

"Bro look at my score" those were the first words I heard from him. He looked quite happy after he made a score higher than mine. I patted on his shoulder as If I was really impressed.

"Are you done playing?" I asked after I realized that his mother wasn't too comfortable seeing her kid play on someone else's phone. She must have been worried in case her kid damaged it and then she would have to pay for the repairs.

"So do you go to school?" I asked.

"Hmmm" He mumbled under his breath. Still, I didn't have his undivided attention.

"Which school?" I asked him.

"VidhyaNikethan High School" maybe a little reluctantly and irritated, he at least started answering my questions.

"Oh that's a nice school, I heard." This time, I didn't get any reply back from him.

He then looked up for a minute and his eyes widened with excitement.

"Brother, Look all the trees are going back faster than us".

"No, Sai trees are not going anywhere, it is just an illusion." I tried answering logically.

"What does illusion mean?" Being a 4-years old kid, he obviously didn't understand the meaning of the word illusion I could have bet this was the first time he had ever heard the word.

"Something that seems to be true but actually isn't." That to me, felt like the easiest definition I could have come up with then. The definition had gone above his head and his expressions were enough of a hint for me.

"Brother, how the bus is faster than others?" was his next question.

"Because the driver uncle is driving fast." it sounded stupid to me but I couldn't have answered better.

"How is he driving?" all his questions throughout the journey were very simple yet very difficult to answer. He was very cute and inquisitive and answering his strange questions made the trip really enjoyable for me. As we reached Medak, I helped Sai and her mom get their luggage from the bus. Before she left in a taxi to her home, I felt like talking to her. I had found Sai very inquisitive at such an early age. I could see how much potential he held in those little eyes to grow up and be a successful man. He had reminded me of a little Shree.

"Didi" I hesitated before presenting her with my suggestion. I knew how suggestions could always be misinterpreted.

"Yes" she replied.

"I see Sai asks lot of questions".

"I apologize for that. He just likes to…" she looked a bit flushed.

"No, no Didi, I didn't mind the talking at all, in fact, I came here to tell you that he is very curious about everything around him. Please make sure to encourage this curiosity to know things. Try answering all the questions he has. The world is full of people who least bother questioning the norm, but only a few dare to ask why? Unlike others, he has a thirst for knowledge. He didn't settle down or stopped asking me why things were the way they were until he was sure he had his answer. "

"Sure, I will keep that in mind" her smile confirmed that she had taken the suggestion in a positive way.

"Now say bye to Bro." she asked her children to bid me goodbye and left to get a taxi for herself and her children.

By the time I reached Medak, the sun was shining at its brightest. I looked at my mobile phone to see if there were any unread messages while Sai was playing on the phone. The screen showed that it was eleven past twenty-two. The bus station was very crowded. I hugged my backpack closer to myself so that I won't get robbed or lose anything. Many were still searching for their buses, many shifting baggage on the top of the bus and many fighting for the window seat. Many were going on a little trip as it was the weekend. As I was just about to make my way out of the station, I saw a weight tracking machine. Since little, it had always been my most anticipated activity in bus and railway station. Whenever we went out of town to meet our relatives on festivals, I would always ask my bother to give me a coin so that I put it in the machine and learned about my future. The excitement and fascination of seeing the machine came to life as soon as the coin was interested was simply out of this world. That wait of one second before a card dropped out of it seemed like forever, the card showed the person's weight on one side and told one's fortune on the other. Many were motivated more by the fortune telling than knowing their weight.

Seeing one at the bus station brought back so many refreshing memories. Even today, I wasn't able to resist that anticipation and decided to let the machine guide me for my journey forward. So I stepped on it and dropped a coin inside. The machine, as always, came to life and dispensed a card showing my weight.

Jeez, I weigh 80 Kg? I thought to myself.

It had been ages since I last weighed myself. I always assumed I weighed less.

"You will miss something most valuable today." The card read. I got a bit furious as I was so sure that it would have something positive to tell me. I stepped down, calling it lame.

There was a security check at the exit gate. I went ahead and stood in queue which was not only long but people also didn't have any concept of personal space. It did not take much time to pass the scanning gate. While I walked out, I thought of calling my mom as promised and update her about my location.

After checking both the pockets of my jeans, I realized that my phone had gone missing.

I rechecked all of my pockets but didn't sense it anywhere. I opened my bag and sneaked in every inch of it but no luck. All of a sudden, I felt as if I lost contact from the entire world.

The person who stole it will also come to know that I hadn't passed even third level of candy crush. OMG!! I immediately went to a public telephone booth. After a second, I realized that I don't remember any of my family members' number and not even friends. Despite countless times trying to recall, my memory failed me.

It sounded a little creepy then. Before there were mobile phones, we all remembered everyone's number by heart. Even those that we saw in advertisements while watching TV.

The only number that I remembered was that of Nandini and even she had changed it. I had no other option except to try. With shivering hands, I dialed her old number, with every ring, my heartbeat fastened.

"Hello" The voice on the other end sounded much mature. It could have passed for Nandini's mother.

"Hi Aunty, is Nandini there?" I knew she told me not to contact her but I had to do it.

"Who are you, by the way?" her voice sounded a little pitched up.

"Adi… My name is Aditya." Never before had I trembled saying my own name.

"You… just stay out of my daughter's life, do you understand?" She started shouting.

"Aunty, I called her because I need a favor. Can you please do it for me?" I tried replying her in a humble tone.

"What's that?" I thought she would slam the phone right away after listening to my name.

"I am on a trip and I have lost my phone. I need you to tell my parents so that they can file a complaint and have it blocked. I don't remember any of the numbers except of Nandu's. I just need my sister's number from her mobile." I finished.

"Okay give me a min." she went on mute for a min.

"9963035507" I noted it down.

"Thanks Aunty." I didn't care if she told Nandini about my trip or not, I had already emailed her about it before leaving home. I had always remained a tech fan but on that day, I hated it for making things so difficult. When introducing mobile phone and the internet, the companies had claimed that it would bring people closer but all it had done as make us more lazy, fake, and isolated.

"Hello Avika" I took a deep breath when she picked up her phone.

"Hey Adi, where are you?" she asked.

"I'm in Medak right now." my voice trembled.

"But whose number is this. Let me guess, you lost your mobile, didn't you?"

"Yes, I just did now."

"Was this attempt planned or unplanned?" I knew she would say that because I had discussed my stupid self-exploration plan with her before. Anyone who heard that would have thought the same.

"No, it happened just now. I called you so that you can block it." She sounded a little convinced then.

"What should I tell to mom and dad?" she asked me.

"Tell them what happened and please stress on the fact that it was not on purpose." I too emphasized on that last part.

"It's okay, just go and get another one, okay?" She suggested.

"Yes I will do that." I thought to have a conversation with mom, but I knew if I told her about the phone myself, she would ask me to come back straight away. So I hung up the call quickly. For a moment, I tried looking at it as an omen, and thought of travelling without a mobile.

As I left the phone booth, I remembered what the fortune telling machine had said. Feeling a little angered at how oddly the trip had began, I promised I would never touch that bloody idiotic thing ever.

As I started walking down the main streets, it felt no different from Hyderabad except for the maintenance. I ate lunch at a restaurant and had a conversation with the owner who sat at the billing counter. I told him that I was a tourist there and asked him if he could suggest me a few places to begin my trip from. Excited, he handed me over a brochure and highly recommended that I visited the Medak fort.

I decided to give the place a visit. After all, it wasn't like I didn't have the time to make the cut; I had time on my hands, money in my pocket and adventure waiting ahead. Going there seemed like a good idea so I stopped an auto and started moving up north to the hills. Medak fort nestled on top of the hill just like Golconda Fort in Hyderabad. It had a short climbing trail from the parking lot to the actual fort's massive doors.

As I made past the large main door, I thought about all the Kakatians and Qutbshahis must have walked through those doors. Thanks to old films on past rulers of India, it was easy for me to imagine how the fort must have looked when people lived here. The grand hall must have been the place where the king sat on a big throne and listened to the pleas of the people coming from afar and wide. The fort reminded me of my trip to Golconda Fort with my own family. I took my time admiring the intricate wood carvings, marble work and the faded red bricks. Elephants and lions had been carved into the sidewalls of the entrance. Sadly, the fort hadn't been maintained or else it would have made a wonderful tourist spot. Most of the trees had either died or were living their last days. Many parts of the fort, especially the back wall needed some attention. After a few more minutes, a few visitors like myself, started to come. Most of them were couples and by the looks of how they held each other's hand and whispered sweet things in each other's ear, they were honeymooning.

The fort was located approximately 90 meters above ground level and in order to reach the top, one had to climb 500 stairs and I would have declared it a waste of time, had I not stepped out of the fort and looked at the view it presented of the city. For a minute, I just stood by the railing, unable to speak. The city below wasn't very developed. Houses were still small and left unpainted. But the view of the mountains encapsulating the little city was simply mesmerizing. It reminded me a lot of Araku Valley but I didn't want to think about much. The top of the mountains were quilted with clouds and lush greenery followed next. The layered patterns blended perfectly within each other giving every mountain its own unique beauty.

I sat on one of the cement benches near the railing. I enjoyed my time looking at the clouds, far away mountains, and greenery. But in the back of my mind, I knew that I would have to leave early as I had to climb down all those stairs and that too —alone.

As I was descending down, I saw a man in deep mediation on one side of the rocky stairway. As I neared him, I became more drawn towards him.

He was the most handsome man I had ever seen. With thick, dark curly black hair that kissed his nape, attractive white skin with high cheekbones and a well-defined jaw line and forehead, he could have easily starred into any of Bollywood's biggest movies and the girls would have lost their minds. He wore a saffron-colored dress which ended till his ankles like that of a Sadhu, and had both his arms casually rest over his knees in front of his torso. He also wore a threaded necklace with only one rudraksha to it.

I thought about moving on, thinking he might be a regular Sadhu and it wasn't right to interrupt his calm meditation posture but I just couldn't. There was something about him that urged me to wait until his meditation session was complete and talk to him. After a while, he opened his eyes and looked at me. As if he wasn't attractive enough already, he even had a pair of deep brown eyes that shone a lighter shade when the sunlight reached them.

"Are you any Swami or Baba?" I had seen many such Swami's back in Hyderabad who would dress up like that and earn money from public. He didn't look like he would do it for money but I still felt like asking him.

"Why do you want to know?" he asked in his silvery voice.

"Your costume says that you're a devotee to some god, but you look so young and handsome with those dazzling eyes and physically fit body? "I mean why sit here all alone at the fort?" In my curiosity, I didn't even realize what I had just said.

"Why would you want to devote yourself to the god when you could model or act in movies?" I instantly realized that instead of doing some damage control, I had actually worsened the situation.

There was a moment of silence, when I recalled what I had just said.

"I'm not gay or anything, just curious." It slipped out of my mouth.

"Hahahaha, how about we have this conversation while we walk?" He asked with a smile.

"Sure, my name is Adi" I stretched out my hand for a handshake. I wasn't sure after the things I had said to him a minute ago, he would want to shake hands with me or not.

"My name is Shiva." He placed his hand in mine for a firm handshake.

So, Sadhus do shake hands, I thought to myself.

I WAS IMPRESSED

"**I**'m no Baba or Swami. It is just that I like meditation so I try spending most of my time doing it." He replied to my question earlier.

"Then what about these saffron-colored clothes? Isn't that like the traditional clothes for all swamis across India?" I asked in a slightly sarcastic tone.

"There are many psychological reasons behind the way I dress, I am sure you will understand what when the right time comes." he didn't mind the sarcastic tone at all and replied casually.

"Shall we have some juice and a chat perhaps?" I became more curious to continue talking with him. I wasn't sure why.

"Sure" he said. We reached a juice stall at the end of the fort stairs. We placed an order for snacks as well and sat down at a table. He sat in front of me and placed his jhola bag in front of him on the table.

"Tell me something about yourself" I was once again curious with many questions in my head.

"What do you want to know about me?" He didn't seem very interested in disclosing personal details about himself. But that didn't stop me.

"Who are you actually; do you live here with your family?"

"I'm an orphan; I don't remember my parents. I was raised in an orphanage here and I don't know anything apart from Yoga, meditation and studying people. Right now, I'm travelling to North."

"You study people?" it sounded weird but also hell interesting.

"Any specific locations you wish to travel up north? " The moment he said north, I thought of asking him to partner me. But since I had made such an awkward first impression, I didn't want to sound too hung up on him. I secretly wished that he were a little mad like myself and going on a journey with no directions or destination to reach to.

"No, I plan on taking an undecided route. I like being in the unknown. It allows me to meditate better. I don't have any deadlines, and I have no one to worry about. So I will take all the time I need. I earn my money at every stop, roam around, observe people and then move on." He would have made an amazing travel buddy. He didn't have a plan or deadline and neither did I. But to trust someone whom I had just met sounded insane. I didn't know anything about him. What if he turned out to be a decoy who robbed people after making friends with them? I was carrying cash with me and I didn't want to risk it —especially after I had already lost my mobile phone.

But then again, he seemed like a nice fellow. Before we could talk further, a little boy brought us our snacks and we started munching onto them. I waited for him to ask about me so that I could share my plans with him too but he didn't seem bothered at all. I thought I needed to start it indirectly.

"You know what, today when I was travelling from Hyderabad to here, I met this young boy called Sai…." I told how well he got connected to me and all his questions.

"What is so special about Sai?" he asked me after listening me talk on for a few minutes about a boy of age 6.

"Ahh, he was very inquisitive. He didn't settle for made-up concepts or theories and kept asking questions until he ran out of topics." I replied.

"Anything more surprising from kids this age you came across?" He expected me to answer with a maybe, but I felt a bit confused as to what he wanted to know.

"No, what's special about kids of his age?" Now I was curious to know.

"Let me tell you something…" he paused for a few seconds and then spoke again. "Kids of his age have such a free soul. They only talk to people with whom they feel comfortable and only do those things they like doing, but as time passes and they grow up, they lose that purity. Sooner or later, they start pretending to like things they hate. They wear masks to pretend to like people even when they don't." What he said made sense. I was more amazed by his thinking and observation.

"During my travels, all I see are people acting different roles and wearing different masks. As time passes, they forget who they actually are.

"Wow that was so philosophical. I'm travelling till J&K without any plan, will you join me?" He seemed to have little wisdom, which most of us didn't have or cared about. All my doubts about him being a forger vanished. I was amazed with his intellect. He was the partner I needed. He would be so much fun to hang out with, I thought.

"Well, should I join you or will you join me?" he started to pick up his Jhola bag.

"Aren't they both the same?" I inquired.

"No, there is a big difference." He didn't provide me any further explanation. May be he expected me to know the difference.

"If you say so?" I didn't want to sound stupid. If he expected me to know the difference I pretended that I knew the difference.

"Can you join me?" I asked.

"Okay, where shall we go from here?" He waited for me to tell. I pulled out my map and started looking for destinations up north. I hadn't really decided where I would head next mainly because I expected to travel alone.

The name *Umri* sounded pretty interesting so I picked that.

"Let's do it." He smiled and we started walking towards the bus stand again. We took a bus to Nornoor as all the buses for Umri that day had already left the station.

"Tell me about yourself" and that was it; I poured everything out every single detail about myself from my childhood to that day.

I hardly remembered anything that he said in between. It took us about 4 hours to reach Nornoor. As soon as we got off and walked out of the station, we decided to share an auto rickshaw.

"Dude, can you take us to Umri." I asked one of the auto drivers.

"He said he would charge 50 rupees," That sounded very fair because in city it took the same to go from one street to the other. It was almost starting to turn dark. As we began the journey, the sky turned darker and half an hour later, all that we saw was through the rickshaw's headlights. All I felt was the bumpy ride that made us jump our seats a few times and almost fall out.

"Adi, we are about to reach the entrance of the village. What do you plan on doing next?" Shiva asked me

"By the looks of it, I don't think we will find a decent hotel to stay in or even a guest house. I think we should go ask some family to take us. We just need to sleep in some place tonight we shall figure out the rest tomorrow morning, sounds good?" I told him the only sensible plan I could have come up with.

To me, it felt like begging others to let us in their homes. Although we were willing to pay, but it still felt a little degrading.

Though it was just 8 p.m., pretty much everyone had locked their doors. In Hyderabad, that only happened when there was curfew in town and people were told to stay within their homes. The streets were pretty congested. Most were huts made of clay, dry hay and branches of trees. We started passing a few streets in hope of securing ourselves a place to spend the night. Luckily, after walking for few minutes, we came across a street where some families were casually sitting outside their homes, chatting amongst themselves under the full moon light, enjoying the cool breeze. They were having their own little bonfire. They had lighted up some branches of old Neem trees in the centre of the road and sat around it, occasionally heating their hands.

"Hello, we are on a trip to north. We kind of landed a little late into this village, can you feed us and allow us to sleep at your place for one night." I asked a lady who was talking to her husband I guess.

"Why would you think we would help to strangers? No, we won't." They walked back inside their house and slammed the door in our faces.

"Shiva, should I feel bad when somebody smashes the door on my face." I felt baffled.

"No Adi, you shouldn't feel bad —even if an unexpected incident hits you hard. Always take it in slow." He said and we headed to the next group of people just a few steps away from us. By the time we reached them, the second family was already looking at us as we if were aliens and had just landed from Mars.

"Hello, we are on a trip and we need food and accommodation for tonight please." I remembered my voice being a little more pleasing that time. I tried to become a better beggar.

"No, we have teen girls at our home. We cannot allow random guys into our home." At least his reason sounded valid from his point of view. By the time we turned towards our left most of the people had already went inside after realizing what we were asking for. I looked around and there remained only one family our last hope, or else we would have been left in this wilderness with no electricity, food, or a pace to rest our heads.

"Shiva, this is our last chance. Do you want to try it this time? I think they don't like me much" I wanted to see if I was the unlucky one.

"No, if you remember I joined your trip. So you will have to go ahead." That was the moment I finally realized what he means when he asked whether I was journeying with him or was I journeying him. He had meant that whoever's journey we picked will be responsible for all such tasks. I cursed myself a little internally. If that family didn't allow us in too, we would have had to stay out in the open with mosquitoes sucking our blood.

I didn't like the idea of that so I became very determined to ensure that I pleased them. Then, I realized how salespersons working on compensation might feel. They too, had to convince strangers to purchase from them. I had turned them down so many times. I promised myself that from that moment onwards, I would stop doing that. The men and women were already looking at us, so I didn't waste any more time and approached them.

"Hello, can you feed us and give us a place to sleep at your place tonight? I can pay if you want." I didn't know if hinting about money was the right thing to do or not. I feared that talking about money might make them feel insulted but I had no other option. The arrow had left the bow and I adjust stood there waiting to see if it had hit him in the heart or the tree behind him.

"No, you don't have to pay son. You can come in." I was amazed at his generosity, without even questioning who we were, where were we from and where were we headed to in detail, he just allowed us to spend a night at his place. He didn't even consult his wife before announcing that we were welcome. Plus, he even refused taking any money from us. His kind-heartedness won my heart. If I were in his place, I would have never allowed two strangers to spend the night in my house. For all I knew, they could be robbers or murderers.

There was no light inside the house; all we could see was through the street light. The man's home was a built with mud. There weren't any designated rooms or partitions, just a big hall. The entire roof was covered with dry Borassus tree leafs. He assumed that we would want to freshen up so he directed us to the hand pump outside his home.

"Please wash your hands and legs here." He then went on to stand at the other side of the hand pump and started pulling and pushing the pump. In a few seconds, water started to pour from it. The water was very cold. We just cleaned our faces, washed our hands and feet and ran back into the warmth of the house. There, I dried myself with the little towel I had brought with myself.

We sat on the floor and the man's wife served us some rice in steel plates. Then she poured some daal and mango pickle on one side of the plate. The food looked ordinary, but as soon as I took the first bite, all my doubts about how bad it might taste changed. It tasted delicious —so delicious that I couldn't stop licking my own finger after each bite. I never did that before, no matter how flavorsome the food was. Once we were done eating, the man set up a little cot that was almost a queen size bed. It was made of wood and ropes.

"Sir, may I know your name please?" Shiva asked him.

"Krishna" he said.

"My name is Shiva and he is Adi." It was then that I realized that I hadn't even told the man my name or asked his. How bad a guest I was.

"You really need not do this; we can sleep on the floor sir." Despite our request, he didn't stop making our beds.

"No, that's okay. You should sleep now. You must be tired from the long journey." "He then dusted a few pillows for dirt and placed them on the bed after spreading a new sheet on it. He even gave us another sheet to cover ourselves from the cold. Strangely, we didn't feel cold inside the home.

As we lay down, we heard in many insects chirping outside. We could see the beautiful star-filled sky from the window beside. It felt so different. There were roughly a hundred or more stars that we saw from that little 3-inch window. I recalled the day's events. I had started on an unknown journey today and had already made two friends. I had visited a couple of places, misplaced my phone, met a sadhu who wasn't really a sadhu, came to this village and then spending the night in someone else's home. I turned to look at Shiva. His orangish dress was fairly distracting; I didn't know why he wore that if he weren't a sadhu. But like he had said, some day he would tell me.

"Shiva" I really wanted to ask him about the dress. I didn't want to wait.

"Yes." He opened his eyes and looked right at me.

"Will you be wearing the same clothes throughout the journey? I mean will you be changing it any time soon?"

"Why?" he asked.

"I have a habit of sleeping awkwardly during my sleep; I like to extend my arms and legs as far as I can. If I were wearing that dress, I wouldn't be able to do that. Don't you feel uncomfortable in it?" I replied honestly about how I felt about his dress.

"Then why don't you buy me a new one?" He might have kidded just then, but I decided that I would buy him a new one anyways. Every time, I talked to him, he would say something would feel very different from how people talked normally —as if he were from another planet and just learning our ways. He would have answers to all my questions, solutions for all my problems and humbleness that made me rethinks my lavishness. Despite his lack of resources he looked much content with his life than myself. in those few minute before sleep, I realized that the more I had, the more worried I was, now that I had no phone on myself, no food and no place to go to, I felt much more relaxed. I shouldn't have felt scared but I did not, I felt relaxed.

I woke up to the sound of chickens and someone using the hand pump. I opened my eyes, looked outside and then at my watch. It was still 5:30 a.m. in the morning, the sun hadn't come out. I turned sides and found the bed empty. I got a little worried as to where he might have gone to and decided to get up and go look for him.

As I stepped outside, I saw another small hut, just beside the main hut. I must have missed it last night, as it was too dark outside. Smoke was coming out of it from a hole in the roof so I assumed it was the kitchen. I walked inside to see Mrs. Krishna boiling water in a big pot. She had lighted a few wooden pieces, stacked them on one another and started a fire. I greeted her and stepped outside. Shiva wasn't in there. I saw a few men chewing onto Neem sticks in their mouth, many women sweeping their front yard and others carrying buckets of water on their head, waist, and hands. I remembered my father using one of those sticks to brush his teeth when we stayed at our grandfather's house. I had never been tempted to try it before but was surely up for it then.

So with some excitement, I pulled a small branch from one of the Neem trees, plucked all its leaves and put it in my mouth, at first, it tasted bitter, but the taste wasn't unbearable. I placed by back against the tree and continued to clean my teeth. I then saw Shiva, walking down the street barefooted.

"Shiva, did you take a bath?" I asked as he approached closer.

"Do I not look fresh to you?" he asked me.

"Ahh actually, I come from a place where if you change and put some perfume that would be enough for people to assume that you took a bath. You are in the same outfit all the time so I really can't guess if you did or you didn't." I tried to joke.

"Don't worry, I did" he chuckled back.

"Where is the bathroom by the way?" I whispered because I couldn't see any around.

"There isn't one here. Just walk down straight to the water pump, I will fetch you some hot water in a bucket. Remove your clothes except for the underpants you have and take the bath. Simple." He said that so nonchalantly.

"Are you serious? I will do no such thing. I'm not going to take a bath in front of all these people and give them a chance to stare at me." I felt a little appalled hearing that. How could he have said that so casually?

"Looks like you are planning your things, aren't you? Then why did you call it an unplanned trip, Adi." Hell he was right; it made me rethink my choice. One of the most exciting things about my trip was experiencing how different life was away from all the luxuries. It was time to live that different life.

"Okay get me water." I undressed myself except for the underwear near the water pump.

"Here you go." Shiva carried a bucket of water filled to the brim from the kitchen. I felt a little embarrassed that many people had stopped to see me take a bath. To them, it was an entertaining show. A young man from the city, trying to mimic the life of a villager.

Using the little mug, I poured some water onto my head. Unexpectedly, the water wasn't that hot, in fact, not hot at all and it sent shivers down my body. I felt as if all my laziness of years got out of me with the weird shimmy dance I did after the first splash. In no time, I heard my teeth grinding against each other.

"I thought you said you were getting me hot water." I became furious. But with my teeth grinding, I looked anything but serious. I had both my hand son my chest with my teeth grinding with cold. He chuckled when he looked at me.

"Oh, so you find that funny…!" I raised my voice a little to property my anger.

"Taking a bath with cold water is good for health, Adi." He laughed back.

I felt all my nerves dancing within me, as I poured more water, mug after mug. After I was down, I dressed as if I had only a few seconds left on the timer.

"Well, I have to admit it. I do feel like a new man now. Shiva stood by the outer fence of the house that was used as a boundary to keep thugs and animals out of the house. He then started walking towards the end of the street, where some other kids were gathered too. I walked there to see what made him and the a few others to stand there like that.

The moment I reached there, I knew exactly why. The view of the fresh harvest and the first rays of sunlight looked spectacular. The chirping of the birds and subtle dancing of the trees on those tunes was simply out of this worried. It looked like everyone was greeting the sun in their own way. The wind was fresh, the sugar cane fields were all set to be reaped and the cattle were happy to explore and wander the grassy lands. So this was why people said that city life was nothing compared to this. There, people might not have the best of resources at hand, but they had this breathtaking view to look at every morning. What we had in Hyderabad or Mumbai was just a yellowish sky, full of dirt, dust, and air pollution. This was heaven when compared to that.

"Oh my... this is amazing." I knew those words didn't do justice to what was in front of me, but they were the only words that my mind conjured up.

"Adi, aren't these people so lucky?" Shiva asked me, still looking at the beautiful scenery.

"Lucky? How?" I asked.

Have you ever seen such a beautiful scene from your apartment balcony?" He then looked at with cynical eyes as if he already knew the answer but wanted me to say it out loud.

"No, I see the bedroom of Shreya from my balcony." I joked. His expressions changed but he didn't laugh. He frowned.

"No seriously, it is worth looking at." I once again tried to make him laugh or at least smile. But he wasn't satisfied with my answer.

"What is the first thing you hear when you wake up every morning?" he started digging more.

"Do you hear birds chirping when you wake up?"

"No; unless I set that as my ringtone." I wasn't going to give up. The man had no sense of humor.

"What do you hear when you sleep with your balcony door open?"

"A vehicle's horns mostly…"

"See… Now don't you think that these people have a chance to interact with the nature all the time? Doesn't that make them luckier than most of the people who live in big cities but miss this calmness and greenery in our lives?" He argued. The man had a valid point but still got no sense of humor. Alas, I thought to myself, now I had to keep all my stupid jokes to myself.

"I think these people are lucky." he continued. He closed his eyes and I breathed in the fresh air. Any other person after that act would have reopened his eyes but he didn't.

"Are you still awake?" I waved my palm in front of his closed eyes to ensure he was okay.

"Adi, did you ever wonder how nature had the power to control our human emotions? No matter how mad or angry you are, you look at nature and it brings down your boiling blood. You feel blue and look at nature and somehow, it makes us joyous, you feel stressed out and it manages to keep you calm. All is its doing. Whatever we learn from life, nature teaches us. The only sad thing is that we humans don't pay attention to it or let it heal us from the inside. I meet so many people on my voyages and I see how they misjudge a good sunrise away from their homes and offices as a great vacation. A vacation isn't only that. It isn't just about waking up into a different hotel room or going to places one has never traveled to before. A vacation means refreshing from everything that holds us back. Things that keep us engrossed on what is insignificant or of no value. Things like money, car, work, and relationships." He seemed upset but he was also right.

"Yes, I see what you are saying." The reason I agreed with him was because I was one of the people he was talking about. My idea of a vacation was the same. Ever since a child, I had traveled to so many places with my parents. What I remembered from these trips were hotel stays, the food and the places —anything but nature. I rarely interacted with it. There hadn't been a day in my life where I had just wandered or gotten lost in this beauty. I always carried with me a list of all the things I wanted to do and all the places I wanted to visit. Never had I put exploring nature on my bucket list. I was a part of that generation who would rather take photographs than admire nature in all its raw beauty.

None of us said anything after that. We just stood there for another 10 minutes looking at how the field changed color as the sun rose, how the birds rushed to hunt an early catch and how the farmers herded their cattle. Everyone looked at peace with themselves. Women didn't rush to the river to have their water buckets filled first. Instead, they all grouped together and waited for everyone to join before heading to the river. They didn't care if anyone had a bigger bucket, they didn't care if anyone walked faster... so unlike what I saw at my office. Everything in the city was a race. A race to get to have the first shower, a race to find the best seat in the bus, a race to get to the office early, a race to impress the bosses, a race to dress better than others and so on. Here, they all were a big family.

We thanked Mr. Krishna and his family for being our host and started our journey forward to Adilabad. People looked at us with weird looks and why not. If I saw a duo that looked completely opposite of each other I would have had the same expressions on my face. Shiva was still dressed in that shaggy orange sadhu outfit while I had changed into new clothes —western ones. Throughout the journey, we talked about a hundred different things and it didn't take me long to realize that his philosophies on life resembled Shree's a lot. Many a times, I even forgot that I was talking to a completely different person and that Shree wasn't there anymore.

As we reached into the city, we decided to shop for a few essentials first and then start touring it. So we headed to RR Mall for shopping.

Every time, we would laugh at something together I would want to put my hands around his shoulders like friends do, but his appearance didn't allow me to do that. As we entered a garment shop in the malls, we were greeted by an unfriendly manager who wasn't a least bit interested in helping us find some good shirts. We asked him to show us their latest collection and he did so with such an uninviting face that we both had an instant dislike for him in our hearts. So after trying a few t-shirts and finding nothing of our interest, we stepped into another shop that sold western wear. As soon as a saw a few good pieces, I become excited to see Shiva trying them. He, however, didn't seem excited at all. I urged him to try a few more and since I was paying, he didn't say no out of respect.

One by one, he tried a few shirts and pants into the changing room. He didn't even look at himself in the mirror. Every time, he came out wearing something new, he would just look at me for approval and see-ing my expressions he would turn back, go back into the changing room and come out wearing something different. He did know how to read people. Finally, after a few failed combinations we finally found an ash grey slim-cut shirt and brown track pants that complimented his physique perfectly. His pumped up muscles looked even fuller in those sleeves and the shirt's width settled perfectly on his abs and perfect waist. Although, he looked more dashing than before, his face still depicted divinity. He may have changed his clothes and appearance but I could still see that orange-colored Sadhu in him.

CROSSED THE STATE BORDER

One reason why the journey was going so smoothly until then was because I was still travelling within my state, I grew up here. I knew the culture and traditions of the place. They were embedded in my core. It felt like being in my comfort zone, but I didn't want to stay in it forever I wanted to explore new places, meet new people, admire nature, and refresh my mind, So we decided to cross the state border and head further north to Nagpur.

The journey from Umri to Adilabad was indeed a pleasurable one. Unlike earlier, the road wasn't bumpy and the view was spectacular. Because we had shopped for a long time, it didn't take long after we boarded the bus that I fell asleep. By the time I woke up, three hours had passed. It looked like the sun had completed its day's journey and the stars were getting ready for their show. There weren't many people on the roads. I assumed it was because the weekend was over. Everyone who was on the road either didn't have a job to go to tomorrow or were business owners who opened their shops late in the afternoon. Since it was dark already, we decided to head straight to some hotel to spend the night. Once we found a decent lodging, we would then decide where to go to next.

"Would you like to walk till we find some hotel to stay at?" Shiva inquired.

"Yes, I can afford walking. I just woke up all energized." As we started walking on the main road we came across many hotels but none of us stopped walking.

"So how are we going to decide which hotel to get into?" My energy was draining out.

"Let's walk until we no longer can and let that be unplanned too." I liked the idea so I didn't refuse. I got more exhausted after every step. On our way many auto rickshaw fellows passed by us and asked if we wanted a ride. I so wanted to rest my legs then but we denied their offers.

I started to feel hungry. The road expanded into an intersection, I decided to turn left and so did Shiva, in that very exact moment. We hadn't planned the turning so we took it as a sign and decided to head straight into the first hotel on the left and see if they had a room available. That was the unplanned intuition we had been looking for and it had happened.

"Can I get a room with two beds?" I pulled out my wallet for ID proof and payment at the reception desk.

"Sure, how long will you be staying sir?" He pulled his registry and started to make a note of the details.

"Only for one night." I handed over my ID.

"300/- sir" he handed over the key to the hotel boy who then led us to our room. It was decent 3-star hotel. The boy smiled at us and waited by the end of the door for his tip. I gave him 200 rupees, requested him to get us some food from the outside and keep the rest for himself.

As we entered, we both let out a little sigh of relief. The room wasn't considerably big but it had two separate beds, air-conditioning and clean mattresses and sheets to sleep on. That was all we needed. I would have wished for a TV, but it was okay. After a quick freshening up session, we both had dinner and rested our backs on the bed facing the ceiling.

"Compared to the feel of this air conditioning, I liked the air much better at Mr. Krishna's home in Umri. Don't you? " I asked.

"Yes, that was much more pleasant." We talked a little about the village and the people over there. That moment reminded me of my sleepover days at my friend's place during which we discussed about life, personal problems, and had many deep conversations.

"It has been long since I had a late night conversation with any of my friends." I told Shiva the same thing.

"Good for you," was all he said. I wanted to keep talking but I was too tired from all the walking and travelling. In that moment I realized that Shiva barely started any conversations. Most of the times, he just responded back to my questions. I called out his name in a very low tone to check whether he was still awake.

"Do you have a girlfriend, Shiva?" I assumed it was quite an obvious topic among friends, especially guys.

"So, if you are the one to ask this question it means you already have one don't you?" he asked.

"Yes, her name is Nandini." I didn't bother giving him more details.

"So, what's wrong in between you both?" his question surprised me.

"How do you know there is a problem?" I became curious.

"You are on a trip all alone; talking to only parents never brought her topic, never called her. So something must have gone wrong?" He observed a lot, I assumed.

"I'm just unsure if we will make it or not." I concluded after disclosing my past to him.

"Don't worry Adi, one day she will knock on your door." I smiled hearing that. It always felt good that someone said something like that.

"But you haven't answered my question yet?" I wanted to know about his love life.

He exhaled and said "No I don't have a girlfriend." I did not feel like asking any further questions on that topic. We discussed about other things like society and meditation. I felt quite impressed with his beliefs and reasoning. After that late night conversation, I felt like I could talk to him about anything. He had wisdom in himself —lots of it. Maybe he could be my guardian, maybe he could tell me what I should do after the trip ends, maybe he can advise me much better about Nandini and how to make things right with her, I thought.

It was the horns of the cars and the noises from the outside that woke me from my peaceful slumber. It seemed as if a fight had broken out among a few drivers and the people behind them were getting impatient. It wasn't something new, it happened nearly every day when going to work. Unlike Shiva, most of us didn't have the patience to wait peacefully and wait for our turn. I finally had to open my eyes, although I wished I could have slept some more. The bright sunlight immediately made me regret my decision and I closed them again. The next time I opened them, I allowed them some time to get used to the sunlight which was seeping through the giant window that opened towards the main road. I turned sides to see if Shiva too had awakened from the noise but as soon as I turned, all I saw was his empty bed and the sheet laid on the mattress without a single crease on them.

Unlike the last time, I didn't get worried. I realized that a man with such a fit body followed a strict exercise regime. To Shiva, his exercise was meditation. I secretly wished some morning I would wake up before him and see him perform yoga. After stretching a couple of times, I finally got the off my bed and headed straight for the shower. Today was going to be our first day in Nagpur and I wanted to start my journey with a fresh mind and body.

After a little while, someone knocked on the door and since Shiva was not in the room, I had to open the door, I wrapped a towel on my stomach and opened the door. It was the same boy from last night who had helped us carry my luggage. He had brought us breakfast in a tray along with that day's newspaper. I thanked him, took the tray from his hands, and closed the door. I placed the tray on Shiva's bed and then went inside to complete taking the shower. I had no idea where Shiva was or when he will return. Watching the fried eggs and toast, I couldn't resist so I started without him. After I was done, I scrolled through the newspaper, looking to find something of interest. It was then that Shiva walked inside the room.

"So what is our next plan?" he asked me.

"Let's wait till we find another omen to lead us." I said, turning to the next page of the newspapers. After sometime, the waiter again knocked on the door. This time it was Shiva who opened the door.

"Sir, I am here to collect the first tray if you are done and offer you tea."

Just a few minutes ago, I had this strong craving for tea. I had already made my mind that as soon as we walked out of the hotel; the first thing we were to do was get a nice cup of tea from any tea stall nearby. Before Shiva could say anything, I got up from the bed and invited him inside. The tray he had in his hands this time had a few empty tea cups, a teapot, and a bowl of sugar. He had just turned around to leave when he remembered something and said.

"Sorry sir, I gave you yesterday's newspaper. Here, please have this, this is today's edition." We both thanked him for the tea and returned the tray along with the newspaper. As soon as I opened the new one, a brochure fell out of it. Shiva was closing the door when I bent down to pick it up. The brochure was an advertisement of the Railway museum in the city.

"Here is the omen we have been looking for." I passed him the brochure.

"This looks fun. Let's check it out then." We started packing and were all dressed for going out. We went downstairs, checked out of your rooms, and stepped outside the hotel.

The weather of Nagpur was beyond hot; it literally felt like someone had put us both in a hot oven. Everyone on the streets and footpaths seemed in a hurry. Many were running late from work and didn't want to get a scolding from their bosses first thing I the morning. Kids were heading to their schools, some happily singing while others sleeping. Most of the buses, rickshaws, and taxis were crowded with housemaids who were heading for work. We started walking towards the bus stop that wasn't far from where we were. By the time we reached there, both of us were in sweats as if returning from an hour's jog. After waiting for a couple of minutes, one bus finally stopped right in front of us. Bit we weren't sure if it was the right one to get on. Therefore, to avoid wasting time, I asked a middle-aged man who was standing next to me.

"Uncle, can you please guide us which bus will take us to Narrow gauge rail Museum?" I asked wiping my face with handkerchief.

"F18" he said and ran on the road to get into his bus. Within 5 min, we saw the bus with F18 on its route board. We boarded the bus. There were no seats available but there was some space in the middle, so we made our way to the middle section and held onto the plastic handles that hung from above.

After 20 minutes, the bus reached one of the main bus stations where a crowd awaited for the bus. There were more than 20 something people so I assumed not all of them would get onto the bus, but how wrong I was. One by one, they all made their way into the bus, filling the empty spaces between us. After another minute, there was not enough space to turn around and I could sense the breathing of the man next to me. He smelled of nicotine as if he just has had a cigarette before getting onto the bus. I hated that smell, but there was no way to avoid that. Besides, it wasn't like others smelled any good. Many smelled like they hadn't taken a bath from a century. I feared that if I tried getting some distance from him, I would enter the ladies section and be charged for misbehavior by the conductor. I dint want to create scene so I tried thinking about something good to distract myself. Nothing good came to my mind and I just held my grip on the handle tighter, counting every minute before we reached our destination.

The conductor came towards us and asked for the tickets. No matter how overcrowded the bus would be, the conductor always managed to sneak and walk in the same to get the tickets. I readjusted my composure, exchanged hands on the handle, managed to pull my wallet out, and took a ticket to the Museum. By the time he gave me the ticket, I felt like I was working in a balancing act at a circus.

He shouted the name of every location wherever the bus stopped which made it a little easier for us to keep track of where we were. My shoulders started feeling the weight my backpack. I saw Shiva standing a few steps away from me. His face looked calm. He didn't look panicked or worried about the lack of personal space. It seemed like he was in a completely different trance. I wondered how he could still maintain the same face. Which made me think that I never saw him tired, angry or dull. He always had that smile on his face.

As many locations passed, many people got off the bus but it still remained packed. The only change was that the man who smelled like smoke was replaced by another man who smelled of sweat. I wasn't sure how long I would take all that before vomiting in the bus. I desperately hoped that the next stop be ours. I needed to get out of here.

"Railway Museum," the conductor shouted from the front door. Finally, my prayers had been answered. Shiva and I made our way out by pushing people. Even though the sun shone aggressively at our temples, I felt better in the sun than the bus. We looked at each other's dresses. They were crushed and folded in different patterns.

"Don't you think people who travel by bus should really take a bath, spray some perfume, iron their clothes and get ready to the office?" I asked.

"I don't think so." He replied.

As we entered through the gates of museum, Green Lawns & Palm trees welcomed us into the museum. I was a bit taken aback how well-maintained the place had been kept. The green grass was being watered and the entry door washed with a cloth for any dirt. We weren't the only ones at the entry gate. A group of school kids, most probably out on a school trip, were gathered in a line with their teachers instructing them to stay quiet. They all looked so excited. I recalled my own time in school. I remembered that the school trip wasn't only the reason why we used to be so excited; a big part of that excitement was of skipping school that day. I sensed the same from those kids. As we walked inside, there was a brief articulation about the museum.

The place was interesting, although not exciting or entertaining. I figured if I had visited this when I was 7, I would have had the time of my life. But now that I had grown out of their age, there wasn't much that interested me. Shiva had the same view. It had different types of steam locomotives —diesel locomotives, and royal carriage. The attractions displayed the models, tools and various communication systems used in railway system over the years very well.

Of all the different models, BNR 677 CC attracted me the most. The red and black freshly painted train was the perfect way to snap a picture.

Many families were getting their pictures taken, some beside the engine while others on it.

We both started walking on the pedestrian footpath. As we were walking, we saw a woman in her mid-40's faint in front of our eyes. I made a run immediately but I was late. Many people had already gathered around her, helped her sit on the bench and sprinkled some water on her face. It was good that she woke up and drank some water. We assumed she fainted because of the hot day.

"People with good hearts still exist on this planet, isn't it?" I shared a thought with Shiva.

"Looks like that." I wondered why all his answers were always short and crisp.

Walking further, we saw a rotating train restaurant with two compartments.

It was only 11:30 a.m., a little early for lunch but we still stepped in. Interior looked like old model train having three tables each on either side of the door. We sat on one side of the door and ordered our food. When it started rotating, we opened our windows to enjoy the view. The ride started from the zero mile station where two giant-sized elephant statues greeted us. Along the way, we saw many multicolored bushes, trees with fruits and flowers hanging from them, kids riding the swings while their parents kept an eye on them from the benches nearby, couples who just wanted some privacy to enjoy a good time and many more delightful sites and statues. It took us around 12 minutes to complete one circle. I didn't particularly like the feeling of eating while in motion. I feared I might get motion sickness. So I barely ate much as we had just started our trip and I didn't want it to end up in vomits.

Shiva was just stared outside the window. There was silence for a long time. The only thing that made any noise was the engine of the train and the occasional horn whenever we reached a different station. I started thinking about my trip so far. On the whole, nothing extraordinary had happened. I thought it was because I didn't stay in one place for long enough. We were moving too fast form one place to another. I'm just moving very fast from place to another? Should I spend more time in each and every place or state? I thought to myself. I had imagined many unexpected situations to take place, but nothing so spectacular had happened.

Then I remembered Shiva telling me that whoever led the trip will make a difference.

Maybe if he led the trip for the rest of the journey something extra ordinary would happen. Besides, I didn't have any set plans.

"What do you think Shiva?" I interrupted him.

"About what?"

"This trip."

"What about it?"

"The way our trip is going on, aren't you bored?" I asked.

"No. Are you?" he asked.

"Yes.".

"Can you plan something good going forward? Nothing exciting has happened for me so far."

"Sure." He was not excited but also not upset. I wondered how he hid all his emotions so well.

By the time we were done with the lunch and the ride, he asked," Shall we make a move?"

"Where are we going?" I asked.

"Not really sure but let's leave it to destiny." He picked his bag and started moving out.

We walked out of the park and started walking towards the north of the city. Grey colored clouds were covering the bright sun offering shade. We reached a flyover and continued walking underneath it. There wasn't a service road underneath that. The ground looked strewn with pebbles and there were many families living underneath it. Some had small camping tents as houses while others didn't even have that. The place smelled bad too. One big portion of the road was covered with trash with everything from chicken feathers to cardboard pieces. Because the families had camped right under the bridge, the maddening sounds of traffic were all they could hear. But they didn't mind that —at least didn't look like it.

Naked kids joyfully ran around. Many women were combing their hair for lice and most of the elderly were asleep on cardboard pieces as beds.

There was one tea stall leaning to one of the pillars. It had two wooden benches. I watched him make tea. Shiva asked me if I needed a cup and I said yes. He then ordered two cups of tea, left the bag and went aside for a couple of minutes. All of a sudden, out of nowhere, a man came running and fell on the mud road as if his foot caught on a small tip. Within no time, two men came looking for him and a terrible fight broke out between the three. The man on the ground tried getting up but the two men with guns in their hand didn't let him. They kept kicking him in the stomach. Anyone who wished to help, didn't out of fear. The two men looked very dangerous and even had weapons in their hands. Most of the people around started running away from the scene. Seeing them run for their life, I too, thought to find myself a hiding spot. The nearest hiding spot was behind the pillar so I made a run for it. Even the tea boy left his stove on.

I saw him bleed but I was too scared to go and help him. After beating him some more, the two armed men ran away from the side, got onto a bike they had parked at a little distance for the flyover. The man tried getting up but didn't have the strength. It was then that Shiva came back from the other end. Seeing an injured man in the mud, he rushed towards him and helped him sit up. But the man was nearly unconscious so he started to fall back on the ground. If only Shiva hadn't held his hand and placed it on his lap, he would have surely hit the floor herd. Watching Shiva help the man, many other came to his rescue too and helped him get up. A few brought him water to drink so that he won't faint. Shiva took out a towel form his saddle bag and wrapped it around the man's arms to stop the bleeding.

Because the two armed men had fled the scene, all of us then came out of hiding. I ran towards Shiva to help him. Shiva and a few other men helped him get up and sit on the tea stall bench. After gulping down a few sips of water, the man slowly opened his eyes. He tried to talk but couldn't due to the kicks he had received in his chest and stomach. Before any of us could ask him who were those men and why were they chasing after him, a car stopped right in front of the stall and a few people stepped outside. It was the man's family members. They all came running towards him, and hugged him. His mother started crying while his brother helped him get up and sit in the car. They talked about taking him to the hospital and left immediately. After the car was out of sight, we all relaxed a little. I started feeling guilty for not helping the man when he needed help. But I had been too scared then, that finding a safe place to hide seemed more sensible. After a few minutes, everyone went back to their works as if nothing had happened the tea stall owner was back making tea, the guy on the barber's seat getting a clean shave, women sweeping fallen down trees from her side of the road and so on. All of it seemed very distributing to me. The visuals of the fight kept running in front of my eyes.

"Here you go," Shiva offered me a cup of tea and sat beside me.

"This place is awful." I said.

"Then I think we should spend the night right here." he said taking his first sip.

"Are you kidding me?" I hope he didn't mean what he said.

"I think I'm not." He said. He wasn't.

"You mean under this flyover?" I remained inquisitive as I knew that when would never suggest something like that. I waited a couple of seconds in case the expressions his face turned and he burst out laughing, but they didn't change.

"There is no point of unplanned trip if you're not willing to come out of the comfort zone which your parents created." I couldn't disagree with his statement. I said yes but only because he was with me. If I had been alone, I would have slept on a park's bend but not in this trashy place. Although, we had been there for about half an hour, my nose still hadn't become accustomed to the smell. I still hated it and every new breeze of wind intensified the feel. But at the same time, it made me wonder how these people spend all their days and night here; didn't they feel yucky at the idea of living there? Did they not find any place better than this? The place was full of diseases, dengue-causing mosquitoes, bugs and other street-roaming pet. Bringing up children in such unhygienic conditions was like inviting diseases to come attack me.

The more thought I put into it and observed their lifestyle, the more worried I got about spending the night under that flyover. But I didn't want to argue with Shiva about changing the place either. I knew what he wanted to stay here. He wanted to show me what life really was away from all the luxuries. I wanted to prove to him that I wasn't a clichéd city boy who couldn't take in all that. So to distract my mind from all such thoughts, I went to join the kids who were playing cricket on the road. The kids gladly agreed to take me and the two captains of the team even had a little fight as they both wanted the man from the city to be on their team. I promised that I will play from both the sides alternatively.

They all rejoiced and we began playing. Although, the kids were very different form the ones I saw in my apartment compound, they had the biggest of hearts. In no time, I realized that the place was their whole world. They loved every dirtied corner of it like their own home. They didn't care about tomorrow. They didn't worry about getting good grades in class; their parents didn't compare them with the other young boys of the community. They all looked after one and other like brothers and sisters. They seemed happy in the moment without worrying about what would happen next.

I and Shiva sat on the uneven floor after I was tired playing. The stones there poked my butt. We had a conversation about the people there and their lifestyle. For most of the time, I did not pay attention to what he said. I felt guilty that I did not help that guy and on the other side I was scared to spend my night here.

"I'm sorry Shiva." I interrupted his conversation to which I wasn't paying any attention to.

"For what?" he asked me.

"I ran away when those two guys nearly beat the guy to death. I felt scared, but you didn't. When I saw you helping him I started feeling bad." I confessed. I needed to get it out of my head.

"It's okay; I know people can be like that." He concluded.

"What do you mean *by that*?" I felt a little insulted. The way he had said that with emphasize on those last two words irritated me.

He inhaled and then exhaled before clarifying. "Do you know anything about impact psychology?" I knew what impact meant and I knew what psychology meant. I didn't however; know what they meant when used mutually. I just shook my head.

"Let me tell you something with the help of a simple example." He paused and looked at me as if waiting for me to give him a go ahead.

"Okay" I gave him a sign to go on.

"You did not help him because you thought that you will become victimized too. Isn't it?"

"Yes" I told him.

"What if you had assumed that you could kick the butts of those two armed men?" His voice was so intense when he said that.

"I don't know. I didn't think I could do it."

"For everything you see and hear, you assume the impact of it. You saw them beating him, you assumed that might happen to you too, but the fact of the matter is that it was just an assumption."

"People see crime happening and assume that they might get into trouble if they try to act against it. Based on certain situations, they estimate the impact and start believing it. Fear is nothing but the outcome of your own imagination. The more bad you imagine the more fear you generate within yourself. Just imagine if we could control our assumptions, no children will ever have fear showing his report card to his parents, no teenager will ever fear to propose, no men or women will ever fear to get married, no employee will fear switching jobs, no young fellow will fear becoming a politician."

"Don't you know it is called being on the safe side?" that was my counter point to his statement.

"Being on the safe side means you are actually afraid. You are afraid to take risks. To challenge the status quo. To stand up against crime."

"Really?" I had not thought about it like that. Maybe he was right. May be I could have helped that man. He was correct; it was just our assumption which was creating it. If we were the one creating it, hell, we had the power to destroy it as well.

"Yes both are pretty much same, except that when you say it indirectly you look dumb." He said it in a sarcastic tone.

"Okay, what do you want to say?" I got a little irritated by that tone. But I didn't want to fight with him over that. Deep within, I had agreed with his point but I didn't want to tell him that.

"Look what I'm just saying is if you don't fear for most of the situations, the way you look at life will change." he concluded.

"Are you trying to get into my head and play with the little brain I have gotten left?" his philosophies really made me feel as if my brain was working very hard, I haven't felt that since long time. A sarcastic smile was his only reply.

I sat alone all by myself doing nothing, while Shiva interacted with the people of the slum. It was really bad on my part for not talking to them, but somehow I was not able to do that. It was around 7 p.m. when the sun finally went down. It was much darker under the flyover than outside. All the adults started to form a group based on the gender. They shouted and laughed in loud. Shiva left the men's group and started walking towards me.

"What are they doing?" I asked.

"You mean them?" he asked.

"Ahan"

"Don't you see they are talking? Idiot" he still hadn't let go of that sarcastic tone.

"I think they are planning on how to kill each other's life partners." I instantly knew it was a very bad joke.

"No, seriously tell me what are they up to?" My curiously increased.

"They were discussing some important family matters about their relatives and their living conditions."

After an hour or so, the ladies finished cooking.

"So the cooking is done. Do you want to have dinner a bit early?" Shiva asked me after one of the belittle boys came up to him to tell him that.

"Yes, I can have it early." The play in the evening had made me hungry.

"Where do you want to have it?" He asked.

I looked round for a second sitting place and then upwards. An orchestra of mosquitoes played above my head. "Do you really mean to ask that question?" I got a little frustrated.

"You can have it inside their home or out here." he so causally told me that as if both the places were out of this world.

"Oh, what is the big difference between the two?" I got all excited and asked in a mocking way.

"Inside, you have less mosquitoes to worry about."

"Okay then I am going in. Are you coming?" I stood up and started walking. I went inside one of them, following the little boy who had come up invite us. The tent wasn't big and resembled that of the one we take to camping minus the cleanliness. It was the only source of light inside the tent was the one lamp that occasionally went out. There, a young girl named Shanti, who apparently dressed a little better than the rest, started serving food. Shiva joined us too. Shanti always referred us as bhaya (brother) which made me a little comfortable. There was just Dal and Rice with pickle on the side. The food didn't look appealing at all but it tested damn well. Once we were done, a boy helped us wash our hands outside the tent with a bucket of water.

All the kids started to fall asleep despite of the noisy traffic. Never in my wildest dreams had I thought that I would spend night under a flyover with those slum people. It wasn't that I hated it; it just felt weird and was a completely different experience for me.

Most of the parents with very young kids slept inside the tents while the rest just on uneven surface.

"Why are you still not asleep?" Shiva asked me.

"Uneven surface, mosquitoes kissing me all over my face, my nose just lost its sense of smell" I blurted.

"Okay, good night." He said and covered himself completely with the blanket.

I forced myself to get into sleep. It was almost midnight and still a few stupid people roamed on the road. I heard the sound of a taxi much closer to my ear. When I tried to open my eyes, two guys wearing mask were trying to pull Shanti into the taxi closing her mouth with their hands.

"Hey" I shouted and all the men woke up. Even I ran along with many to beat them up, they ran away with a few injuries. People looked at me. I expected them to thank me for my bravery but not one of them patted me on my back or even smiled. Everyone just went back to sleep as if nothing just happened. I wondered whether these people knew how to react?

"It seems like you have little less fear in you now" Shiva who had seen my heroic attempt from saving Shanti from being kidnapped said and slept.

After a while, someone started tapping on my shoulder.

"Bhaya....Bhaya" it was Shanti.

"Hey Shanti, what happened?" I knew she came there to thank me for saving her life.

"Thanks a lot Bhaya" She said.

"It's okay, tell me, why did no one react much after that, how come they could they all just go and sleep as if nothing happened?" I wondered.

"They are all awake, right?" I asked, she laughed.

"This is quite common here." Even she sounded very casual about it.

"What do you mean?" I was horrified listening to her.

"Well everyone on this earth is a survivor, but it is just that we are the survivors on the road side. We never know when one of us will be grabbed and smuggled in the name of human trafficking. Even gang rapes happen here." For a moment, my brain just stopped functioning. I couldn't imagine all those things she said sitting right there.

"Why can't you go somewhere and live, where it is more secure?" I asked worriedly. I felt like helping her out, taking her away from this, she didn't deserve to life like this —her only two future options being gang raped or smuggled for trafficking.

"We don't own any place, we don't have any livelihood. Government threw us here last month."

"From where?" I inquired.

"From another flyover, which is two streets away." she said.

"Oh", there was not much I could have said other than that. All such things happened to these people on a daily basis. They were so genuinely nice. They let us in their homes, gave us food to eat and a place to sleep. They might have been poor but they had bigger hearts than many rich people I met in my circle. They were in deep shit, yet they cared for us like their own. They didn't despise us for our middle-class lifestyle, or begged us to help them. They presented us with the best that they had without expecting anything in return. In that moment, I felt more and guiltier of not talking to more of such men and women an hour ago when Shiva has asked me to.

"One day a drunken driver crashed his truck on this way and squashed my elder sister right underneath it, near that pillar you see. We didn't even have a place or the money for a proper burial. So we just buried her near the pillar. The driver didn't seem guilty at all. He said that she came out of nowhere. He said that it was her fault to roam around like this on the road, but many of us saw it with our own eyes. It wasn't her fault. She was just standing on the footpath waiting for the signal to go red so she could sell the remaining flowers in her hands. But because we are poor, no one came to our aid. There was no case made and the driver wasn't charged." She seemed stressed and as soon as she closed her eyes, two tears rolled down her cheeks.

"I'm sorry for that, come on don't cry, please." I tried to console her. I didn't know what else to do. I was so taken aback then with her tragedy. I didn't know what would make her feel better. There wasn't really much I could have done. If it had been my sister, I couldn't even imagine anything happening to Avika. But she kept on going after that.

"Sorry for disturbing you bhaya, I didn't mean to upset you. It's just that I miss her very much today. She was so good to me all the time. She looked after me and we two were very close. I will just leave now, good night." Such was her generosity that after surviving and almost kidnap attempt, she was worried that she had upset me with her story. I was sure that many of them had similar stories to tell about. The more time I spend under that flyover, the more respect I gained for them in my heart.

I felt like doing something for them, but there wasn't much that I could have done. I had no job and didn't even belong to a very wealthy family. Besides, they had not once asked for my help so I feared if I offered it myself, they might have felt insulted.

After listening to all that, there was no way I could sleep. A hundred thoughts circulated in my mind. Those people were holding their lives in their hands, not sure when a threat might come along their way. We, on the other hand, had everything we wanted, were living a secured life and lacking common sense day by day. I knew that if I kept thinking about it all I wouldn't get any sleep at all.

I turned the other way to get away from my thoughts. The pillar where her sister was buried was straight in my view. I experienced conscious sleep throughout whole night for the first time in my life. It was terrible; every sound seemed scary especially after seeing the pillar. Every time, I turned and some stone touched body, I felt like Shanti's sister was poking me from the underground, telling me how sad she was there. It was almost dawn when some of my fear left me. I thought finally now I would get some sleep. I had just closed my eyes Shiva nudged me.

"Adi"

"What?" I shouted aloud. He scared me with his high voice.

"What?" He asked.

"You didn't have to shout it like that." I told him.

"I thought you were sleeping. It's almost dawn. Let's take a shower and make a move." Shiva said. Thank god it was morning again.

"Bath? You mean same as we did in Umri?" I asked.

"Yes, Get up, let's go!" he took out a small hand towel and soap from his bag and started moving. I just followed him to see the bathing location. He stopped after crossing a couple of pillars.

There was only a municipal water tap. It was right in front of the road and traffic was starting to crowd them. But the crowd had nothing to do with my dislike. It was the stinking smell that was thrusting deep into my nostrils with every wind breeze. Many had already taken a bath earlier than us and a pool of soapy black water had gathered in the place. The water was mixing with the trash that was piled up against the wall, each time bringing another empty bag of chips, a baby's pamper, some rotten fruit peels and what not. The water had mixed with sewer water running down the street and had therefore turned all black and smelly. No way was I putting my feet in that place let along take a bath. I looked at Shiva who was busy taking off his clothes. How could he not feel yucky, taking a bath in that dirty water was equivalent to not taking a bath? It wasn't like we could get all pure and tidy after that, In fact, I was sure that we were going much worse than what we already did then. Umri had been much better than that. At least, they had kept the place clean.

"If you still want to live in your comfort zone, it's okay." He used those words as a weapon. It felt weird but I made my mind to take the bath. It was just that I had more audience now. Shiva held my bathing towel as I took a bath in that water. I was just in my underwear. It want the first time I had taken a bath in one, I had bathed like that multiple times when on a trip to the beach or private pool party. But somehow, taking a bath there in the same underwear felt invasion of privacy. I closed my eyes to avoid the humiliation. Every time the dirty water underneath my feet splashed, I put soap again and rewash myself. When I was sure, I was clean, I asked Shiva to hand me my towel. The water as usual had been cold. In the back of my mind, I had already prepared myself for that. I knew I wasn't going to bathe in hot water unless we stayed in a hotel. Well, the toughest part was to dress up in such an open area.

Before we were about to leave, Shanti tied a talisman on my hand. "What is that for Shanti?" I asked. "It just brings you good luck bhaya." I didn't believe in those things but I didn't have the heart to turn her down. So, I decided to keep it.

BLOOD ON MY SHIRT

We decided to head to Sagar in Madhya Pradesh. We took a train then. Because it was weekday, not many people were in the compartment. I and Shiva both occupied the window seats in the hope of enjoying some greenery after those last two days at Umri and under the flyover. I didn't mind staying under the flyover or at Umri, I still felt like I needed to stay someone place better the next time, but since I had agreed that Shiva lead the trip from then onwards, I wasn't sure how much of a say would I get in the accommodation matter. Shiva was just string outside the window when I was reminded me something that he had said last night.

"Why did you say last night that I had little less fear in me?" I asked.

"Because I felt so," he said, still looking outside.

How can you say so?" that one line answer wasn't what I was looking for. I wanted to know what compelled him to say that and I wasn't letting it go by until I got my answer.

"Because you shouted and ran after those guys in the taxi."

"No, I shouted because I was scared and that made everyone wakeup."

"Didn't you go along with them?" He inquired.

"Yes. I did"

"Why did that happen?" he asked, raising his eyebrow.

I had no answer to that.

"Why did you not assume that you will get beaten up this time?" he asked.

"I had everyone else along with me."

"Well, if you had made an attempt yesterday afternoon, who knows many others, might have joined you and you could have saved that man from getting beaten up." It made sense to me.

"Fear is nothing but a made-up theory of our negative assumptions." I knew that it was almost impossible to argue with his opinions. And I wasn't in a mood of doing it either. I was exhausted due to lack of sleep last night; my eyes started feeling lazy and I slipped into sleep.

By the time I opened my eyes, my head was resting in Shiva's lap. I got up and sat back. I looked outside the window. It was almost past afternoon as the sun was spreading its golden rays over the paddy fields.

"Did I drool over you?" I checked my mouth.

"No, you didn't." he said.

"How was your sleep?" he asked me.

"I have to be honest, it was one of the most comfortable sleeps I had recently. But wait, how did I end on your lap?" I asked.

"I think you are habituated to sleeping with a pillow. I saw you with one in Umri and then under the flyover. You were not able to sleep so ..." he stated.

"Oh, okay thanks for that."

The train started to slow down, may be some station ahead was near. After a few minutes, the train reached a station called Bina, which was the name of a small town in Madhya Pradesh.

"Get up let's get down here." Shiva stood up and started gathering his things and bag.

"But weren't we headed to Sagar?" I inquired as we had purchased tickets for Sagar.

"Does it matter? It's not like anyone is waiting for us or expecting us to come visit. We can go wherever we want. Can't we?" he was right, it didn't matter which place we went to. We got down at the station and started walking. But instead of taking a taxi or auto, we started walking on the railway track.

I felt relaxed watching the multi-colored sky. It was a little warm but the cool breeze made it harsh. We kept walking on the road parallel to the railway track. There were no homes nearby. The calmness felt good. Shiva didn't speak anything either. I think I needed that quiet time. I liked the feeling of not having anything on my mind to worry me about.

It was then that heard someone moaning from some distance. As another gust of wind blew, I heard the same sound again. I started moving in the direction of the sound. The closer I got, the clearer the voice became. Shiva had started following me, but didn't ask any questions.

"Shiva, do you hear anything?" I stopped walking and started to focus. I just wanted to make sure that I wasn't hearing voices.

"Yes, I hear someone crying." We both then started following the sound. We walked towards the long bushes which were right beside the railway track.

I was leading the way and Shiva was following me, he collapsed against my back when I suddenly stopped in the tracks. A little annoyed, he showed his irritation in the form of a grunt under his breath. But even if I had wanted it, I couldn't have moved. I was lost for words or sense when I saw what I saw. A women less than my age was the one making the noise. The only thing covered in her bare body was her own blood. She had been brutally beaten and her left knee had turned the shade blue, as if someone had hit her with stones. She was turned on her side, with most of her hair covered her face and her bosom. She was in so much pain that she wasn't even able to raise her voice for help.

Sanity returned and I immediately took out a towel from my backpack and wrapped it around her. The moment I touched her, she panicked a little. But I calmed her down. Seeing me kneel, Shiva finally saw what I was doing and ran towards the nearest road to stop a car and get help. My whole body was trembling. My mind had stopped working. Seeing those bruises and cuts on her body, I felt like crying. Who would do such a thing? Had humanity completely died? I tried helping her up but she was not in a condition to sit up straight, let along walk. So I decided to carry her in my arms and tried lifting her, my hand might have pressed against some bruise as she let out a little painful sigh. Her breathing was worsening by the second and I didn't want her to die in my arms like that. If she did, I would have never forgiven myself or gotten that image out of my head. Thinking that, I stood up, holding her firmly in my arms and started walking towards the road.

"We will take you to hospital, please don't close your eyes, and stay with us." I kept telling her. Just to make sure, I kept tapping on her cheek so that she won't fall unconscious. I could hear Shiva shouting at people to stop their vehicles. I stood by the roadside, in hope that the next vehicle would stop and help us. But it passed right by us without a care in the world. I looked down and she was staring right at my face. She smiled a half smile. I didn't know what that smile meant. Did it mean that the torture was finally over and that she was going to enter heaven any time soon or did she smile because she knew she was in safe hands?

But in the very next moment, she started closing her eyes gradually. I tried keeping her engaged so that she won't; fall asleep but my efforts didn't seem to be working at all.

"Shiva…Shiva" I screamed.

"What happened?" he came back running and panting.

"We are losing her; we have to take her to the hospital like RIGHT NOW!" I said.

"Let us carry her to the other side of the road and get a cab to drive us there." I did as Shiva had told me to. As we reached the other side of the road, I sat down wither head in my lap. Looking at us, an auto rickshaw stopped. We immediately carried her in. We both never gave up on keeping her awake. The driver told us that the government hospital was very far from there, so we decided to take her to the nearest private hospital.

Once we reached the hospital, Shiva ran in to fetch a stretcher. We rushed in; pushing the stretcher forward and a couple of other nurses joined us. Thankfully, the hospital took her in. We were asked to wait outside the room. After a while, I walked into the restroom to splash some water on my face. I got a bit stunned looking at my own reflection in the mirror. The image looked nothing like me. I was covered in sweat and blood. Most of my shirt was dripping with the blood of that girl and that very moment reminded me of the last time I stood in front of a mirror into a hospital's restroom. It was the day I had last seen Shree alive.

The whole thing happened that night with Shree replayed in my mind. As I recalled more and more details of that night, tears started rolling down my cheeks.

"I didn't know, who she was or what had happened with her I didn't even know why I was chosen to help her? Why did she come to me? Why did I hear her little cries?" I started speaking to myself.

Maybe she came to me for a reason. Maybe life was giving me a second chance to save someone's life. I tried my best saving Shree but I couldn't. But I won't let this girl die. Saving her felt like giving a tribute to Shree. I continued talking to the image in the mirror.

"Are you okay?" Shiva walked in.

"Yes, I'm alright. How is she?" As I returned back to reality I got concerned about the girl.

"Luckily, there are no major head injuries so she is not in the red zone."

I let out a sigh of relief and almost sank down into the floor. Shiva picked me up immediately and told me to stay strong.

"What happened to you? Why do you look so heartbroken?" He seemed a bit concerned.

"Her blood on me reminds me of Shree. I did nothing to save him. I might not know who is she but I don't want to lose her. Not another person's life through my hands." I knew I struggled to sound right but it felt as if my voice had been caught in my throat.

"It's okay, everything will be alright. You don't have to blame yourself for what happened. Doctors are saying that she will be fine." He put his arm around my shoulder and we both walked out of the restroom. We sat on a bench in the waiting room, expecting doctors to come up and report us about the girl's condition.

"Who could have left her there like that in such a deplorable condition?" I kept asking myself. I was sure that she had been attacked but by who? There were other weird thought going on in my mind but I didn't want to keep myself from thinking about them.

"Adi, have some water." Shiva fetched me a glass of water.

As I was about to take a sip, one of the senior doctors walked towards us.

"How is she doctor? Will she be okay? Can we go see her?" I had a tone of requests to make. The doctor seemed calmer than me and put his hand over my arm, signally me to calm down a little.

"We are happy that she is responding to the antibiotics but..." there were hardly a few things that I hated more than the "but" suspense. As of then, I hated it to the very core.

"Because of the rape she went through, there are a few minor injuries we are worried about. In order for us to operate on them, she needs to stabilize a little and regain some physical strength. We have kept her on the ventilator for now to observe her recovery. Let's hope for the best." The glass from my hand slipped and the water spread all over the tiled floor.

I was stuck at the word rape, "What the hell, she had been raped?" so my assumption had been true. My worst fears were going to be the story of someone's life now. She would always have to live with it. But it wasn't fair, she didn't ask for it. Then, why her?

My heart started to beat faster and my breathing quickened. I collapsed on the chair and didn't hear any of the things the doctor said afterwards.

"Adi... Adi... are you okay?" Shiva shook me.

"I don't know who she is. But I tell you Shiva, there is something other than blood, which urged me to help her. I feel so terrible for her. She is going to wake up only to die every minute of her life. She will never move on from what happened with her. The society is going to eat her alive." I started crying as soon as I remembered the way she had smiled at me as I was running towards the road to get help.

Even Shiva didn't speak a word. There prevailed complete silence. The only thing that made any sound was the ringing of the phone at the reception desk that kept ringing after every one minute.

It had been few hours and almost dinner time for the hospital staff.

"Shiva, can I trouble you for a bottle of water." I asked for the favor in a low tone.

"Sure, let me go and get it for you." He walked fast and got a water bottle from the wending machine. I nearly drank half the bottle and passed it to Shiva. We both stood up as we saw the doctor walking towards us from the ICU.

"She is responding to the medicines very well now. We are going to operate on her now. I know you are nowhere related to her, but In order to operate on her, you need to deposit a certain amount in the hospital it is against the policies of the hospital to use its machinery and equipment without payment. If you can just deposit some amount until someone comes looking for her, we can start with the operation." I knew that the operation was very important for her. If she didn't get it then, her chances of survival would decline.

"How much does the treatment cost?" I saw some hope of saving her.

"It may cost around 1.8 lac including her medicines. Just take your time and see if you can arrange for the cash. Just let me know if you have any more questions. " He walked away.

"My dad deposited 2 lac in my account. I have already used 15,000 for the hotel and traveling. I will still be able to pay for her though I knew that I will be left with 5000 only." I hoped that Shiva would offer some advice.

"Let me tell you something, if you feel what you're doing is good, then never rely on anyone's advice." It felt like an indirect way of telling me that what I was doing was right. I walked inside the doctor's room, filled in the form, had the doctor sign it and made my way to the cash counter. I withdrew cash using my card.

"We will operate on her early in the morning. If you wish, you can go see her." The doctor told us. I looked at Shiva, and he just showed me the way towards the ICU —again giving me the go ahead sign indirectly. At first, I felt a bit afraid to go in. I didn't know what I was going to say to her when she looked at me. What if she didn't remember what had happened with her and I had to be the one to tell her?

A nurse gave me an infection control mask before I entered the ICU. I followed her. The entire room has this smell of alcohol pads. There was nobody inside the room expect for the nurse, me and the girl lying on the table. Her head was covered in a doctor's cap. Although she wore an oxygen mask on her face, it was the first time I actually looked at her face. All the wounds had been cleaned and dirt washed. She was dressed in a patient's gown and looked as calm as ever. There were still a few open wounds on her arms and legs, but none of them bled. She was hooked to different machines and tubes that went inside her chest, hand and mouth. She was breathing... just breathing and nothing else. There was no sign of movement in her body.

"How is she?" Shiva asked as I came back out.

"Alive." That was the only truth I knew. We did not even have food that night. Every time I tried closing my eyes, the flashes of a lady being raped and then later thrown into the bushes to die occupied my mind. Those flashes didn't let me have any sleep at all.

Even Shiva stayed awake but we rarely talked. We sat idle. The doctors performed a couple of operations on her. After the second surgery, the doctor told us to wait another hour before she woke up.

Hearing that, tears of joy rolled out of my eyes. I had not lost another life. I had finally saved her. I felt like a heavy burden had been lifted from my shoulders the burden of Shree's death. I knew he would be happy watching me from above. Shiva hugged me to console me a little.

"I'm really proud of you Adi for all that you did." for the first time since our journey began, I saw tears in his eyes. They weren't rolling down his cheeks but still, there were in his eyes.

"Sir, you can see her, but please don't make her speak much for a few hours." One of the nurses asked if we were interested in meeting her. Shiva was not ready for ICU. But I was eager to see her this time. I followed the nurse inside the room. As she heard the door close, she moved her hands and feet a little.

"She is still under anesthesia," the nurse said.

I was more than happy; joyful was how I would put it. Seeing her alive, I experienced a magical feeling inside me. I didn't know how to put those feelings into words. I felt as if Shree had come back to life.

I made sure that there were no dues in her payment. While we were sitting outside hoping to talk to her when she wakes up, a family rushed in from the in gate, stopped at the reception desk and then went inside the girl's room.

"Who are they?" I asked a nurse who just walked into the ICU.

"They are her family." She told me. Now that someone had come to her, I didn't feel the need to talk to her.

"Shiva let's go." I said standing up. I had made my decision. I didn't want to give her a hero kind of a feeling and remind what happened to her again and again, she was already in much pain. All she needed was good support, for which the right people were around.

"Are you sure, you don't want to talk to her?" He asked me. He knew how much I had wanted to see her as soon as she woke up. My decision made him question me.

"No, I don't want to, especially now that her family is here. I helped her without expecting any credits; I don't want to spoil that feeling." He agreed and we walked out of the hospital without acknowledging anyone.

WORKING AT RESTAURANT

I was happy that she had woken up and had her family beside her to console, but what happened to her was not something she will easily forget. The very thought didn't leave my mind for hours and left me restless. I didn't want to think about it I knew that whenever I over thought things, I ended up doing something stupid. Shiva decided that we both head straight to Agra and I didn't question him. After having breakfast at a local dhabba, we both headed for the bus station. In about an hour, we were on the route to Agra.

My body ached and I felt exhausted from head to toe. The inconsistent sleep pattern gave me a headache, so strong that I felt like someone was hammering it twice every second. But despite all that tiredness, sleep wasn't coming to me, every time I tried to close my eyes, the face of that young girl would appear in front of me and how I had found her. I placed my head on Shiva's shoulder and he didn't mind. Even a blind man could have felt the exhaustion on my face. I closed my eyes in anticipation that sleep might come, even if for a few minutes. The only sound I heard was that of the wind outside, banging against the cracked window sill. The continuous thud felt a bit irritating but I didn't mind it as it kept me distracted from the thoughts of the girl.

We got off the bus when the sun was setting by the time we gathered our luggage and freshened up; the sun had gone down completely. Shiva was still in the public washroom. I had freshened up and I felt much better after that brief sleep on his shoulder. To my surprise, the bus station was empty —not a single soul. Before I could go back in and call Shiva, I saw a young beautiful woman walking alone on the road. She felt out of place like she didn't belong there. She wore high heels and the strong wind was making her walk a little difficult. Her hair were flowing which made it difficult for me to look at her face. All of a sudden, a van stopped near her, and a few masked guys stepped out. They pulled her into the van and started ripping off her clothes. She started to cry for help but they shut her mouth with a piece of cloth and started torturing her.

The van started moving and in order to save her, I started following it I ran as hard as I could but the van's speed only increased. I was running out of breath and the van was just getting out of sight. The girl's scream-ing had stopped too. In that moment I knew she was gone. I knew what those guys meant to do with her. I stopped as there was no point running. After a few seconds, the same van approached towards me, this time from behind. As it neared, the back door opened and the girl who had been abducted was tossed out of it. It being a moving car, she rolled over sev-eral times on the road and stopped near my feet. It was then that I saw her face for the first time. She was the same girl.

I woke up instantly, panting for air. Thankfully, it had been a dream. My heart had nearly stopped; I had sweat all over my forehead and neck. The image had been so frightening that I wasn't able to get it out of my head for a fair amount of time.

"What is it? What's wrong?" Shiva asked, looking at how disoriented I looked.

"Nothing, I'm fine. It was just a bad dream about her." I confessed.

"Come on, let's get off here." He decided that I needed some fresh air and asked the conductor to stop the bus right away in the middle of the road. Right from the point where Shiva had started to lead the plan I had been experienc-ing very uncertain circumstances. I hated it, but still, I felt as if it was making me a better person. I trusted Shiva, so I did not resist getting off the bus.

We got down and started walking on the road. I remained silent and didn't bother him about where we were going. He started walking towards a village, but before reaching the village, he stopped at a point and started walking behind a pile of rocks and then into the bushes.

The view form there was spectacular. Most of it was rarely visible as the sun was starting to set, but as far as we could see, it was breathtaking. Greenery was spread over many acres and the crops were dancing with the winds. There were many Borassusflabellifer trees. We sat there on the rock under the shade of a tree.

"Just look the fields, the birds, and the movement of the tree leaves due to the wind." I said. I knew it was worth looking and something I desperately needed to see. Just being there instilled calmness in me. I took my time staring at the landscape, listening to the chirping birds heading back home and just allowing the cool wind to touch me.

"How are you feeling now?" Shiva asked.

"I feel a little better. What you said was correct, looking at nature when we were unstable helps a lot." I wondered the science of it but I couldn't come up with an explanation.

"Let me tell you something, do you know that the weather has a certain impact on human emotions? Our skull needs to absorb certain amount of sunlight to perform specific chemical reactions which keep our body clock proper. If we spend our day with insufficient light we tend to be lazy, drowsy all that day. On a rainy day people tend to get depressed or frustrated than on a sunny day. In the similar way, nature also has a certain impact on our moods. In whatever mood you are, just walk down to any vista point nearby. Sit and watch and think what's wrong and miracles will happen. It has the power to bring down your negative moods and cheer you up more when you're happy. You just need to interact with Mother Nature; she will take care of the rest."

"What do you mean by interact with it?" I doubted.

"Getting lost while looking at the beauty of nature is itself interacting." I wondered where he got those kind of thoughts from. There was lot of wisdom in his head, each time he started explaining any of his philosophies, he had something new to teach me.

He helped me come out of my comfort zone at Umri village, what he told me about fear was correct. He was there supporting me to enjoy the joy of helping others. The more I realized and recalled, the more blessed I felt to have him in my life then. I had never met someone who had influenced me so much with their words. The odd thing was that none of his philosophies on life had been wrong.

After spending a few more minutes, we started walking back on the highway. We walked in hope that a bus would stop for us. I had experienced that many times. Every time I waited for something, everything else would show up except that. The same happened with us then.

"Shall we rest here under this tree for a while? I'm running out of energy" I requested Shiva because he never felt tired. I didn't know where he got all that energy from.

"Okay." He said looking at my exhausted face.

I just leaned to the tree. I felt thirsty after all that walking but we didn't have any water with us. There was no sign of it around either. I opened my bag and pulled my diary to update it.

"What is it?" he asked me.

"It is my personal diary." I said.

"Oh, I didn't know you have a habit of writing diaries. I haven't seen you writing one since we met." He was little surprised and I could hear it in his tone.

"Well, I don't write it on a daily basis and I usually write in mornings, coincidentally when you do yoga and meditations." I explained.

"Hmm okay." That tone was not usual, it seemed like he wanted to have a conversation about it, but didn't.

"Is there anything wrong about this?" I extended the topic.

"Let me tell you something." There it is. I knew another life philosophy was on its way.

"Come on, even for this?" I joked.

"What do you write in your diary?" He kept his tone serious.

"My feelings, thoughts, special events, unusual events." Those were the very first things on top of my mind.

"Human brain has terrific capabilities. One of them is remembering. Do you know that?"

"Ha ha, very funny." I didn't really get what he meant by that.

"Look, if any special events touch you very deeply, whatsoever may happen you will remember it forever. Many events in our life are periodic. They look special only for that moment. Recollecting them doesn't give you the feel back. So, firstly if you forget some event, it indicates that it was worth to be forgotten. Secondly, no matter how hard you try you cannot erase memories of special events which mean the world to you. If we talk about your bad events, why do you want to make a note of them?" he paused.

"Oh, it is because you can learn a lot from those mistakes." I wanted to sound a little intellectual.

"Learning from mistakes is a psychological process, not a document-ing one. Either you do something bad or it happens to you. Whichever it is, it will make you feel terrible at some points whenever you recall them. Then you learn what went wrong and never do that again."

"But it gives you us a better feeling to share." I knew I couldn't against him, but I still wanted to try.

"Good point. Let us say Nandini breaks up with you and you are depressed. You open your diary and write down about how you feel. Does it help? Does it make all things better? Does it make all the pain go away?" He asked.

"Uh, May be." I didn't know what he was getting onto.

"Can your book be a crying shoulder for you? Or can it give you sug-gestions in return to get over it? Or does it console you?"

"It didn't really console me. It just... I can't really explain what it does." I was starting to get a little frustrated now. I knew he was right but I also knew that I wasn't completely wrong either. The journal might not tell me what to do next, but writing it all done felt like venting out my sadness, anger or desperation. I felt light-hearted after writing, like my mind cleared up and I could think better but explaining all this to Shiva who was hell-bound on proving me wrong was very difficult.

"Then why do you want it. Suppose if you have a best friend who is in depression. How would you feel if he chooses to share his grief, sorrow, sadness or anxiety with a book and not with you, how would you have you felt it he had chosen a book over you?" He said. I didn't have anything to say to that. So I stayed quiet.

"You feel something is wrong with your friend and if he shares his problems with you, there is a scope of reducing the depression. There is some scope to come out of it, of course if he wants to."

"Share your feelings and thoughts with people so that you can improve yourself. You are going to remember the most important event in of your life, good or bad. You don't need to capture them in a diary. All the things that hold some value will never leave your mind, leaving little space for the unnecessary. Can you recall any moment in your life that wasn't significant but you still remembered it? Probably not! You either got hurt or was your happiest. That is the reason why you remember them, because they were important to you and you will remember them like they happened yesterday whether you write it down or don't. So, instead of complicating things, live simple."

There might be some advantages of writing diary, but I was convinced enough to stop my pen in between and put back the diary in my backpack.

"You are good at convincing people aren't you?" I genuinely was amazed by his persuasion skills.

"Maybe." He didn't think it was a quality worth praising. To him, it just felt like common sense.

We saw a bus approaching our way. As it neared, we saw that the board on the front said that it was going to Agra. That was the bus we had been waiting for almost half an hour. We signaled it to stop, got on it and started our journey towards Agra.

"Hey, did you feel bad when I said if you and Nandini broke up?" asking that his voice seemed apologetic. He felt like he had said something that might have hurt me.

"Well, no I know we won't, so it doesn't matter." And I believed it.

"How did you feel when you were in love with Nandini?" That was a strange question to ask. Anyone who was in love felt the same —loved. How else anyone would put it.

"First, I never expected that she would say yes to me. Once we are there I enjoyed each and every moment like all other couples who are in love do. I started paying attention to the lyrics of romantic songs and not only that; I actually started understanding those lyrics. I know she is the one."

"I'm happy for you." Thank god he did not start anything on love. I hoped that Nandini saw my email I send the before leaving. I knew it might have upset her a bit as I had quit my job and had nothing planned for the future. But I also knew that she would understand my frustration. If she knew me at all, she knew that I was free spirit; I wasn't the kind to be caged. The thought of Nandini brought back many happy memories. Many even made me smile.

It was almost 3 p.m. by the time we reached Agra. Whenever someone mentioned Agra, the very first thought that came too everyone's mind was of the Taj Mahal —one of the greatest wonders of the world. Taj Mahal too, was designed as a symbol of love by a Mughal emperor. Today, it not only held sentimental value, but was also the hotspot for all tourists. Even I had visited it once with my family when I was young.

"Let me call my parents first."

"Okay."

"Hi, Mom. Adi here. How are you?"

Adi, my son. Her voice on the phone told me how happy she was to hear from me.

"We are all good, how are you and where are you?" Before I could say anything, she went on asking a hundred questions about how I was, where I was, what I was doing how was my trip going, was I eating right etc. etc.

"Mon relax. We are in Agra." I told my family about Shiva when we were in Adilabad. My mom was kind of relieved that I had some company. I spoke to my mom and dad for about 15 minutes. I didn't speak too openly about my journey or all that had happened. I wanted to tell them face to face and see the excitement on their faces when I went back. I didn't want to miss out on those valuable expressions on call, so I just told them a little bit about where I was and where were we planning to go next.

I paid my last note on the call. I realized I was running out of money. I knew Shiva didn't have a job, just wanted to know whether he has any for rest of our journey.

"Shiva, I have run out of cash, I only have 5000 more in my account. I don't think it would be sufficient for the journey ahead. Any idea what we should do?" I was hoping he will have some idea as always.

"Why can't we do a job here for a week and continue the journey with that money." It sounded cool, but I wasn't sure what job is he talking about. Who would give two complete strangers a job and that too only for a week or so? Finding a job these days was fining a needle in a haystack. The completion was tough and there weren't many jobs for the fresher.

"I visited Agra in one of my travels before. I have earned here for my living for few months. We can go there and try." It sounded good and a little relieving that he knew someone in the city. Besides, it wasn't like I had any other option. We started walking to the place where he worked.

The streets of Agra hadn't changed much, the houses were still built in old style, and the roads were covered with auto rickshaw. It wasn't very different from Hyderabad, just a little crowded.

"What is the place you worked at?" I was curious to know.

"It was a restaurant." That didn't sound any good. Did he work as a waiter there?

Finally after a long walk, he went into a restaurant called "Priyan's Restaurant" and asked me to standout for a few minutes. I was dying out of thirst.

"Adi..." Shiva called my name from the entrance door of the restaurant. He took me to the manager of the hotel.

A man with a French beard on his face put forward his hand for a handshake. He looked like he was in his late thirties. Most of his hair was gone and in its place was shiny bald front yard. He was wearing a suit minus the coat with an odd colored tie That tie was the only piece of clothing that made him look superior than the rest of the staff. I shook his hand but he didn't seem very courteous.

"Vijay, he is Adi my friend." Shiva introduced me to him as we shook hands.

"Hi, nice meeting you." His accent was little country side. And that was it. Shiva had already told him that we would be working here and the manager had gladly agreed. No wonder he needed more people on his staff. I had never worked at a restaurant before. I felt a bit excited. The manager started walking us through all the rules and regulations. It was decent 3-star hotel. The best part was that it had air-conditioning and the bad part was that I felt a little degraded working as a waiter in a restaurant. It would have been much easier to ask dad to deposit some more cash in to my account but I knew that Shiva wouldn't have liked that. He would have lectured me on it several times to make me feel awful and I didn't want that.

"Here are the keys for the room, go to the kitchen eat some food. Then go to your room, and get some rest. Then around 7 p.m., get dressed for the evening shift we are expecting a big crowd tonight." Saying that, he walked back to his counter.

"What room is he talking about?" I questioned Shiva.

"These people have rooms on the roof for workers."

"Wow that's so nice of these people." that was such a nice gesture. It was the first time I had walked into a room which read "Employees only" in any restaurant. After stepping in, I knew why they said so. The room was anything but clean. The floor seemed slippery and wet at the same time. We were then served microwave food from the kitchen downstairs.

The room was located on the terrace of the same building. It was a 5-story building, where each floor had different business units. The restaurant was located on the 1st floor of the building. As we had climbed the stairs, I couldn't help but notice many pan peaks on the side of the stairs. In fact, it wouldn't be wrong to say that they were almost painted with a brownish red. The rest of the stairs had countless cigarette remains but all if it was not something that I hadn't seen before. As we were going to our rooms, I thought me and Shiva will be sharing the room but I couldn't have been more wrong. Shiva knocked on the door and a man of our age opened the door on the third knock. He didn't seem very happy as we had just woke him up from peaceful lumber. It looked like half of India was living in that room, the room was just a few square inches bigger than my bathroom at home and there were already eight men lying on the floor covered with a rug sleeping.

"Shiva I think we should think again about doing job or at least here." I didn't want to share that room with 10 people. It smelled horrible too. Like the room of a local drug addict. I didn't even want to look how the bathroom looked as I was sure if I did, I would vomit.

"Let me tell you something." Not again please, a voice in my head shouted.

"Many of us just live our life, we don't even find time to look into other people's life and help them. This is an opportunity for you to live and experience their life. This will help you, just trust me." I agreed only because of him.

We were told that we would have to start the evening shift after three hours so we better get some sleep and be dressed by the time it starts. Shiva sat down on one corner of the room. I didn't feel like sleeping on those filthy mats, god knows what they were infected with. So I rested on one of the empty chairs placed on the other end of the room. I slept for almost an hour before I was woken up by the noise in the room. All the other men who were sleeping an hour ago were getting dressed in the room. They were sharing everything from a comb to a sock. Many of them had already taken a bath, while others were waiting for their turn, just sitting and playing games on their mobiles. The bathroom was located on the terrace too, but wasn't attached in the room. My turn came 4th before Shiva's. Thank god, I had carried my own soap as the one in the bathroom had hair on it. The mirror was cracked and reflected a distorted image of the person. There was a bucket filled with water and a mug with no holder surfacing on it. I took off my clothes and bathed. I had slept in that room, it didn't matter to me where I bathed. Besides, it was much better than bathing in front of a hundred people. It may not have been the cleanest of rooms but at least it was private.

By the time I got out. Shiva was holding two aprons in his hand. One for me and one for himself he then got inside and quickly took a bath. Most of the guys in the room had already left for downstairs. After getting dressed I tied the not so new apron around my wait and headed downstairs with Shiva too.

"Are we going to cook or help the chefs down there in the kitchen?" I asked Shiva as we were heading down the stairs.

"Ha ha, you are going to clean the dishes and I'm going to serve the food." I had a "what the hell" kind of feeling in my head, but I went for it. When I walked into the kitchen, they directed me to the dish wash section.

"This is a water spray tool. It blows pressurized water. Use this to clean the dishes in case any food remains are on it. But don't clean it with the detergent. We have a dishwashing machine for that. Once you are done spraying the dishes with the eater, I will then put them in the dishwasher where they will be cleaned and dried. Soak the spoons in the container containing the cleaning agent. Once you rinse everything I will put them in the machine which cleans and then dries them up." One of the men in the kitchen instructed me of my role.

"Cool that is not at all work." I thought.

I started at 7 p.m. standing there, waiting for plates to come in. No men around me wished me good luck as it was my first day on the job. They were busy in their work. I knew no one except Shiva and he wasn't here in this section. He was in the main kitchen with others. I wished he was there. I just stood there playing with the water spray thing. After an hour, a couple of plates turned it.

As the clock started ticking, the count of the incoming plates raised. I felt uncomfortable to even touch some of the plates that had gravy spread all over it. There was too much work and the colleagues who had instructed me to do the dished was standing at my back shouting and instructing everyone to move their hands faster as we didn't have all night. By the time the load of the dishes lessened, I looked at the clock which had spider web round it. It was 9 p.m., the manager had told us that the restaurant closes at 10 which meant I only had to work for an hour before getting off. I felt a bit relieved as my knees weren't able to carry my weight any longer.

After a while, one of the guys who looked like the head chef came in the back of the kitchen room and asked me what I would like to have for dinner. The thought of dinner reminded me that I hadn't eaten anything since the last 5 hours. It was my first day of work, so I didn't want to sound too picky. I went for biryani as that was most of the others guys in the room had agreed to eat.

"Can I get Chicken Biryani too?" I asked with a little hesitation.

"Okay." He smiled. He looked friendly.

"Hi, how are you doing here?" Shiva walked in.

"Oh boy, I missed you like hell in the last three hours." I said and he chuckled.

We collected our food and went upstairs to the so-called room. We were having food on the terrace looking at the moon irritated by the music mosquitoes were humming in our ears.

"Does your back hurt?" I asked.

"Just a little but that's fine." He replied.

"How is your biryani?" He asked.

"I'm hungry so it doesn't matter. But to be honest, I hate it as it is nowhere near to what Hyderabad Biryani tastes like." Although, we both were physically tired, we still chatted for a long time. As we walked inside the room, many of the guys had already fallen asleep. There was so concept of personal space there as they were laterally piled up against each other. Finding a space was not less of a challenge. But none of them seemed to care. It seemed like they all had practice sleeping like that to me, it felt like sleeping in a coffin where you had to share a place with someone else. There was no place to make any movements for let alone turn like I was accustomed to during sleep. I looked at Shiva in a sad desperate way and he gave me his own spot to sleep on. This was much better. Instead of trying to adjust in between two people there was a wall on one side of it. After staring at the ceiling fan for some time, I dozed off into deep slumber.

The next morning we woke up around 7 a.m. to start the morning shift. The thought of working for more than 10 hours scared me a little. I wondered how my mom used to wash all the dishes when we were young and couldn't afford a maid. The pain I was in for just standing for 6 hours was nothing compared to what my mother or any mother felt when she had to spend all day in the kitchen preparing food, washing the dishes etc.

I never washed a plate in my home, may be that was why I was doing it then. By the end of the day I had two strong feelings. First, that I might have washed plates from other restaurant too and second, I might need a wheelchair for tomorrow's shift.

"Can I ask you a question?" We were just sitting out in the cool air after the lunch shift had ended.

"Yes sure go ahead." Shiva said.

"How much are we getting paid?" I never bothered asking before but my physical pain forced me to ask.

"150 rupees per day." He said very casually.

"It better be a joke or else I will jump from the roof." I said.

"Ha ha ha" Not sure why he laughed.

"Don't laugh Shiva; I spent 150 on a coffee at the Barista Cafe. I cannot work anymore here. Let's go."

"Let me tell you something." And there it was.

"No stop right there don't say anything." I wasn't in a mood to be lectured. I was furious, all that hard work for just a hundred and fifty rupees.

"Listen buddy, you still have 5000 in your account and you can have more money with just one phone call. But what if you didn't have both of those options?"

"Why do you think these people working here for more or less the same money leave their families in the rural areas and come here?"

"You have to respect every type of job, Adi. There should not be a social status taboo in labor." What he said was right, this job made me realize the efforts of my mom and also that there are people who are making a living out of this. I should have showed some respect for them.

I remembered my last job; I still felt that it was much worse. In it, I felt like a robot.

"Can I ask you something?" I wanted to know his opinion on it. I wanted to know if he would approve of me leaving my job because I wasn't enjoying it there.

"Initially I waited to get into a project, and when I got into one, I felt excited, like over the moon, but then eventually, I started hating it. I felt like a robot, it was very boring. I keep thinking if quitting was the right thing to do?"

"Let me tell you something, people who love money more than their job will sooner or later start hating what they do. People who value the job more than money... they never get bored of their job."

"What about people who are in between?" I was intrigued.

"That is much worst, their life passes by right in front of their eyes and they aren't able to do anything except regret the past."

"You are right, but I seriously can't stand in a place for almost 10 hours a day. I start to feel like I have been trapped and my survival instincts kick in, and I need to get out of there. Like when I was doing the dishes today, all day I felt like that little room was a prison cell. I didn't like it."

"Okay, I will talk to Vijay, we will switch roles." He smiled.

"The most important thing is having a smile on your face, interact with customers with a smile, get the food from the kitchen when the bell rings and serve them. Keep an eye on the water needs of the customers. Clean up immediately if any of them or the kids has made a mess. Don't wait for them to call you. Once they are done eating, clean up the table, drop the food leftover in the trash and wipe the tables and arrange everything back to normal." Vijay gave me a brief lecture on my role.

For what I am being paid, all I can promise is a half-smile, I thought, but of course I didn't tell Vijay that. He had already figured out that I belonged to a well-off family by my clothes, may be that was why he thought it was important to remind me that I was working for him. Anyways, I didn't want to get in any debate with him. It was difficult for me to respect a job that I hated. I knew how badly customers behaved with servers. I didn't do it myself but I had seen many others insulting and humiliating them. Until today, I never felt how they must feel.

Our next shift began at 6 pm in the evening. I had just wiped the washed dishes with a cloth and was waiting for customers to start rolling in. The first customer of that night was a couple with two young kids. The man was Caucasian and the woman perhaps Chinese or Korean – I could never tell the difference, the two little boys were not more than 5 years of age. I started towards them with a tray of water and the menu card in my hand. The camera in the man's hand told me that they were tourists. The man was ordering for everyone.

"How spicy would you like your food today, sir?" I asked politely. He turned to his wife and started asking her the same but in sign language. I realized she was deaf. I felt a little sorry for her but also felt interested at the same time. The way the man's fingers moved, coupled with the expressions on his face, it looked like he had taken proper training of sign language just for his wife. They made such a cute couple, I thought. They looked genuinely happy and in love –something that I hadn't seen for some time. I took their order and went back to the kitchen. Since they were the first ones and having an early supper, their food was prepared in less than 15 minutes. I went out with the food tray in my hand and served them. The man thanked me verbally while the lady gestured. A smile came onto my lips genuinely. They were so well-mannered and humble. Every time I went up to them, they treated me with courtesy – so much that I felt like sitting down with them and hearing their love story. They reminded me that true love didn't need any words to be expressed. It could easily be done when one is kind to one another. It was the first time that I understood the meaning of what it was like to be silent yet still have yourself heard.

I wanted to ask how they were so happy, but I feared that my questions might seem too personal and intervening. But I also knew that If I didn't ask them, my brain will keep thinking about them for god knows how long so I built up some courage and walked after them as they started their way out of the entrance.

"Excuse me sir. Can I ask you something?" My voice was a little hesitant.

"Yes please."

"You both look great together. I was really amazed by your bonding. The question I am about to ask may be a bit personal but I need to ask you this. How did you know that she was the right one for you?" she smiled when he explained what I had asked.

"It is because I love her for who she is and not for what she is or what she has." I understood that sentence in parts but not together.

"How do you adjust if something cracks up between you two?" I made up my mind that this was the last question I was going to bother them with.

"Adjustment between couple comes into play only when one is not willing to let it go. It is not fair to ask her to change her way of dealing with life that is based on the psychological thinking she developed since the past 30 years. Just because she became my wife didn't mean that she had to change any of her interests unless she wanted to on her own. If you know the original person and love her originality then there is no scope for adjusting."

"Thank you sir, it was nice meeting you." His answer was lovely. How pure of him to accept her for who she was. I thought that was what was lacking in India. Whenever people went at the girl's house of with a marriage proposal, they expected too much from her. Asking her to give up her job, her lifestyle, her unique personality, and her interests wasn't fair; it was like stripping her of her originality. The couple restored my faith in humanity. No one would have loved or married the woman if she were born here. It wasn't her fault that she was born that way. But people here wouldn't have acknowledged that. I loved the small talk. None of them flinched or seemed irritated, considering a waiter was asking them such personal questions, a waiter they didn't even know or met before. I saw a little glimpse of Shiva in the man. It was a very nice experience to work there, though initially I hated it, we earned 2100 for those seven days. We thought it would be sufficient for then, so we moved on further.

AN ADDICT

We entered the state of the five rivers "Punjab" through Patiala. Everything about Punjab was staunchly traditional. The women were dressed in a shirt and Salwar with beautifully set Dupattas on their heads. The fields on both sides of the roads had a harvest that bloomed and many men and women cutting them down. The air was fresher without the dust and air pollution. All men were seen wearing turbans on their heads. We got off on the bus station with no idea what we were going to do now that we were there. I had always wanted to see Punjab. We started following the people who had gotten off the bus. We came across a playground where a group of kids were playing cricket. We decided to sit down for a while and watch their play. We thought that would give us some the time to think about what our plan was. We found a place under the shade of a big tree. I requested Shiva to sit down. Since the playground was acres long, there were many matches going on simultaneously. I tried focusing on the one nearest to me.

It was a bit confusing in the start as none of the boys were wearing any uniforms. The enthusiasm of the boys reminded me of my old school. I was not a fantastic player though but I enjoyed playing the game If I were to rate my cricket skills, I would call myself an average all-rounder. I felt that my strongest suite was bowling; I wouldn't say that I was the greatest.

I didn't take any wickets but didn't deliver an expensive over either; my batting skills were good but not as good as my wicket keeping skills.

I always believe the reason why cricket was in the blood of this country was because it was so adaptable. All one needed was a bat and ball. It could also be played with an exam pad and a paper ball if one was playing in a room. I sat there, watching them for another few minutes. Then I felt nature calling.

"Hey, I need to pee. I will be right back." I informed him, while he watched the game.

"Okay" he nodded without even looking at me; I knew that would happen with that game. It was so addictive and nerve-wrecking if both the teams had equal chances of winning. I looked around for a suitable place to pee, a little hidden from the crowd. I spotted a few trees in the woods nearby and decided to head for them.

I found a nice spot. When I was done, and about to turn back, I saw glimpses of a building from the branches of the tree in front of me. I followed the view, in the hope of getting a good look. As I neared, I realized the building had been demolished. Realizing that I had just wasted a few minutes on this, I started walking back but something stopped me in the tracks. I heard someone; laughter. I turned around to see if I had missed seeing something. There was no one. I got a little scared. I didn't believe in ghosts but then there wasn't anyone in sight either. I rejected the thought, I must have imagined the voices, and turned back again. The voices were heard again, this time louder than the last time. I was sure about it this time. My curiosity urged me to take a closer look and I started stepping on the knocked down bricks in the direction from where the voices had come. The building was a two-room single-story house. The rooms were filled with construction waste that had been left there to rot. The insides were dark and since there wasn't any electricity or direct sunlight seeping inside, it looked haunted. Many bare steel roads were hanging from the ceiling and the walls still standing were covered in uncountable cracks. The room portrayed the perfect picture of the one's shown in horror films.

I heard the voices again; they were coming from the other side of the room. When I moved closer, I saw a bunch of guys, younger than myself, chatting amongst themselves. I hid behind a pillar to see what they were so happy about. They were six in total. They were doing some crazy stuff. One of them pulled out a plastic bag filled with some bronze colored liquid form his pocket. All boys cheered at the sight of it. As soon as he opened the rubber band, I knew it was petrol by the stench of it. One by one, the boys started transferring that petrol in six different plastic bags. I didn't know why they did that and I wasn't going to leave until I found out why. Once all the guys had a plastic bag in their hands, they started shaking it. The petrol started to dry out in the open air, why would they waste petrol like that, I thought to myself and then they did something I would have never imaged them doing. As the petrol dried from the plastic bags, they put it on their heads and covered their faces in it. Oh god, are they attempting suicide was my very first thought. Then, all the guys started breathing in the scent. After doing that for a minute, they pulled away the plastic bag and started smoking something. All of it looked weird and made no sense. After a few seconds, one of them started to act weird followed by the others. Then one of them pulled out an injection syringe filled with some liquid. He injected that in his elbow and the other guys followed suit.

"OMG, they are taking drugs," I thought and I was shocked to see petrol being used in such a way as a drug. The air around them started to smell weird. They all were younger than me but I was afraid to look at them. They looked like drug addicts in movies with unkempt beards and dirty hair. No bath for a long time.

"Hey, who are you?" someone just pushed me into their space from behind and I fell down on the mud.

"I was watching cricket and I came to pee this way and I heard you guys talking so I came to check." I said with a breaking voice. Surprisingly, I saw fear in their eyes instead of anger.

"I'm not a snitch, don't worry I will just leave." I felt scared at the bottom because of their looks. One of the guys, who looked like he was seventeen or eighteen, looked the most scared, but he also looked cleaner and smarter than the other guys. He was almost the same height as me, had a fair complexion and wore a turban on his head just like all the other guys.

"Just go from here." They shouted out of fear. I walked back and Shiva was still watching the match.

"Let's go," I said. I didn't feel like sharing what had happened with him because he might go there and be on a mission to change their minds.

Punjab was a place which had great taste in food. We had a chat with the locals while we were having our lunch regarding accommodations. We came to know that many families in the town accepted paying guests.

We walked around many streets bargaining prices for paying guest. Finally a man in his 50's agreed to keep us in for the amount we were willing to pay. He was wearing a regular Punjabi kurta which hung down to his thighs, loose-fitting pajamas, and had a turban wrapped loosely around the head. He had a white beard and mustache, serious eyes, and you could see all the Punjabi food in his stomach.

They were a big joint family. The family consisted of three brothers who ran a family business and their wives and children ran the households. There roamed many children for of all ages in the big ground below. The bungalow was a decent middle class building, almost as big as my own house. It was a two-story house. The ground floor had a big kitchen and a living room area while all the bedrooms were on the first floor of the bungalow. We were allotted the room on the roof. Thankfully, it was well-furnished. I wouldn't call it completely furnished as the walls had a few cracks and the bathroom wasn't very big or clean. But it was much better than what we have lived in when working at the restaurant. After freshening up, we both walked a little on the roof, casually talking about the journey. I couldn't help but notice that majority of the homes surrounding were poorly kept. Almost all of them had some unfinished construction. Some were missing paint, while others had a bricked wall smacked down in half with the debris still lying on the floor. Most of them were on the same level and close enough that one could easily walk from roof to roof by climbing the 3 inch walls dividing them. We walked for some time and then came back into our room for some rest. We were offered lassi by one of the kids in the family. The lassi was chilled and refreshing. It had been made using buttermilk and therefore was a little heavy. We both fell into a deep slumber after that.

We were invited for an early dinner because all the men and boys took their food first followed by the girls and women in the house. This custom in Punjab was as old as Punjab itself. People believed that since men worked all day outside their homes and were the breadwinner of their families, they should be offered the food first. As I was making my way into the dining hall after washing my hands, I saw a familiar face in the crowd of men and women. It was one of the boys I had seen earlier, injecting drugs. I looked a bit closely just to be sure.

Yes, he was the young boy who was taking drugs this morning, I uttered under my breath. I saw the reflection of fear on his face as our eyes met. He had also recognized me from the morning. My presence made him uncomfortable all throughout the dinner. But he wasn't the only one uncomfortable. I was in a dilemma too. The right thing would have been to talk to his father about his drug issue but then something stopped me. At that age, we all had been stupid. Maybe calling out on him would make him take them more in retaliation. I gobbled down my food and went to my room without saying a word.

Somebody knocked on our door while we were having a conversation about where to head from here.

"Hi" it was him; I closed the door and stepped out. Because I hadn't discussed it with Shiva yet, I decided to keep it between him and me for then.

"Please don't tell to my family about it." He requested.

"About what?" I acted naïve and decided to tease him a little about it. I had already made up my mind that I wouldn't tell on him. But I didn't want to give him the satisfaction of knowing that.

"What you saw this morning." He really looked scared then.

"Hmm, I will try my level best." I don't know why I behaved like it but I kind of liked it. He was angry when I said that but he couldn't do anything.

"By the way, what's your name?" I asked.

"Anup" he replied and left the place.

It was a pleasant morning when I stepped out of the room. Looking at the trees, long farming fields, birds, I thought what Shiva said was correct, people who woke up to this were indeed very lucky. The air was cold but the sun was giving a warm feeling.

I saw Anup at home, while we went for breakfast, which was a bit surprising as he did not go to either college or to his secret spot. He was constantly staring at me. I knew he was afraid that I might reveal the drug secret. We visited the farms in the day time and reached home by the evening. We followed the same routine for two days, and even Anup did, he never left the home.

On the third day evening, I was just sitting alone on the terrace, while Shiva was taking his nap. All of a sudden something bit me, I pulled my hand and held my finger very tightly, Anup came running and killed the scorpion with his foot.

"Hold your finger tight, I will be right back." He said and ran downstairs. The pain was excruciating but not completely unbearable. I kept holding my finger like I had been told. He came to me with a match box and a very small bowl which had a few drops of water in it.

He started to take off the non-toxic red phosphorus off their heads and mixed it with water. He started applying it at the bitten area. Slowly the pain started to alleviate and I felt a little better. All the color that had left my body came back.

"What is that?" I wondered.

"This will reduce the poison effect. Don't worry; it is not from the dangerous breeds." He said, still holding my hand tight.

"How can you say not to worry? How do you know that it is not poisonous?" I was still in a little bit of shock. Everything had happened so quickly that I didn't even have the time to scream.

"That is "Opistophthalmusadustus" belongs to the family 'ScorpionidaeIschnuridae', it is non-venomous." That was a whole new language to me.

"Now, it feels better. If you know all of this, I think you should become a doctor." As I uttered those words, he looked at me with a pained expression on his face. I didn't know what I had said wrong.

"Just let it dry and then wash it, you will be good." He left the place.

That night while Shiva was having conversation with the family downstairs, I was in my room alone.

Knock, knock.

"Hey, come on in." It was Anup.

"Thanks for your immediate reaction in the morning." I said. He did not reply. He just sat on Shiva's bed looking down on the floor.

"Don't worry, I will not tell anything." I promised him.

"I wanted to become a doctor from my school days." He started to speak out in a slow voice. He continued.

"Out of my interest, I started reading medical books and almost read everything available in my school library. My hunger towards it grew even more; so I became a member of the public library and started reading."

"When I talked to my parents about it, they did not agree."

"Why?" I asked.

"They said it is an expensive degree, and that they want me to look after their farms and family business. After schooling, I never visited the college again. I was very depressed, I wanted to become a doctor but my parents were against it. I have no idea what can be done. My family never believed my medical suggestions. That was even more heartbreaking. You are the first one to say that I should actually become a doctor. So, I got a little emotional." He said and wiped his tears.

"But how did you land into the drug trap?" I asked.

"When I visited one of my friend's birthday parties, my friends forced me to drink alcohol. I kind of liked it, all the time when I was high it made to forget all these things and most importantly that night I did not judge my life or think about my future. I just slipped into sleep as soon as my head was on the pillow. It gave me a much better feeling to forget what was going on. I started consuming alcohol regularly. Then slowly drugs got introduced my some other common friends and I liked them even more. The day you saw me was my third time taking drugs." He confessed.

"We do few things repetitively because they make us feel better. It might be nicotine, alcohol, drugs, sweets, food, and sex whatever. If something makes you feel better than worst you tend to like it, if something makes you feel best than better you will love it, if something makes you to feel greatest then best, you will start craving for it again and again. It is addiction –the only thing which can cheat both brain and heart at the same time. If we won't react at the right time to overcome it, it will swallow us completely." he said. I was amazed by his observation and philosophy.

"You are very smart Anup, you know it all, and I don't think I need to tell you to control your addictions."

"Regarding the doctor dream of yours, I can tell you one thing. Only enormous amounts of passion and patience can keep one's dream alive till it is achieved. Don't give up on your dream. Everyone in this world will have a dream, only 50% will start to make an effort, out of which only 20% will make half the journey. 10% will give up just before the end. 5% will try their best but luck might not be with them, but these 5% will try again, they won't let it go. Only 5% people achieve their dreams. Have tons of patience and put your best." I said.

"Thanks for giving the confidence; I will talk to my parents again." He said and left the room.

HER NAME IS KEERTHI

We decided to go further north form there onwards. We travelled a little on foot first and then were given a lift by one of the tractor drivers who were also heading for the city. We requested him to drop us off at the railway satiation and he gladly agreed. As we were getting off from the tractor we heard a train's whistle. It was followed by a lady's announcement that the train heading o Ludhiana would leave in 5 minutes and that it was the final call. I and Shiva looked at each other and without saying another word we rushed to the train ticket counter and bought two tickets for Ludhiana. Since the train was almost full with passengers, I and Shiva didn't get seats side by side this time. We did, however, sat in one compartment.

The seat in front of me was still empty, I secretly wished that the person it had been allotted to miss the train so that Shiva could come and sit there. Or else, I would have to keep quiet all the way to Ludhiana or talk to the men and women around me. There only remained 5 minutes before the train left the station. By then, I was sure that no one was coming so I motioned Shiva to change his seat. He smiled at me and gestured me to wait with his hand.

"But I don't think anyone is coming here." I said in a low voice.

But before Shiva could get up from his seat, the compartment door opened and in came a girl. She took the seat I had been eyeing for Shiva from the last 10 minutes. She looked out of breath as if she had run the last mile on foot.

She was busy in herself, drinking water from her bottle, then setting up her hair and then checking her luggage's pockets as if she had left something at home. She was doing it all in such a cute way that I couldn't help but notice. I wouldn't call her beautiful but she was very cute. She had midnight black hairs that were cut in layers, the last one ending till her shoulders; she had the same colored eyes with thick eyebrows. She had a heart-shaped face in a whitish shade and a slim body. By her dressing, I assumed that she belonged to an educated family; she looked much younger than me. After a long whistle that nearly left us all deaf, the train started to lag slowly away from the platform. And then it sped up. No one in the train spoke in the first 30 minutes of the journey.

I was reading The Alchemist to kill time since Shiva was sitting very far from me and I had no one else to talk to. I had the book placed right in front of my face.

I continued to hear the voice of bangles clashing against each other in the hands of the girl sitting in front of me. An urge to look at her again, made me drop down the book to my eye level so that I could see her face every now and then. As I neared the end of one page and shifting to the next, I stole a quick glance. I had planned to keep the glancing to a minimum and I would have kept going with the plan but something odd happened. The girl was crying. Every time, she would wipe off a tear from her face, her bangles clashed with each other.

"Oh no! What happened to her?" I thought to myself. She was weeping but not aloud. Most of the people around her had already fallen asleep or were busy listening to songs on their cell phones. Because she was doing it very silently, no one noticed. I wouldn't have noticed it either had I not been sitting in front of her.

I wanted to ask her what was wrong but I didn't have the guts too. A hundred thoughts ran through my mind. Perhaps she lost something important, perhaps she was missing someone, perhaps she had run away from home, or lost someone close to her recently etc. I pretended to bypass what I just saw and continued reading the book.

Later, I kept my book aside as I couldn't concentrate on it at all. Her crying face kept running through my mind. I started looking at her whenever I got a chance, indirectly. She had stopped crying but still didn't look happy. The sadness didn't suite her beautiful face.

"Are you okay?" I couldn't resist asking so I broke the silence. The look she gave me reminded me that I was a stranger to her.

"Oh sorry, I'm Adi" I offered my hand for a shake. Maybe I didn't look trustworthy as she took a couple of seconds to place her hand in mine for a handshake.

"I'm Keerthi."

"I saw you crying a while ago. I am sorry but I couldn't help but notice that you still look a little gloomy; I just want you to know if everything is alright or not. If you need any help, please don't hesitate asking." I thought that clarification was needed as it eased the frown she had on her face while shaking my hand.

"No, absolutely fine, thank you for asking." She gave me a fake smile. Then there was no talk again for some time. We still had 5 hours of journey left, and since I couldn't sleep because there was no empty seat next to me where I could rest my head or lay down, I had to stay up. But staying up and that too, silent, was going to be a b little hard. Unlike others, I didn't have my cell phone on me or else I would have listened to some good old Bollywood songs myself.

"So, what do you do?" I tried initiating the conversation once again, hoping she would think of me as a creep.

"I work as a designer for a textile firm." she replied. I waited for her to elaborate about her job description a little but since I was still a stranger to her, she didn't feel comfortable sharing with me those details. If I had been in her place, by now, I would have told everything about myself.

"In Ludhiana?" I don't know why I was bothered to know.

"Yes." Then came the one-word answer. It was a clear sign that she wasn't interested in talking with me, but I wanted to make her happy.

Her "mind your own business" attitude put a stop on my efforts to make her happy.

"So, are you going to Ludhiana?" this time, it was her who started the conversation after remaining silent for two minutes.

"Well, yes."

"Where in Ludhiana?" she seemed interested now, maybe she too realized that she was stuck in the train for about 5 hours and had nothing to do other than stare out of the window and see the fields, the rivers and the small villages that the train passed by.

"I don't know."

"What ...What do you mean by I don't know." She looked confused, I guess.

"Well, I can clarify that but it will take about an hour." I said.

"Well, I'm all ears." I started with my job, told her how frustrated I was from the robotic life, Shree's death and what compelled me to go on a trip, how I met Shiva, the places we had visited etc. I stopped when I realized that I had been talking for about half an hour. She hadn't uttered a single word, just looked at me with her eyes wide open.

I am sorry, you must be bored hearing all that." I said apologetically.

Are you kidding me? I can't believe you are actually doing this?" she genuinely looked amazed and not bored at all.

"Actually even I did not believe that I could do it, but with Shiva it was very easy and fun."

"Where is your friend Shiva?" she asked. I would have pointed at his seat but he had gone to the bathroom.

"He got another seat right in the next lot of the compartment."

"That's nice; it must have been exciting all the time right?"

"Yes it has been very exciting, you wouldn't believe the things we saw or went through, I told her about the almost kidnapping of the girl, the life in the restaurant, the girl I found in the bushes." hearing all that she once again became a little gloomy.

"I still can't believe that you actually slept under flyovers, worked in a restaurant and saved that girl's life. I salute you for helping that girl.

You are a good man at heart Adi." Her smile was very distractive. I barely listened to any of that.

It was so beautiful and addictive. Anyone who saw it was completely captivated by it. It was the kind that pulled you into it, almost hypnotizing. The kind that makes you happy even if you were at your lowest. At times, I felt like blushing, other times just smiling back.

Though it was me who did most of the talking, I could see that she was becoming more and more comfortable talking to me. I felt after almost half an hour, we were at a stage where she could tell me why she was crying as soon as she boarded the train.

"Can I ask you something?"

"Yes, sure"

"I saw you crying…. Why?" The moment I asked her, the smile disappeared from her lips and she started to look outside. She took a deep breath in and then exhaled it.

"Please don't share if it is that personal." She took a while before she hit the road.

"I'm a girl, who loves going to school a lot." May be she was just missing her school, nothing big I thought.

"It is because I hate going home."Um-hmm I didn't see that coming.

"I'm the only daughter to my parents. I was brought up by my grandparents until I turned 6. They brought me back for a better school. My mom used to visit me, but I hardly had any interactions with my dad." She was taking long gaps between her lines.

"I used to pretend to sleep early every night. I heard my parents screaming and having a fight almost on a daily basis, I cried out of fear every night, my mom used to come back and put me to bed. She knew that I was pretending. I was never aware of the reason why they fought so much. My mom used to get me ready for school and she used to talk like nothing happened when I got back from school. I never was never on good terms with my dad. He was not a normal father; I hardly ever talked to him."

"I tried asking my mom the reason behind the fights but she was not ready to answer my questions. I saw her burst into tears whenever I tried to know, so I gave up further."

"When I was 8, one day the yelling between my parents became intense and loud. I heard the sound of things crashing onto the floor. I knew it was definitely my dad; He had a habit of destroying things when he was angry. But it was never that loud, I couldn't pretend anymore.

I got up and sat on my bed. I waited for the screaming to lower but they only increased. More things landed into bits and pieces on the floor, urging me to get up and check. But I thought what if that made it worse? Then I heard my mother scream aloud. Not the kind where you are mad and screaming but the kind where you are calling for help. I immediately pulled the covers away, got down from the bed and started walking towards the door. Every step I took, some part of me told me that I shouldn't dare. But I did. I opened my bed room door and saw..." She then mumbled the last line and started crying.

"What did you see?" I was so in the moment that the words came out of my mouth. Of course, I wouldn't have asked her if what she saw made her that sad. But nothing could have been done then.

"I saw with my own eyes, my dad stabbed my mom with a knife. Not just once, but several times, right through her heart. I had never seen anyone kill. Every time, there was some scene on TV where an animal killed another, my mom would change it saying I was too young to see all that. Can you imagine how I must have felt when I saw a man killing another for the first time and that too, my own father?

"I am sorry to hear that." I said.

"Don't be." she replied and continued.

For a moment, I thought it was a bad dream. But the moment he saw me and started walking towards me with the knife which had my mother; blood on it, I completely lost it. On those few second, I didn't know how I got the courage to run when I felt like there was no life in my bones. All the while, I screamed aloud. I unlocked the main gate and before running out on the road, I looked at my mother one last time. She lay motionless on the carpeted floor in a pool of her blood. I knew she wasn't dead then. But I couldn't save her as I had to save myself first. I knew that one of my uncle lived nearby as the school van passed by his home on a daily basis. I ran barefooted to his home in the middle of the night, screaming for him to open the door and save me. I didn't know if my father was still following me, but I didn't have the guts to look back and see. I pounded on the door until my little hands no longer could. The light of the hallway lit up and the front door was opened.

"I told my uncle all that I had witnessed. He was there for me that night trying to control my tears. I don't remember when I fell asleep but by the time I woke up the next morning, my whole life had changed. As I opened my eyes, I saw my uncle resting on the armchair in the room. The bed squeaked a little as I tried shifting the side. He woke up instantly. Your mom is dead and they have arrested your father. Without any hesitation he shot that news at me —like without any disclaimer or comforting. He did not even give me any time to cry. In a few hours from then, I was told to get dressed as he would drop me off into an orphanage. He lived alone and was mostly out of town on business so he couldn't have kept me at his place. I couldn't go back home as the place had been seized by the police. He said that it would be best for me to enroll in some orphanage in another state so that I would escape the thought and forget about the incident."

"I said okay, we started from Bihar to Punjab. We travelled in the train. That was the only day in my life when my eyes were drip throughout the journey. Now every time I ride the train, I am reminded of that day. How scared and alone I had felt, I was going to live in another state —a place where I didn't know anyone. I was to be moved into an orphanage. I knew how terrible they were. It was all so new to me one night I was in my own house, enjoying a glass of lime water after returning from school and the next morning I was headed to Punjab. I completed my schooling in the orphanage and enrolled in a government institution for my college. Now I'm working in Ludhiana." That was her story. It took a while for me to make sense of it all. I tried being in her place and it wasn't where I wouldn't wish my worst enemy even.

"Wow cool!!!" that shouldn't have come out of my mouth, but it did.

"What?" she sounded a little confused at my reaction.

"Don't take me wrong. I know how painful that must have been. You never knew why that happened. It just happened like a flash. I know it is important to have family around, but I said wow for some other reason."

"Do you mind telling me?" she wasn't convinced. She felt like I had just made fun of her whole existence but I really hadn't meant to.

"For most of the kids, parents build a protective layer so that they can protect them from making mistakes. We all make silly mistakes till we enter our teen ages —many even don't learn till then. We never know how the world would react if we weren't bound to that protection. What if they had not been their shielding us, teaching us and correcting us? Correct?"

She just nodded.

"You were on your own. Many things might have hurt you and you too, must have made many mistakes but you learned from them on your own. You matured long before you should have. It is not so easy to become a successful person under your circumstances. If you look at the brighter side, this made you independent and strong."

"If that were the case; why only a few people talk to me?" She said.

"It might be because of variation in maturity levels. You might not have been exposed to some sensible emotions and they might have not been exposed to some hard emotions. So you aren't compatible with each other. That should be fine. Usually men start living by their own terms when they get married, but women never get a chance to live by their own terms. But you have lived on your terms since 8 years old. That is no easy one, Keerthi."

The smile was back on her face. "I saw all of them feeling sorry for me, but you're the first one to say Cool. Even I never thought of the brighter side like you. I have to admit, it did teach me a lot."

"See, that was the wow I talked about!!" I chuckled.

We chatted about many topics and shared our common thoughts. I was glad to see her smiling again. We almost reached our destination.

"I never thought my train journey will be so happy. Thanks Adi." She was right; even I had an amazing time with her. I couldn't believe that 5 hours had passed. I felt like I had just met her an hour ago.

Once we reached Ludhiana, we both gathered our luggage and got off the train; I introduced her to Shiva then. I briefed him about her awful childhood but warned him not to ask anything about it until she willingly told him. He agreed. We all got on the platform. We all bid goodbye and Keerthi started walking in the other direction. We had just walked for a few minutes when I heard someone calling my name from behind. Since the platform was crowded, it was hard to see who it was. Then I saw someone's hand waving at me and a second later, I spotted Keerthi coming towards us with half of her luggage on her shoulders and some of the platform's floor that she was dragging. We both started walking towards her so that we can meet half way.

"What happened, Keerthi?"

"I just wanted to ask you something." she was out of breath so I offered her some water to drink first. She took it, thanking me in the same buffed tone.

"What is it?"

"If you want, you guys can stay at my place, till whenever you want." I did not see that coming. I looked at Shiva. He gave me the "it's up to you man, you decide" look.

"Thanks for the generous offer Keerthi, but we should be fine." I replied.

"Why do you want to spend money on expensive hotels while I am offering you to live for free? Stay in my home till you see Ludhiana." she had a good point to make but it still felt a bit awkward.

"Are you sure about this thing?" I was not so comfortable to say yes, because I was not aware the comfort level we might have staying under the same roof.

"You said that I'm independent and it is not so easy to come to this level. Do you think I will make a mess at judgment?" This time, she had both her hands on her waist and a slightly angered look on her face.

"After you, ma'am." We started following her.

Her apartment was on the 5th floor. She opened the door of the suite 509.

"Sorry for the mess, just before my travel I had to search for something and I was in a rush so..." Saying that, she directed us to the guest bedroom, which was pretty much empty except for the comforters that lay on the floor.

Keerthi started dinner preparations as we both freshened up. It had almost become a custom in India that if the TV was not in the dining room, but the living room, no family would ever have dinner in the dining room. We always preferred to sit down and eat while watching TV. Dining table will be saved for special guests. So we made ourselves comfortable on the floor in front of the TV.

A woman on the TV started was saying "We all knew about a young lady being rapped and thrown from the running train in Bina, Madhya Pradesh." The news made me stop eating any further. Although the new channel had clouded the face of the young woman, but I knew they were talking about the same girl as I recognized the doctor and the hospital.

Finally the guilty had been arrested. As it turned out, it had been her ex-boyfriend who raped her as revenge for breaking up with her.

"Is she the same girl you were talking about?" Keerthi asked. I heard her but didn't respond. Shiva did. That was an incomplete dinner for all of us. After we wrapped up and helped Keerthi clean the dishes, I requested Shiva that we go somewhere for some time. I was still thinking about the girl —but not in a sad way. I was angry at the boyfriend who did this to her. The way she had been raped and then thrown to rot in the bushes without anyone finding her body for days, I wanted to kill that man.

"Can we go out? It really worked for me the last time."

"Hmm, Keerthi do we have an open terrace on this building?" Shiva asked.

"Yes there is, we can go and sit on the water tank." She picked up the house keys.

We went on the roof, and then climbed onto the water tank with the help of a ladder that had been placed there. Sitting on the water tank facing the city, it felt relaxing. There were city lights all around. It looked really amazing; it did bring back the feelings of my college days.

"How one can do such thing to his girlfriend?" I asked.

"Let it go, Adi, she is fine now and he is arrested." That was not enough.

"Why do we have animals in humans?" My voice was rising bit by bit.

"Let me tell you something" I was expecting that, anything starting with those words had the power to control my thoughts.

"Desire is fuel for human brain. Desire drives our daily life. Desire isn't bad but it is also important that one plays with it consciously."

"You need to elaborate."

"Let us say his desire was to get his girlfriend back in his life. But he chose the wrong way to fulfill it. Whenever you have a desire, you will know the intensity of it, how badly you want it or how far are you going to go to get it. Your desire should never dominate your intellect. When you're in a highly emotional state, don't let it overshadow your common sense. Your common sense helps you to assume the pros and cons of any situation and therefore helps you to decide in a better way."

"He was not able to assess that assaulting her can make things worse. Now, his entire life will be on police records."

"Every human emotion has its own extremes within it. It is very difficult to find and understand that thin line between like and love, love and lust, love and hate, hate and dislike. You can only see that line wide and clear if you put your mind to it. You use intelligence and your common sense to know the difference between the two sides."

"Wow!! How do you know all these things?" she was amazed listening to Shiva's philosophy.

"Exploring life in all possible means teaches you a lot. One just needs to have a clear and clutter-free mind to see that." Keerthi too, went on to explain how she felt about the incident with the girl. Talking to them that night on the roof helped me feel a little better and a lot less angry.

I wanted to thank her for letting us stay. Most of the night, we talked more about our lives, our childhoods and our current standing in the society. We talked about our future goals too and I was impressed by the decisions Keerthi had made for herself on her own. She also turned out to be a very fun person despite her troubled childhood. She was one of those people who saw the silver lining in everything, those who didn't back down when hit but stay on their feet and face the challenge with shoulders high.

HER SECRET

The crust around my eyes had been a bit irritating when I woke up. I started rubbing my eyes to get rid of it. There was a piece of sticky notes in a striking blue color on the wall straight to me.

"Coffee and breakfast on the dining table, I will be back at 6 p.m." The note instantly brought a smile on my face. It was such a nice thing to do for someone especially on a busy working day. When I thought about it, everything about this newly-formed friendship was different. We have just met in the train yesterday and there she was, inviting us into her home, in her life and making breakfast for us. She really had a heart of gold. Who did that for anyone in today's world. I decided that I would do something for her too. To repay her for her gratitude. But nothing popped up in my still-a-little-sleepy head. It was a good thing she made coffee, I thought to myself. I got out of bed, freshened up and then headed outside the guest bedroom. Shiva was as usual up before me. He had even completed his morning meditation session and was reading the newspaper placed on the coffee table.

I poured out some coffee in one of the mugs that hanged on the little hooks near the sink. Next, I gathered the breakfast which consisted of Paratha and Aloo curry.

"I think that we should do something for her in return when she comes back from her office today. What do you think?" I asked him.

"You can do the same for her."

"What?"

"Cook dinner for her." He said while turning to another page. It was a good idea, but I wasn't very confident about it. Cooking wasn't my forte but it wasn't like I was really bad at it either. I thought it was time I honed my skills a bit and decided to give it a try. But before doing so, I thought about cleaning after the place a little. There was so much paper waste in her house that I knew she didn't need any more, there were magazine and newspapers with last year's dates on it. She had briefly talked about getting rid of it all last night but she didn't have the time to do so. Since me and Shiva didn't have anything on our hand all day, we decided to get busy decluttering the place. I asked Shiva to start with the newspapers cabinet while I cleaned the dishes in the sink.

I washed them first and later dried them with a kitchen towel. As I was cleaning, I saw through the glass of a cabinet that the dishes inside were place awkwardly —like they had just been placed one onto another. I feared that the next time the cabinet was opened, they might fall. So I decided to organize it. As I had feared, the moment I opened the cabinet door, a plastic bowl fell out and dropped on the floor. The lid had opened and was rolling like a tire on the road before coming to a halt. I knelled down to pick up whatever was in the box. To my surprise, the box wasn't filled with any food item, but with photographs. Something inside me told me that it was wrong to go through someone's personal stuff, but as I was picking them up, my eyes dawned on a few of them. It was of Keerthi cutting a birthday cake. All her friends were gathered around her and she looked really happy. The digital date on the side of the photograph caught my attention; it was dated 14-02-2011.

That day was 13th Feb, which meant tomorrow was her birthday. Now that we had discovered it, there was no way we were going to act surprised when she told us about it. I decided I was going to celebrate her birthday. Yes, that was going to be how I repaid her gratitude, I thought to myself.

I for once was very excited as celebrating and organizing events was my forte. I knew a lot about it, especially when it came to celebrating a girl's birthday. I had done it for many of my college friends. I had once celebrated Nandini's birthday too.

"Shiva, tomorrow is her birthday, why don't we celebrate the party?" I showed him the picture with the date on it.

"I never did any such celebrations for anyone so I don't know much about them. If you are confident that we can pull this off then I am with you. You do all the planning and I will help you execute the plan." Shiva made it very clear.

It took me almost couple of hour to plan the whole thing. While I was making the house look good, I found a few other things about Keerthi that gave me a few new ideas. I found her phonebook, which looked pretty old, but had many numbers written on it. I also found an old camera which we could use for her party. Thankfully, it was working when I turned it on.

I got so involved into the planning that I forgot that I hadn't eaten anything since afternoon. It was almost time for her to return. I was desperately waiting to see the look on her face when she saw the house all cleaned up. And the moment finally came. She was more ashamed than surprised that we had to do the cleaning. She said that we were her guests and therefore shouldn't have done it. Later, she thanked us by buying us drinks which we enjoyed after dinner at the water tank, playing cards. We all were become really good friends and it felt like we all had known each other for ages and not merely some days.

We did not wish her on the day; as I wanted her to tell us about it. She didn't and left for her office as usual. I was all set for her birthday. At around 6:30 in the evening, we heard footsteps approaching the door. I had placed a sticky note on the door for her that she wasn't aware of. The footsteps stopped as soon as they were on the welcome mat outside. I assumed she was reading the note which read, "You may have celebrated your birthday with many of your friends but I believe we are a bit special. Go to Tipsy & Topsy bakery now."

I heard the sound of the footsteps fading out. The bakery was at a distance of 10 minutes from the place. As she went inside to collect the cake, she was handed another sticky note by the manager of the bakery who first wished her happy birthday and then handed her the note which read, "A cake has been ordered in your name, but you will have to pay for it yourself. Once you have collected the cake, wait for me I outside the apartment gate. I know you must be wondering why you had to pay for it. Shiva says that we only remember things that are unusual. If we had paid for the cake ourselves, you wouldn't have remembered it."

I hoped she would not misinterpret what I had tried saying. I was already waiting for her at the apartment gate told Shiva to stay at her apartment to handle the other surprises. I saw her walking towards me holding the cake. There was big smile on her face. I took the cake from her hands and placed another sticky note on it.

"Can you read it loud?" I requested and started recording her video.

"I can never imagine what it must have taken to get to this stage where you are now. But I am sure of one thing. You didn't do it all alone. There must have been many people who supported you along the way —people who didn't have to, but did. They watched over you, kept you safe and held your hand in all your worries. It is only fair that you thank them on this very special day. Let's start with those who protected you indirectly." She read it aloud. She looked a bit confused but understood as I signaled her to thank the watchman of the building with my eyes. She felt a bit overwhelmed.

I recorded the whole thing on the camera by standing beside her. She reached the security guard of the apartment who was in his late 50's and thanked him. He had been like a father figure to her.

"Thank you Uncle." she said with teary eyes.

"Happy Birthday, Keerthi. God bless you." He said placing his hands on her head and then handing her another note.

The note read, "Walk into your apartment, somebody is waiting for you." We got into the elevator and got off at the 5th floor when she entered her apartment, the lights of the entire house had been turned off. I asked her to turn on the lights and when she did, the whole house was decorated with Christmas lights, colorful ribbons and balloons.

Once when she turned on the light switch, the entire living room came to life. Shiva stood in front of her and took the cake from my hands and handed Keerthi yet another note.

"There is still more?" She looked genuinely happy.

"Thank these people for keeping you happy all the time," read the note.

As soon as she read that aloud, a bunch of people entered the living room saying surprise. Some had been hiding behind the couch while others had been waiting in her bedroom. They were her friends and colleagues. At first, I thought her friends might not come because we were here. But even then, I called the ones who seemed closest to her and they all showed up.

"Thank you friends, thank you very much for being a part of my life." She hugged all her folks one by one. Then another note was handed to her by one of her friends.

"Go to your room." She started walking and I followed behind her with the lens.

One of her friends held a laptop in her hand about to make a Skype call to someone. Once when she sat in front of the machine, her friend just clicked the dial button.

It was her caretaker in the orphanage she had been brought up in. She was so happy to see her that she almost screamed aloud.

"Thank you, ma." Her voice was shaking out of joy. They had a chat for about 5min, and then said her goodbyes. Then I requested her that she closed her eyes so that we can blindfold her. Next, her friends took her to the roof where all the arrangement for the party had been made. There was food and drinks and some cushions and mattresses on the ground for the guests to sit on.

I then opened the blindfold. I handed over the camera to one of her friends and handed her the last slip myself.

"There is one person in your life, whom you should thank. Without him, we don't even want to imagine what would have happened to you. Thank him when you turn around."

She turned around to see who it was and busted into tears when she finally saw who had made it to her birthday party. It was her uncle Sudhakar, who had enrolled her in the orphanage and supported her both financially and emotionally whenever needed. His was the only contact in the book that had any family relative words. I came to know that they had not met from long. It took me some time to convince him to come over for an hour as he turned out to be a very busy man.

"Thank you uncle! Thank you for everything." That came out in bits and pieces. We had the party for an hour and then everybody left early as it was a weekday.

"Thank you Adi. This will always remain the best day of my life." I was expecting that from her but not with a hug. I was flattered with her words and the hug reflected that she truly meant what she said. I felt like my efforts had just paid off.

We had Chinese food on the water tank after cleaning up the place under the moonlight facing the city as always.

"Do you have any opinion on secrets, Shiva?" I don't know if she asked Shiva that because she wanted to share something with us or for her own peace of mind. But because she had brought that up pout of the blue, I assumed the former was true.

"Yes, I do" he started off right away.

"Wait wait…" to listen something like this it should start in your style." I interrupted.

"Let me tell you something."

Now that's more like it. I said excitedly.

"Secret is nothing but another form of fear. You decide something should be kept a secret because its impact scares you. A married man who has extramarital affairs will keep it a secret because he knows the outcome it can have on his family and his societal standing. If he thinks no one will care if he had an affair or not, he won't hide it."

That made sense as always.

"And secret is not decided based on the content; it is actually decided based on the other person. If I have an affair, I can share it with you because you don't know my family; you are no threat to me. So it is a secret for my wife but not for you. People should not keep any secrets only because they fear the outcome. They should just face it. Fear generates secret, so if a person has many secrets then he/she is not very daring person."

Shiva was very good at these talks. He always had an answer for everything. I was not sure why Keerthi asked that question. But there was no further talk on this topic. We all went to bed later.

I began hearing someone cough indistinctively. It was so aloud and persistent that I lost my sleep. I tried to ignore for a while and sleep back but I couldn't. I just lay conscious on the bed. The sound of the coughing was coming from Keerthi's room. I wondered if she was okay.

I walked into the living room, and grabbed a bottle of water and started walking towards her room. I hesitated a little before knocking.

"Knock knock, Keerthi?" Once she saw me I completely walked in and switched on the light.

"Are you alright? Please have some water." I placed my hand on her forehead to check if she had fever. Her temperature seemed normal. After taking a few sips her cough went away and she calmed down a little.

"Thank you very much, and I am so sorry that I woke you up in the middle of the night."

"It's okay, you don't have to apologize. Try to have a nice sleep." I was about to off the light and walk away.

"Adi?" her voice sounded worried to me.

"Can we talk for a while?" she requested. Maybe it was hard for her to get back to sleep.

"Sure, tell me." I grabbed a bean bag and sat beside her. I sensed that she felt a little troubled by some thought of thing. She was trying to find the right words to start the conversation but was failing miserably. She pulled away the blanket and placed her feet on the floor facing me.

"I have something to share with you. I wanted to keep it a secret but what Shiva said tonight was right. It will not make sense or reap any fruitful outcomes if I never say it fearful of the outcome." She hesitated a little.

"I know this would sound weird but I Love You Adi" when she said that, our eyes met. The look she had in them told me that she really meant it.

"Wha-what?" It was hard for me to even manage to make out those words.

I took a deep breath and said "I respect your feelings and I love you too, but not in the same way as you do. I already have someone in my life. We are waiting for our parents to agree so that we can get married." I told her.

"Oh... wha wha what's her name?" she was trying hard to control her feelings. I should have told her about Nandini before but the topic never came up. Besides, it had only been two days that we had known each other, so it came as a shock to me that she would confess her love for someone she had just met.

"Nandini" I said.

"Nice name, she is very lucky." She smiled.

I hope so..." I didn't know what else to say, I had just broken he heart in a million pieces. I wanted to comfort her, but it would have only made the situation even weirder than it already was.

"Is it really possible to fall in love with a person within two days?" And there it was. I had spoken my thought aloud and made her even more uncomfortable. She must have thought that I was making fun of her and her feelings. I instantly recalled the first time I had seen Nandini, it had been love at first sight for me too. Then why wasn't it possible for her to fall in love with someone she met a while ago? I wanted to tell her about Nandu and myself but it would have made things awkward. I had already broken her heart, telling her more about me and Nandini would have been like putting salt on an already-burning injury. She broke the silence and told me not to worry about it.

"I hope you get married to her very soon." She said after hearing me out.

"Okay now, try to get some sleep." I got up from the bean bag and left her room.

"Adi" she stood up from the bed, but kept her eyes lowered. "Can I hug you for one last time please?"

I actually felt sad for her. If I had been in her place and someone had rejected my proposal, I would have been heartbroken too. Without making any delay I hugged her. I moved from there after a while, but this time quickly.

I felt bad for hurting her feelings. I didn't get any sleep all night, I just couldn't. I thought of staying for a week with my new friend whom I really liked, but after what happened tonight, it was best to move out soon My stay there would have reminded her of her naïve confession in the middle of the night and make her feel awkward in front t of me. I didn't want that. I wanted to leave on a good note and thought moving out first thing in the morning was the right thing to do. When feelings between two people start clashing, it is better to stay away from them, I thought.

It was past 6 when I was awakened by some movement in the room. Sleep had just come to me 15 minutes earlier as I looked at the wall clock. Shiva had gotten up for his meditation. I thought of telling him about last night. I just wanted to make sure that the decision I had taken last night was right. I shared with him all about last night, and he too felt that leaving would be the best thing, so we both started packing up so that we can leave early. We had wanted to leave before she got up and left her a note writing down the reason, but surprisingly, she woke up early too. I assumed she wanted for office before we got up so that she won't have to face the embarrassment. But as we were making our way out of the guest room, she stopped us.

"Are you guys leaving?" she stopped asked.

"Yes, I think it is time for us to carry on with our journey." I said.

"Is it because of me?" I know she would think that, damn she should not have felt guilty about it.

"Someday or the other we had to move on right? And no it isn't because of you Keerthi"

"Yes, but why today?" I had nothing to say to that. I looked at Shiva.

"Keerthi, come sit here." He sat on the couch along with her.

"Listen Adi told me what all happened last night." She didn't look surprised with that statement.

"Let me tell you something" Here it comes now she will be convinced, I thought.

"Any attempt to fulfill our desire is a beautiful journey. You might get it or you might lose it. But never ever give importance to the destination or outcome, it will break you down and prevent you from trying again. Always enjoy the journey irrespective of the destination.

"We know that Adi is in love with Nandini. You met someone special like him in this journey; you had some special feelings for him. Aren't those feelings and times beautiful? If you remember just his No to your proposal, you will hate this beautiful journey." It is very surprising that she was listening without tearing up.

"Even you are special to me, Shiva." She said.

"Can I get your phone number?" she asked me.

"No, Keerthi we had a very good relationship. It is better to leave on a good note... a good memory." I don't know why I sounded like a rock to myself, but I believe what I did was right.

THIS IS IT

We reached the bus station in Ludhiana. Shiva was yet to decide which our next destination would be. I just slipped into the restroom to pee before getting on the bus and holding it in for another hour or two before the bus made a stop.

"Oh boy!! After holding the pressure for so long, the feeling you get when you let it go from your bladder is the best," was what I thought while peeing in the restroom.

By the time I walked out, Shiva was not there. I looked around but there was no sign. I started to get a little panicked.

"Adi….Adi" I looked around from to see where the voice was coming from. He was calling me from a bus he had already gotten onto, putting his head out of the window and gesturing me to come fast. The bus started moving and so did I. I just made it in time before the bus driver hit his foot on the accelerator and left without me. I saw him in the bus, but there no seat available beside him.

There was only one seat available in the bus and luckily it was a window seat. Beside me, sat a man in who looked in his early 50s. The sun was shining its brightest as usual. Now that I wasn't seated next to Shiva, I had some free time on my own. I wouldn't have wanted that as with no one to talk to, I started thinking about Keerthi and recalling last night.

I didn't want to think about it, but my mind didn't let me think of anything else. I did not want to lose a person like Keerthi, but I had to. When something happened against my will my attitude turned apathetic. I turned into the Alexander Rybak song- "Leave Me Alone".

I knew that we could still be friends, if we acted mature enough to take it easy and move on but I just wanted to avoid any further complication. I couldn't watch her get hurt every time she talked to me. I always believed that it was impossible to stay friends with someone for whom you had feelings for, regardless of the bullshit people said. How can you stop loving someone or see them with someone else when you clearly have feelings for them. The only way you can get rid of those feelings if you move away from that person. Staying friends would only remind what could have been and the person in love will never be able to move on. At least, that was what I believed in.

"Where are you going sir?" the man beside me interrupted my thoughts. I wasn't really in a mood to carry a conversation.

"I don't know." I answered with a fake smile and started avoiding him. He should have taken that as a sign that I wasn't interested but he went on introducing himself.

"My name is Samba and I'm going to Samba, isn't that funny?" He continued to interrupt and mess with me. I was like dude..... "If your mouth has a remote, please put it on mute."

"My name is Adi." I tried being nice to him. Later, I realized that this man had taken me for granted and went on probing questions like do you work? You look so young, what is your age? Where are you from?

"Look man, can't you see I am not interested in talking to you? Can you not just shut up? It would be best if you mind your own business like I am trying to mind mine. "I shouted loud enough. Everyone in the bus stared at me; I just turned my head towards the window and shut my eyes.

Later when I woke up from my forceful sleep, he was no more interested in talking to me. I did not care much about that. I started watching the movie that was playing in the bus. The man sneezed loud and spread all his germs on my hand. I knew he hadn't done that intentionally, but it literally boiled my blood.

"That's enough, don't you have any manners to at least cover-up your mouth when you sneeze." I became the center of everyone's attention again.

"Sir, can you go and sit over there." Shiva came and requested the man.

"Thank you Shiva." I felt relaxed.

"Let me tell you something"

"Now you don't start please. Like I said earlier, I am not in a mood to talk to anyone." I think for the first time, I had opposed him.

"Just listen" even his voice was sharp and serious. I never saw Shiva this serious before. I couldn't interrupt him any further.

"Did you read Ramayana?" he asked.

"No, but I know the story a little, not in detail though."

"There is one incident in the Ramayana which you need to know." Stating that, he started.

"When Raavan abducted Sita and took her to his Kingdom Lanka, she started dropping her jewels one by one, leaving the sign for King Ram, her husband to find her. Based on those jewels he had only one clue that Sita has been taken somewhere towards South."

"He along with his brother Lakshman started to march towards south. They were travelling with no rest, no bath, and no proper sleep. While they were travelling in a forest, an old tribal woman who lived in that forest stopped them. She said you look so tired, just sit down for a while. They agreed and Ram sat down on a rock and his brother stood behind him. I can see that you haven't had anything from a long time. I have berries with me. Have them so that you can get some energy and you can carry on with your work. They did not oppose her. She took first berry out from her basket and had a bite and gave it to Ram. He took the berry from her. She took another one and did the same, but she threw away. She did the same to the third berry and gave it to Lakshman. He got furious. How dare you to give a fruit which has your saliva on it. Don't you know any manners? You gave the spittle fruit to Ayodhya king Ram. He became so angry that she was horrified. Looking at his brother speak in that way Ram smiled at him. What's wrong brother? Why are you laughing? He wondered. What I saw was far different from what you saw. To have a conversation with two armed men in this forest she should have been brave. She saw our state and offered us food which tells me that she is generous and she tasted them to make sure they are sweet enough so that we can enjoy them, making her a good host. Lakshman understood. How do you expect her to know the manners, which you were taught in the palace? She has never been there; she doesn't even know what a palace looks like. Lakshman realized what his brother was saying; he apologized to the old lady and had the fruit. Her name was Shabari.

"I know why you are telling me this; I shouldn't have behaved with the man in the rude way."

"Remember Adi, this is very important in life. If you habituate to think from other's point of view and then talk, you can cut off maximum nonsense people's talk. It sounds a little tricky but it so easy."

"A person may be rude to you; but you never know what made him to be so. You should not expect people to react the way you want. You should not try to control of someone's thought process." He explained to me calmly.

"What if he/she is doing wrong, do we need to leave instead of changing him." I doubted.

"You should never try to change a person. For every good or bad work we do, it has its own consequences. You cannot decide whether it is right or wrong without being into his shoes. Judging other people might be the easiest thing to do on earth, but at the same time it is also the most foolish thing to do on the planet. Let us assume, one of your friends did a robbery. Police will arrest him or he will know for sure what he did was wrong. There is no reason for you to hate him. The way he was brought up made him to take decisions like this or may be the situation." I still wasn't convinced.

"Irrespective of situation he should not get this idea in the first place." I said.

"That is what I'm trying to say, who are you to predict and dictate his thought process. Doing certain things to control their thought process is nothing but human hacking. Never say a word without thinking it all through. We all teach our kids how to talk and behave with other, but we never teach them how to react. That is the reason as they grow they become less sensitive and more complicated."

It was all starting me make sense to me now. He might be the person who interacts with people in all his journeys. I shouldn't have reacted so rude. I walked up to him immediately and apologized to him. People around me looked at me and smiled. It gave me such a good feeling.

It was almost lunch time when the bus stopped at one of the dhabbas on the highway. It had been a while since I had my favorite Chicken Biryani. I remembered days when my dad used to take us on trips. Back then, Dhabbas used to be a small shack where most of the customers were bus drivers. But now, nearly all the dhabbas we had seen on the highway were air-conditioned and had a family seating area. I felt it lost its authenticity of look at least.

Any authentic biryani can be smelled when it is getting steamed, but I didn't even smell the aroma when it was right in front of me.

Ahh No!! This is much worse than I expected. It was just a mixture of chicken curry and colored rice. I just wanted to call the cook and tear him apart. Sitting with Shiva reminded me what he had just told me, I thought I would give it a try.

"Okay, so may be North Indian Biryani has a different recipe. Or maybe people around here like this better than Hyderabadi. It was not gross but not as good as Hyderabadi biryani either. I didn't need to be mad at him for that." Shiva's words were already changing me into a better human being. I just skipped from saying a few bad words.

"Hey, it is working Shiva, I thought of scolding the cook for the food, but now I'm not doing that." I had to tell him that.

After a lunch break of almost an hour, the bus started to move again and it didn't stop until after sun had lost all its brightness and was turning the sky pinkish. I was not bothered much about it. I was enjoying the blue sky and the Mountain View. After sunset, the driver finally turned off the engine and people started to get down.

As we were walking towards the exit, I saw a board that read "Jammu & Kashmir State Road Transportation Corporation Srinagar."

For a brief moment, a smile crossed my lips. I had finally made it to Kashmir, the place that I had planned to go. But then in the next second, it was gone as it reminded me that this was our last stop. I will be returning back home after this and not be with Shiva everyday like I had been for the past few days.

Then suddenly, my whole body shivered as if all my veins had frozen. It felt strange, almost funny that all the way I hadn't felt the cold. But as soon as I read the board, if felt it. The very thought made me crack up a little. Shiva turned to look at me but I gestured him to continue moving as it wasn't that important. I just walked along with him.

"How long are we going to walk like this?' I did not realize the day became dark and all the street lights were on. The nerves in my legs had tightened from the cold and the walk.

"Just two more kilometers." He said very casually.

"Two kilometers? What?" I was surprised.

"Wait, how long have we walked since leaving the bus station?" I felt I already missed a day.

"We have walked about 9 km." he said.

"We walked what? I can't walk anymore Shiva."

"Oh yes you can, come on now." He never stopped even for a while. My pace slowed down as we started to take the mountainous road. When he stopped to say we are here, I didn't even see where. I just collapsed on the floor.

There was a temple in front of me. By the looks of it, I assumed that it must have been some hundred years ago. But we were still no way near the entrance gate. We still had like a million stairs to cross as the top ache of the temple looked like it was touching the sky.

"Are we going up?" I asked.

"No, it is closed now; we will rest here for today."

"Are you kidding me? It is freezing here; we can't stay the whole night out here."

"No, we have free accommodation for the temple members. I can take a room for us." That sounded pretty better.

"The room came to an end as soon as I walked in. It was so small; it could fit only two of us."

"So, this is it, huh?" I couldn't stay longer holding it in my head.

"Yes, it is time for you to go back home and live a much happier life."

"Why can't you come and stay with me." He had no one and we had become such close friends, I thought he might agree.

"No Adi, I'm going further north with a few saints here. It will take time for me to come back." He looked pretty serious when he told me that. I assumed it must have been. I never bothered him with that again.

"I wish I had my cell phone." I had said that loud.

"Why?"

"So I could have taken a picture of us together." I really meant it.

"Let me tell you something…" in that very moment, I realized how much I was going to miss his philosophies or quotes from now onwards.

"The best camera in this world is your eyes. It just burns the image along with feelings in your brain. Don't cut off the feelings by storing it in the memory card."

"Tell me your favorite moment in your life with friends?" It was a very different question form out of the blue, but I didn't hesitate answering. I have had so many great memories that I easily recalled.

"When I had alcohol for the first time with Tinu and Shree."

"Did you take any pictures of it?" He asked.

"No"

"See, even after several months you still remember that day. It even brought a smile on your face. This entire journey is within you. You may forget a few faces as time passes, but you will never miss the feel or value of it." He was right. Every time, he started something with the words let me tell you something, I knew he would convince me. I had started to blindly believe in everything that came later.

Next day, I thought of starting the day with Shiva, so I got up very early. Surprisingly, Shiva was all ready by then. He was in his saffron saint wear. It had been so long since I last saw I saw him in those. He had looked very different that day. His face was glowing with charm. I couldn't believe that I had been with a Swamy for the last three weeks.

"I'm ready." Call it a coincidence, but even I had chosen to wear the same dress I had worn when I had met him the first time at the fort.

"Adi, Let me tell you one last thing."

"What is that?"

"A man's life is not all how rich is he, it is about how wise he is." Saying that, he hugged me and told me that we will meet again. I did not react to any of that, not sure why.

As promised, Shiva started towards the stairs of the temple. Now that I looked at it in bright daylight, it looked more artistic than before. Even thought it had been constructed purely of cemented bricks, there was some intricate work of art on each. Some engravings were of local animals, some of quotations in Arabic, Sanskrit and Hindi. When we had started on those stairs, there were a hardly a few other show were on the same journey. But as we continued to make our way up, more and more people joined in, many wearing saint attires. Shiva sat on the first rock stair and shut his eyes for meditating. All the other saints sat in front of him and started the same thing.

"What the hell is happening, why all these people are looking up to Shiva?" I sat down almost at the last.

"Om NamahShivaya" all the saints started chanting the mantra. I didn't what urged me to meditate like them.

I crossed my legs one over the other, and rested my hands on my knees. I started chanting "Om NamahShivaya". The more I was chanted the mantra something inside me changed. I felt some energy pumping into me. Some sort of cleansing was happening to my brain, but I really couldn't put it into words. All I knew was that it felt peaceful.

"Adi, you need to come home now, it's time now." It was my mom. I opened my eyes all of a sudden. No one was there around me. I got scared and ran around looking for Shiva. There was no sign of him. I saw a priest walking back out of temple.

"Swamy, why there is no one here?" I asked him, still panting from the search.

"We haven't opened the temple yet, it is just 8 am in the morning." I was horrified. He was a priest, why was he lying to me?

"Do you know Shiva, the man who was mediating on that first stair a while ago?" I hoped he would know something.

"No my child, by the time I came here to open the temple no one was here except you. You were the only one meditating. " I just collapsed right there. I couldn't think. I went completely blank for a while as if all the cells in my brain just died. I don't know why tears were not rolling out of my eyes.

My legs trembled yet I tried to get back up on my feet. Once, up, I started roaming around the temple like a lost child looking for its mother. I looked all over the place but there was no sign of him. I sat where I saw Shiva for the last time. When I shut my eyes again, "Just go home, we will meet again." his words played in my mind.

I trusted him. When he said we will meet again, so he will. I picked up my bag from the room and started walking down the hill. My mind was occupied with a thousand questions, so I least bothered where I was going or what I was doing.

Where is he? Why did he just disappear? Why didn't he meet me before he took off? A question popped in my mind then. How did I meditate for so long? What was so special about that mantra? Did it make me fall asleep? I re-imagined my journey back all alone. I couldn't even think for one moment. I went to the airport and took a flight to Hyderabad.

BACK AGAIN

I was trying to pacify my feelings looking at the long spread white clouds through the flight window. I was silent throughout the journey. I did not inform my family that I was returning home. I wanted to surprise them, especially my mom.

I took a taxi from the airport. "Welcome to Radio Mirchi: *Idi chala hot guru*", that was my favorite radio station on the machine. I instinctively sang along like I used to back in college. Certain smells, houses, faces, noisy roads, and apartment buildings even certain angles of sunset gave me a feeling of the familiar things.

I got off the taxi, paid the driver and walked towards the elevator. It took me a second to recall the right floor.

"Knock knock"

Avika opened the door and shouted in full excitement. My mom came running from her room; her excitement on a scale from one to ten hitting the top number.

"I missed you a lot Adi." Happy tears rolled out of her eyes.

"How was your trip?" Avika asked me.

I knew it had been the best 30 days of my life but as soon as I recalled Shiva and the way he had left me there in Kashmir, my heart kind of sank a little. I forged a smile and politely lied "It's was great!"

"Where is dad? I don't see him around." I asked.

"He went out to take the groceries, he will be returning any minute now." He walked in as soon as Avika uttered those words.

"Hey Adi, how are you my boy? How was your trip?" He asked me while hugging me.

"It was great, dad. I will fresh up and take some rest." I was really tired both physically and mentally.

My room was had been cleaned. I thought "don't worry I'm back."

"Adi, here is your mobile, you did not lose it." She tossed it on my bed while I was lazy to get out of bed.

"What?" Looking at the cell made me mad. How could this happen? "Where did you find it?"

"It was in your backpack, folded in with one of your shirt." I still couldn't believe it. How can a phone from my pocket get into my bag? Questions started to pile up in my head, but they were only questions, I had answer s of none of them.

After taking a shower, my mom readied my favorite breakfast. "Oh mom, I guess you missed me a lot, right?" After finishing, I took my plate to the kitchen and saw that the sink was already piled up with dishes from last night's dinner.

I started to clean them up, "Why are you doing this? Leave it, Adi." She even tried to pull me out from there. "It's okay mom, there was a time when I did this in a hotel for money. I kind of liked it."

"What do you mean for money? Did you spend all the money?" she looked surprised. After my dad and sister went to office, I told her everything.

"I still can't figure out where did he go or why did he leave without meeting me?" she went speechless for a moment.

"Don't worry Adi; you will meet him again for sure." She tried to console me. She couldn't see me depressed.

I felt the nerves in my brain tighten whenever I thought about that. I wanted to check if I had got any reply from Nandu. There was an email from her; it was received a day ago.

Hi Adi,

I hope your trip is going on well. I just want to tell you that I'm almost there to become your significant other.

Hope to see you soon.

Yours lovingly,
Nandini.

Instead of feeling happy, I felt as if more questions had been added to my mystery queue. Question and answers make a beautiful pair together, I thought. Questions make us dead, and finding answers to them kept us alive. They wouldn't mean anything they were separated from each other.

"Well said, Adi". I thought in my head, may be if I had to tell anyone I will start with Let me tell you something.

"We are planning Avika's marriage this year and next year it will be yours." Dad kind of made an announcement. Marriage? With whom? I wasn't mentally prepared to marry anyone but Nandini. Maybe it was time I told them that. But I feared if they refused. "Fear is just your assumptions, don't fall into trap." I remembered Shiva's saying.

"Dad, I'm in love with Nandini for the past three years." I spit it out.

"Oh, is it?" There was silence in the dining room for a long time. The only thing making noise was the silverware.

"Okay, let us talk to their parents, and then we will see." He said. I had not seen that coming.

One day one of my uncle's families came for dinner. His son was a software engineer and working in a very reputed software firm. I expected that the topic of my career would soon be discussed and I hadn't been wrong.

"So, are you looking for a job?" My uncle asked me.

Yes, I'm looking for one was the first thought I got, but before saying that I thought why lie.

"No, uncle I haven't decided on a career yet. I am still evaluating a few options" He chuckled.

"What are doing at home?" he extended.

"I'm helping my mom in the kitchen. Spending some time with my family."

"If you want, you can take career advice from my son. He can get you a job in his company." I knew it was coming.

"I'm happy and I see my mom is always happy when I spend some time in kitchen. I think I need this time to decide what I should go for next. I have worked in the software industry and to be honest, I didn't like it very much. I have decided I don't want to work for money anymore. I want to do something that makes me happy. I know life is driven by money, but when you believe only money can drive your life, it's too late." That was quiet a good speech, I thought. No one said another word after that or tried to convince me of otherwise.

"Always think from other's point of view and then speak." His words splashed in my head. I ran up to him in the parking lot while the family was on their way.

"Uncle, I'm sorry I shouldn't have reacted that way." I knew he was very proud of his son. He had to be. Unlike me, he was good at what he did. His pride had driven him to compare his son with me and that was okay. I shouldn't have taken it up with my ego. Those thoughts had made me apologize.

"No Adi, you're right. I see my son earning round the clock, but he doesn't have a minute for us." Aunty said and she was not interrupted by her husband. They both got into their car, his son Anoj still waited outside.

"Thanks Adi, I think it is time I start behaving like a human with emotions." He left.

It was hard to think from other's point of view before speaking but it wasn't impossible. In fact, doing so changed the way I looked at others and in general. The more I practiced caution before speaking, the wiser I became. People started looking up to me. All that Shiva had taught me made my life easier and joyful.

One night, I busted in tears when I was in my room. My parents heard the sound of my running nose. They walked into my bedroom and Avika followed after them.

"What happened, Adi?" Avika consoled me by placing my head on her shoulder.

"I'm missing Shiva." I said. I thought it would be better to spill it out than die internally.

"He is the one who changed the way I used to think. The way I look at my mistakes have changed, I can see a visible difference. Now people are looking up to me, they are happier with me. For everything good or bad happening to me, it is all because of Shiva. He was the reason for this new me."

"We can understand you, Adi... don't worry you will definitely meet him again." They all tried to cheer me up. I knew I was not going to be okay for a little while but I have pretended to be so. I wanted to pursue my MBA. But because the college I had chosen was very far from where I lived, commute was going to cost me a lot and both in monetary terms and time. So I convinced my parents that I move out and live in a rental room near the college. My mother hadn't been happy about my decision but she agreed for my sake.

The time I spend with him had made me a better person on the whole. I became more fearless, less talkative but frank. Every time, I tried doing something the old Adi would have done, Shiva's voice would just pop into my head and I would abstain from doing it. I wanted to tell him all that, but where was he?

Today I'm fearless, frank, less talkative enjoying my new me. I give the entire credit to Shiva, but where is he. Thoughts about my trip always played in my head. Every thought ended up with a question. I knew sooner or later, those questions were going to kill me if I didn't get answers to them. I decided to deviate myself from the present so that I can detach from my past.

At first, the only solution I found to not think about him was alcohol. It relieved me of those now- painful times. But then, surprisingly, the same solution started to remind me more of him. It broke my heart that I had let go of such a great friend in my life.

That is when you knocked on the door.

"Wow!" Nandini took a deep breath.

"Now I understand why you were weeping for him."

"I have spoken enough. Now you tell me, what you are up to?" I thought I should get answers from her now about the email she sent me.

"Like every other parents, even mine did not agree for our marriage. They were mad at me. They did not spoke to me for some time. Now everything is okay".

"Oh wow, it must have been tough to convince them right?"

"No no Adi, I never tried to convince them, I made them believe that you were the one for me."

"Our parents are meeting tomorrow at my place." She said very casually.

"What? I was not aware of that. Why didn't they tell me?"

"Are your parents not worried about my settlement? I mean I have no job, no house other than my parents and no future —at least for now. How are they okay with that?"

"Come here." She came closer by placing her hands over my shoulders and mine on her hips.

"I love you for what you are not for what you have. No matter what you do, I will be there for you." Those were usually the words a hero in a movie would say to the heroine. In my case, the roles had been reversed. But I didn't care about it as long as she was beside me. Our parents did agree for our marriage when we were ready. It was the day before her flight to Delhi. We sorted out what I could probably do. Going into a teaching profession, completing my MBA, taking up some old hobby and turning it into a career etc. were among the few top options we decided on.

"You know what?"

"I think Shiva is god." She said.

"Come one, what are you talking? You may be a devotee of Lord Shiva but not me." I denied her comments.

"Never say I don't know and answer my question. Doesn't it make more sense?" I didn't answer which she took as a sign to continue.

"Where did you lose your mobile?"

"Medak".

"Where did you meet Shiva?"

"Medak".

"How come? Even after you told Avika to have your number blocked?"

"I don't know" was all I could say.

"Why would any saint travel with an anonymous person?" It was my time to raise a question.

"He might have taught you many things, but out of all those did you observe about Ignorance, limitations and fear."

"Yes I'm aware of them." I wanted her to get to her point.

"Did you ever hear them before?" she wanted me to really think.

"No, I have no idea."

"Do you remember the Swamy at Borra Caves; he said the same things to us."

"Shiva being a saint, he might know of those things" I still didn't seem convinced of what Nandini was trying to say

"Where did he finally disappear?"

"At Shankaracharya temple." My voice slowed down.

"It is another form of Lord Shiva."

"No, no, no! I cannot buy your explanation." I may not have answers yet but I was sure that Shiva was no god but an actual human being.

"Let me tell you something" she started with that.

"It was our last day of college; we both along with our friends were having a blast in KFC at Narayanguda. We were the last to leave on the day before of the state bandh. Your bike wasn't starting. Being a day before bandh, all shops were closed pretty early and all the roads were empty. You tried hard to get it started but there was no luck. There were not even auto rickshaws on the road. We started to walk while you were dragging the bike. It was not light-weight, so you were taking breaks in between. What happened, brother? A man's voice from behind had almost scared us to death, remember? He looked like a mechanic, he tried for a while, but still there was no luck. There is problem with the spark plug, I can replace it. My mechanic store is very near. Saying that, he had taken the trouble to drag the bike till his shop. He opened the shutter, fixed your bike and didn't even charge you for it. Do you remember what did you say to me then?"

"We can call him god, who came out of nowhere to help. Not the one in the statue." she repeated along with me. I remembered saying those words.

"Do you remember what happened on the day after bandh?" she asked me.

"I went to the mechanic shop to thank him, but the real owner said that no one like him worked there. That really bugged us for a long time, remember? But eventually we forgot about it, because it only happened for a brief moment. You spent over a month with this mysterious man or god. It won't be so easy to come out of."

Even though, I was an atheist, she had convinced me to think of the possibility.

Adi, I can't see you lost like this in bits and pieces. I think you should find him first and then think about what you need to do.

"Where can I find him? I know a person with no shadow. I have no details about him."

"Hey, you said you recorded Keerthi birthday party right, if you really met him, he must be in the video?" Nandini was right. How on earth had I not thought about it myself?

"But you both did not exchange any contacts, how will you contact her?" she asked.

"Uh actually, I do know her number." I replied.

"Wow! Interesting, tell me more about it." She was serious but still cute to me.

"No, nothing like what you think. While I was making calls from her old landline phone, her number was written and tapped on it. So I kind of remembered it."

"Then go ahead and call her now." She said.

"I was all excited and ran to get my phone."

"Wow! You seem to be so excited to talk to her." She teased me again. That made me to slow down. While the phone was ringing, my heart raced up.

"Hello" It was voice of a women but not Keerthi for sure. It was an old women's voice.

"Is Keerthi there at home?" I asked

"Sorry, there is no Keerthi here." I started to hear my heartbeat when she said that.

"Is this 25245568?" I wanted to confirm myself.

"Yes it is, but there is no one by the name of Keerthi here. I have been using this number her for the past 10 years. " She hung up the phone. I was in shock.

"Was that a wrong number?" Nandini asked.

"No, I'm sure about the number. This can't be happening." Now Nandini's god theory was popping in my head. I wanted to prove it to myself that I was correct and that Shiva was an actual person.

"Yes, we worked in Hotel Priyan's, the manager knows about Shiva." I opened my laptop and started to type in Google.

"Yes, I found the number." But it said "The number you are dialing is out of order."

"I should find answer for this Nandu, now after what you have told me, if I won't, the questions will kill me for sure. I have no idea where to begin from but I have to."

It was a kind of feeling where people assume you're dead but you're still alive. I went to a trip with a person called Shiva, but there is no proof of him. Was my entire trip a lie?

"I know you cannot withstand questions in your way. So just go and find the answers you need. I will wait for you. This time make sure you have your mobile safe." She kissed me and left for Delhi.

I was all set to leave my home again in search of Shiva. As I thought more and more, the questions were fighting with one another to become dominant. By the time, I locked my home and stepped outside I had only one question on my mind. **Who is Shiva?"**

To Be Continued....